SCARLETT M. HONEY

FAE QUEEN RISING

AN EPIC ROMANTIC FANTASY

CROWN OF EVERGUARD
BOOK I

First printing, 2025

Print paperback ISBN 979-8-9922964-0-2

Print hardcover ISBN 979-8-9922964-2-6

EBOOK ISBN 979-8-9922964-1-9

Cover design by INK Designs

Edited by Claire Bradshaw & Khloe Cain

For the love of my life. Who believed in me before I believed in myself.

To all my fellow thirty-somethings and beyond who grew up immersed in fantasy worlds and now yearn for those worlds to evolve alongside you—
I see you.

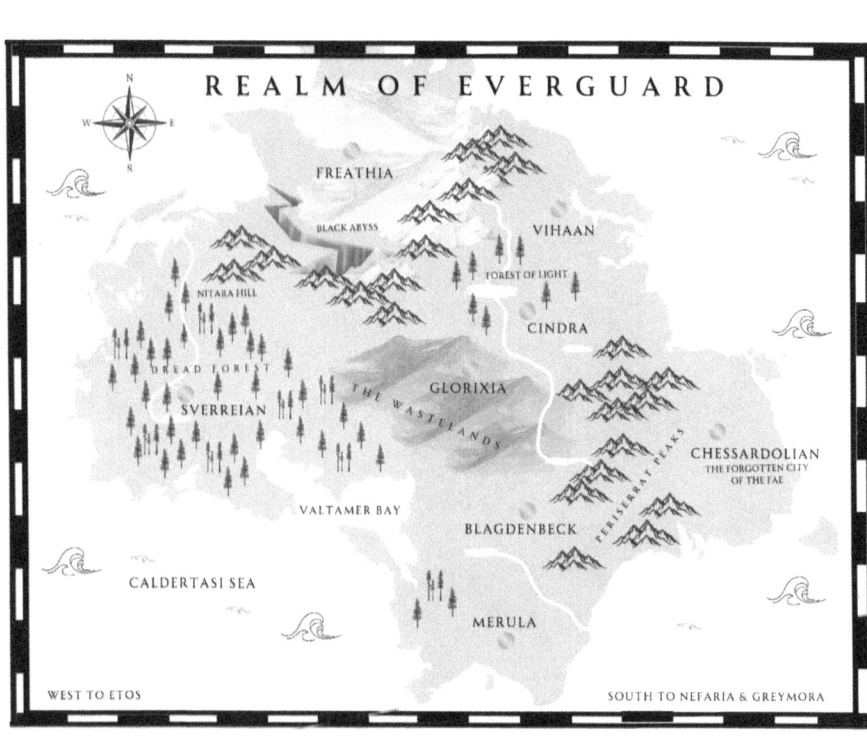

A NOTE FROM THE AUTHOR

Hey there, reader!

Just a heads-up: this book has some spicy scenes, some intense fight scenes, and a few characters might not make it out alive. So, if you're looking for something light and fluffy, this might not be the book for you.

But if you're up for an epic fantasy adventure with some sizzling scenes and maybe a few tears along the way, then buckle up!

Fair warning: There's gonna be some steamy stuff, so you know... reader discretion is advised.

I hope you enjoy the ride!

CHAPTER ONE

I'm glad he's gone.

The thought jolts me awake. Either the thought itself or was it the squeak of the carriage door opening that wakes me? My hands fling out to steady myself but only meet with the soft, velvet cushions surrounding me.

"Leave it to you to be late for your own homecoming." I melt into the seat; relief floods my body as Licia's delicate features come into view. She sticks her head into the carriage even as it's still coming to a halt. I take two deep breaths, the only thing that seems to work lately with the nightmares plaguing me ever since...

The fear tries to rear its ugly head but I swallow it down, happily replacing it with a swell of excitement; I'm home. I rush to gather my things and follow Licia back out of the carriage, eagerly glancing around to see who else awaits my arrival. Are Father and Mother here? Or perhaps Killian with my new nieces? Or Gryphon?

Licia pulls me into a warm embrace before I even have two feet on the ground. "It's been too long, sister." Despite the chill in the air, her arms are full of warmth and I sink into her. Tears threaten to spill at this small show of affection after such a whirlwind of the past few days, but now is not the time for me to fall apart. Stepping back, I glance around, noticing the only other people out here are the servants bustling around unpacking all my trunks from the carriage.

Surrounding us, the backdrop of the white travertine castle walls gleams to perfection. The walls themselves must be older than time itself—a reminder of the Fae people who ruled here before our family. But even now, the walls are an impressive combination of welcoming and imposing.

"Take these to our chambers," Licia calls over her shoulder with all the authority of a princess old enough to know her worth and young enough to retain the confidence and air of someone in charge without consequences.

I turn toward the servants who are gathering the bags and trunks, thanking them quietly before following Licia. It will take time to get used to this.

Being back at the castle is so different from how things were in our cottage where I carried my own bags and made my own meals alongside Avicii. Licia though, doesn't give the people scurrying around us much thought as she pulls me along into the castle.

The carriage did run later than expected. Father and Mother have a schedule to keep, so it makes sense they couldn't await my late arrival. Killian barely leaves Father's side, so I can imagine he's busy as well. And there's no way Gryphon would sit still waiting for a late carriage; I doubt these last ten years have tamed him. She tugs harder on our interwoven hands but then notices the confusion clear on my face. "They're all at dinner. If we hurry, maybe we'll get a small morsel. Of course, Father thought you'd be here hours ago. You should see tonight's crowd." She looks over her shoulder, making sure I'm keeping up. Her cheeks are full of a rosy hue that wasn't there a moment before and a smile growing even wider than the one she gave me at my arrival. "Killian says Father has a big announcement."

Did Father wait for my arrival to announce Licia's match? I can't believe it's taken this long, but he must finally be satisfied he's found someone who'll bring great advantage to our family. Everyone, until now, has fallen short of his mark. And now at thirty-four-years-old, I secretly worry she'll live her entire life without marrying. Although in our letters, her retellings of her trysts would leave me blushing and out of breath, so I know she's made every moment of her young and unattached life count for something, and there's no cause to worry.

My feet move at their own accord as I take in the larger-than-life walls and their eloquence. The exact opposite of the small space and green hills where Avicii and I built our quiet life. I already feel lost. "I didn't mean to inconvenience anyone, especially here at the castle. I wasn't sure where else to go after—I didn't mind staying at the cottage, but Father—" I'm babbling and I know it, but now, returning to the castle after all this time, feels like a failure. And returning as a failure to the entire village of Merula is a harrowing thought.

"Of course you had to come home, Rowandine. Don't worry, you know Father. He has plans for his plans, and from what I hear, the next one is already in the works." She bounces along toward the great hall, unphased by my hesitance.

"I was hoping I'd be able to retire to the healer's ward," I volunteer, missing the days spent helping courtiers and villagers alike. "Perhaps be there full time. I figured it'd be the best place for me, since, you know..." I repeat the words I've said to myself the whole ride here, knowing I've done my duty to my family and my kingdom, and now, this would be another way to do what I must for my people, but at least this time, working in the healer's ward is something I want to do.

Licia looks over her shoulder at me. Even by her one glance I can tell she's not as convinced as I am that this is my calling. "We'll figure out what you really want. You've been gone for ten years, Roe. A lot has changed. You've changed. We'll figure it all out before we're both sent off into the world again, on the arms of new matches." She looks wistfully over my shoulder, no doubt picturing hours from now when Father announces her match and the cheers ring out, toasting a new happy couple. I think to ask about who she's recently been courting but she barrels on ahead, eager to weave through the impeccably clean, yet rather stark hallways to reach the feast that awaits us.

"I'm sure you're right. Being back at the castle will make it easier." Without missing a beat, I continue ambling behind Licia's precise footsteps. But even as I agree with her, a sinking feeling begins in my stomach. I'm still unable to voice what "it" is. I don't want to think about it at all. But being around family will certainly make for an easier transition.

Her loose curls bounce as she makes her way up another stairwell, leading us up several levels toward the magnificent feasting halls. With each rising step, my anticipation grows. From the top, the view from the halls looking out over the Caldertasi Bay is as breathtaking as I remember, a view unmatched by any other.

That was, until our cottage. The brilliant, close-up view of the Periserrat peaks stole my breath the first time Avicii led me up the narrow path serpentining back and forth across the peaks to our new home. The daunting mountain range loomed over our small plot. Even with the cottage positioned half-way up the western face of it, we still looked straight up into a rock face deemed nearly impassable to even the most adept travelers, which is why so many passed just by our home. It was as if our cottage was at the end of the world, the furthest western point of Everguard you could go before—if the stories are to be believed—the last of the Fae who've made those lands their home would snatch you up.

Licia turns, the flickering torchlight highlighting what the darkness outside did not. Her eyes narrow as they take in what they see.

My fingers travel up to my hair, attempting to twist some semblance of order through it. I know it's in vain, though. Licia has always had the better hair. Although similar in color, hers always fell just the right way, and when Marlys would curl it for us, only Licia's would behave.

"You look..." Her gaze travels from my messy hair, to my face, to my rumpled dress. I wait as she no doubt flips through all the words that would define how I look, trying to come up with one that isn't too unkind. Her face falls and she sighs, unable to find something suitable. "You look like your husband just died." Her tone fills with sympathy. "I wish we had time for you to settle in, but with the way the evenings have been going..." She lets me fill in the blanks. She licks her thumb and begins wiping the dirt smudges off my face.

"Licia! We're not ten anymore!" I fail in the attempt to push her off me and concede to her ministrations. She makes quick work of taming my curls into submission by combing her fingers through them. "Well, good luck with that mess," I grumble.

"It's not so bad. But honestly, when was the last time you brushed this?" A laugh escapes me while she works. My hand comes to my mouth, stifling the sound but Licia doesn't notice as she pulls and tugs strands into place.

When's the last time I laughed out loud? The thought startles me.

Everything used to make me laugh. Even Avicii. Before everything fell apart.

She steps back, tilting her head and assessing her work. She pulls two strands out to frame my face and then turns back down the hall, satisfied. I hesitantly touch my hair, using my hands as eyes to see what she's done, amazed by what she's able to do with so little time, and then hurry after her.

If only I had a cupful of her natural beauty in instances like this.

It always surprises everyone when they find out we're twins. Or at least, that I'm the twin to the beautiful and angelic Princess Licia. And every time, their look of disbelief is a dagger to my heart. It's clear what they're thinking. With her delicate features and pale skin, she favors our mother and brother much more than I do. And both her and Killian look so distinguished with Father's strong nose. While I've always been a bit thicker and more awkward, traits that no one else in our family has and neither of which is smiled upon in a court that praises girls for their looks and quiet obedience.

I follow in my learned obedience. As a child, I could never run out of questions, always needing to know why or what for. But somewhere along the way, the importance of following along took precedence over my inquisitiveness. And now, we continue on our way. A nervousness rises within me for what we'll find in the dining hall. "If only we could call Marlys to work her magic or at least wash the rest of the road off of you, but we'd miss dinner for sure if we did so." Framed by the massive windows overlooking the ships docked in the bay, she turns back to me. Her deep blue eyes are apologetic, tracing over my dusty and wrinkled skirts, the mourning black now more of a gray at this point. I pause, attempting to brush out my skirts and tidy my appearance, but Licia grabs my elbow, encouraging me along.

"I'm sorry. For your loss, by the way." She slows her pace to match mine and then reaches for my hand as if I never left. She's looking at me, but I keep my eyes straight ahead. This is the part I've grown to hate. The sympathy in their eyes when they say those words to me. I can't take their sympathy and I can't take their sadness.

Not when it was all my fault.

I nod in acknowledgement of her condolences and squeeze her hand, but nothing more.

We wind our way through the castle halls and I'm only dimly aware of how everything looks exactly the same as when I left it. Golden banners drape haphazardly over the brilliant Fae murals spanning the walls as if only a temporary fix, even after all this time. A long, dark red carpet covers the blue mosaic tiles swirling with the majesty of a grand river beneath our feet every few strides. Extravagant riches hide the ornate beauty of our home, created by the monstrous creatures who once ruled here.

Licia turns left at the end of the fine hallway and I pause, instead wishing myself on the main level, ready to pass down the darkly lit hallway and travel past old office rooms and unused libraries down to the healer's ward.

With one look at my face, she reads my mind. "Not even you would choose applying salves and changing bandages over a hot meal after your days on the road. Hurry, Rowandine."

"Of course you're right." But that doesn't stop my mind from wandering to the ward and what Thaliya is doing right now or if there's been an influx of villagers since autumn's arrival. But she's right. There's some place else I must be.

And as I turn, I hear it.

CHAPTER TWO

The melody pulls me down the hall. Upbeat and lively notes float past us, but the singer's voice tells another story. The musician is still too far down the hall to decipher the lyrics, but his smooth, raspy tone hints at a long, haunted life of disappointment after disappointment. As my silent slippered feet pad down the last bit of hallway, I don't spare another glance at the brightly colored tapestries lining the walls, knowing they paint gruesome pictures of Hadeon's glory. The Human King who was able to take down the entire court of Fae before us. Instead, I'm pulled as if in a trance toward the great hall, where this bard must have the entire court hanging on each note he drops.

"That music—" I whisper as Licia's hand closes around my wrist.

"Oh. He's just recently arrived at court." Licia's head tilts to the side, assessing me. "Are you alright?"

I shake off the odd hold the music has on me. Clearly, I'm exhausted from traveling. "Yes, of course." But the need to join the room full of music overcomes me.

As I close the distance between myself and the great hall, the lyrics become clearer. Not surprisingly, he belts out another ballad about conquest and a people saved. But unlike the hundreds I've heard in this hall before him, I can tell there's something different about this song. I just can't put my finger on what exactly. This old soul of a voice, so rich in knowledge of the world and many lives lived, dances around me, tugging me closer, tugging at an unknown part of me.

More lyrics spill out into the room, telling of bravery and hard choices. The words and melody list through the air in a way that can only be described as joyfully melancholy. So bright with truth that he paints such vivid pictures.

I swallow a scoff at the thought. Everyone knows there is little truth in the words of a bard, especially one so lucky as to grace the court of King Hadeon. There's clearly nothing here but pomp and praise to an old king whose seen better days.

Licia and I round the corner into the great hall, waving off the callers. Even after all this time, I can't seem to arrive when I'm supposed to and we don't need them to draw attention to it. We cling to the fringes of the room, my hand still tightly grasped in Licia's as she expertly weaves us unseen through the crowd toward the high table.

I can't yet make out the bard. The crowd is heavy tonight, no doubt to get a peek at the poor widow's return, but in my mind's eye I've already cast him as a man so worn with age and travel. His bright, resonant voice is haunting in the way he hints at all the hardships lived and many loves lost.

The cold of the marble pillar leaks through my thin dress as I try to find a good vantage point of both King Hadeon and the bard.

"You should hear all they're saying about him." My eyes widen at Licia's whisper when I take in the scene before us.

"All who says?" She gives me an impatient look and I realize how absurd my question is. Licia always places herself in the middle of conversations at court. She's always the first to hear something, so much so that even before I left, Killian started looping her into some of his more local strategy meetings and asking her what conversations about the realm she's heard, especially when the people at court are involved. So, I try again, "What do your song birds say?"

"Most importantly, it sounds like he's a real monster between the sheets." A knowing smile plays across her lips as I try desperately to turn my laugh into a cough, causing those closest to us to cast disapproving glances over their shoulders. I missed her frank bawdiness. "For another, he's dangerous. There's just something about him that isn't right."

Bouncing on the tips of my toes, I try to move just enough to fully view this man with a voice of such sticky physicality that I can barely stand still, but I can't picture someone with such a beautiful gift to be bad.

From here, I can see Father and Mother seated at the high table. The king and queen look, for the most part, unchanged. The king, my father, still has an air about him that whispers of his past as a conqueror, but court life has softened him. Tristana has retreated further within herself, even in the way she sinks into her chair, trying to appear invisible to the crowd before her.

It shocks me to see that the king does not have the same reaction to the bard's alluring words. Instead, Hadeon sits tall in his seat, his hawk eyes moving from courtier to courtier, not missing a single interaction, and evidently not even hearing the melody before him. My mother is beside him, wilting into the shadows. Even more so than the last time I saw her.

Before we move to join the king and queen, along with our brother, Killian, and his small family, I finally have the right vantage point to the singer who holds everyone else within his spell.

Blinking at the man before me, I try to reconcile what I see with what my mind has already decided of him. The bard is not old and definitely not weary. Quite the contrary.

The man singing and strumming along on his four-string is in his prime. My eyes must be playing tricks on me because the voice is so powerful and expressive—deep with an agile sadness, but the man himself—well—he is not old nor weary. In fact, the only word that comes to mind at the moment is beautiful.

I gasp audibly; my courtly ability to hide my every thought completely forgotten after all this time away.

Licia nudges my shoulder with her own as we settle into our seats. "He's fairly enchanting, hm?"

"He's beautiful," I manage to whisper as I drink him in.

The way the candlelight dances across his deeply bronzed skin only serves to further entrance me. And the manner in which his hair twists around itself and is pulled back by a thick headband so it doesn't fall into his eyes while he plays embodies an artist full of soul—and maybe full of himself as well. I miss his last few lines, but as his lyrics spin a new tale, one of darkness and shadows, his eyes drift up to the crowd.

My heart flutters. Something I thought was impossible after all these years of stamping all the feeling out of it. Yet I float with hope his glance will fall on me. And it does. He doesn't even sweep the room. He looks up as if there's a question on his lips, and I am the answer. He continues his lyrical ballad of darkness, but his eyes travel over me, searching for an answer I can't give. As a glint sparks in his pale green eyes and the corner of his mouth lifts in the hint of a smile, I realize I'm not only staring, but my mouth has fallen open. I quickly close it and try to dissolve into the marble behind me. Only to remember Licia and I have taken our place at the high table already and the eyes of the entire court will soon fall to us. Instead, I focus on trying to steady my breath before anyone notices.

Notices what? That I'm late? That the bard's tale moves me? I look around and can tell his words have ensnared many in the crowd. And many others are just as lost as I am in his looks as well.

My lips curve into a smile, surprised that I can even still have feelings. I suppose they just don't dissolve into nothingness, but it seems like maybe they should've. It'll be easier if they do after all this past month has shown.

I shake off the memories before they surface. Now is not the time.

Killian, on my other side, clears his throat to draw my attention. It's been too long since I've seen my brother. I tear my gaze away from the bard, expecting to meet Killan's expressive eyes filled with dreams and ideas for the realm. The same eyes I would watch as they pored over the tales he'd read me when I couldn't sleep and found him in the library. His big arms would scoop me up without hesitation, placing a contemplative finger on his chin, pretending to select the perfect book that would carry me into sleep.

Instead, his kind eyes have sharpened into something else. Deep frown lines appear at his brow, making his disappointment at my late arrival clear. I pause my hand mid-air, almost clasping it atop his own in a subtle way to say I missed him. But I quickly place it back into my lap, my smile replaced to mirror his formal facade.

As the singer strums his final chords, the crowd erupts with cheers. I put all my energy into clapping for him, glad for the distraction. The servants swoop in with trays and full flagons of ale before the crowd calms. As everyone turns toward the food in front of them, the bard swaggers into the shadows, already forgotten by those around him.

"How does it feel to be back?" Licia motions to the crowd before us dancing and eating. I turn in my seat to fully face her, putting my back toward Killian's chilly greeting.

She seems content, so I try to show the same. "It's really something. It's so different from how it used to be. But I suppose that's just me." I shrug, hoping my response is adequate.

It *is* good to be back, even if so much is unknown at the moment. For this small time before my father decides my next fate, I'm here with Licia, and being together again feels like home.

Home. It's strange to call a place I haven't seen in over ten years my home. But sitting here with Licia, that is what I feel. Even the first few happy years with Avicii never felt like this. Licia has always been easy.

Dinner passes slowly and uneventful. I use this time to reacquaint myself with court life. The sounds alone are so much more than I'm used to. Avicii and my small estate, if one could call it that, was well out of the way of anything and more than a day's travel back into Merula. While Avicii always described our house as an estate, I always described it as cottage-like, painting its size and location as a magical place. I loved the way the rolling hills peaked just as our home came into view, nestled snugly between two hills and lined with tall conifers on either side of the sand-colored pebbled path. And the way the Perriserrat Peaks pierced into the clouds in the background. As we first traveled up the golden path the garden appeared small, just visible. But over the years, I learned much and expanded across the side yard and into the back. Avicii always said it was too much for the two of us, but I enjoyed sharing with surrounding neighbors, always hoping it would soon be more than just us two there.

Until the hope disappeared, of course. Until I knew it could never be.

The thrumming celebrations abruptly bring me back into the present. I have a hard time focusing on any one conversation before my attention is pulled elsewhere. Thankfully, very few people approach me at the high table. From the few darting glances I receive, I wonder if people are unable to place me.

Am I that changed? A quick glance down and, yes, perhaps I am.

My sun-kissed skin is even darker from the hours upon hours spent in the garden. My hair, from years of not having to bother with it, is now curly and unruly, and despite Licia's earlier efforts, flows loosely down my back. Doing a quick sweep of the room, maybe Licia should have pulled it up more in the latest court fashion rather than just out of my face. Instead, I'm left sticking out like an overgrown weed in a bed of roses.

My thoughts, and thankfully also the surrounding chatter, are suddenly hushed by mellow strums. The bard strides back to his perch in the center of the room and continues his songs on his four-string, gaining listeners as he does. As the servants make one last sweep, gathering empty plates and filling empty mugs, the bard begins his evening with a slow, moving ballad.

He plays incredibly well. Especially since he can't be more than forty-years-old, yet the speed in which his fingers dance across the strings is something I'm sure only the most experienced musicians master. He, on the other hand, makes his level of skill look like something he was born with rather than spent a lifetime trying to acquire.

When the words spill from his lips, his bright tenor resonates somewhere low and deep within me. I can't help but focus on his features. Besides being younger than I'd first imagined, and more attractive, his features have a sharpness to them that echo Licia's earlier warnings, which I dismiss as soon as the thought comes because he's a bard for goodness sake. How dangerous could a man with a four-string possibly be?

Just as I attempt to stifle a laugh while imagining the man in front of me fighting off a dragon with only his lute for a weapon, he looks up, and his pale green eyes find mine once again. In that instant, I am no longer laughing. Far from it.

A strong jolt yanks at me, and at the same time, I am rooted deeply in place. It doesn't hurt, exactly, but it's what I imagine my seedlings feel when I take them from their small cups in my warm windowsill and replant them into my garden at the beginning of each spring.

An unmistakable feeling of familiarity winds its way around me, yet even as I think it, I dismiss it. Impossible. But his eyes are still on me, and while the pull isn't as strong as it first was, it's still there, like the bees who buzz around the periphery of the garden while I work on.

His eyes are questioning, searching my face while he continues his musical tale of the stars only know what, as if he feels it, too, which is absurd. I shake the thought off before it's able to take root.

His song ends and before he begins another, he looks toward King Hadeon who stands and raises his glass. The strumming falls quiet and the crowd follows. The sea of faces all turn toward the high table and Hadeon waits expectantly. When silence falls, he waits a beat more until he knows every eye in the room is on him.

Licia is positively vibrating beside me. Here comes the announcement she's been waiting for. It's finally her time. I clasp her hand and squeeze, just as excited for her as she is.

"Tonight, we gather here to welcome my daughter, Rowandine Aeronwick, home as well as help shoulder her burden of losing her husband, Lord Avicii Sintinell, too soon. As we all know..." As he sweeps his cup to include the onlookers in his ramblings, I can't help but tense when he mentions my late husband, someone it took entirely too long for me to realize was nothing more than the king's dark blade but I quickly shrug off the thought when Licia's grip tightens on my own and I can't help but wonder why Father hasn't mentioned her yet. "The best way to ensure moving on is to continue forward with your duty. Let's all raise our glasses in celebration of second chances. Rowandine will surely prove a successful match this time to our neighbors to the west, in Etos."

Beside me, Licia chokes on her wine, quickly bringing a napkin to her mouth to catch what spills out. Clearly we both thought she would be next.

My eyes slide sideways. Her eyes find mine. The incredulity that this was Father's big announcement written plain in the tilt of her eyes and the way her mouth is slightly open.

Ten years have gone by and there's already a wedge before I can mend the chasm of time. I smile politely at the crowd but I hope my shock is clear to her, because with all eyes on us, there's little else I can do at this moment.

Etos? He's shipping me off as soon as I've arrived? Nothing good can come from a match with Etos. From what I hear, it's even worse off than Nefaria was before Hadeon trampled his way into Everguard. Or the rumor he's a complete monster. Pick any of the stories, none paint him in a positive light.

Everyone raises their glasses and I belatedly realize they're waiting for me to join in. I try to control my shaking hand as it reaches toward the full cup in front of me. Rather than gracefully scooping it up to join my family in celebration, the glass tumbles over. I look up to meet my father's eyes and am met with a hint of rage at my inability to meet even the simplest request.

Before I have a chance to apologize, a servant places another glass before me, taking time to even wrap my fingers around the stem before stepping away. Their attention to detail is admirable. As I raise my glass, I silently toast the nameless servant standing at the ready behind me, instead of my supposed second chance.

A collective exhale fills the room as everyone takes a sip and returns their glasses. The wine tastes sour in my mouth but I dutifully swallow it, outwardly showing my support for the king's plans.

He seems satisfied and continues. "Lysander Sturdevant is crossing the Caldertasi Sea as we speak. Unfortunately, as spring surrenders to the autumn storms, his crossing becomes unpredictable. We'll have a better idea of his arrival in the coming weeks. Until then, we'll begin preparations for the wedding of the year." His voice booms across the table and hits me like a physical blow. His words reverberate through my body, causing me to wince. As I catch myself, I almost miss the unreadable look between Licia and Gryphon, who is seated at an honored table just beside ours.

Distracted momentarily from my impending marriage, I look between the two of them, trying to read their communication. The look on his narrow, bright face is unreadable in response to Licia's shoulder shrug. Is she angry? Relieved?

Just the fact that I can't read the silent conversation between my sister and my best friend speaks volumes. Before, it was always Gryphon and me with Licia joining in only when she could find nothing better to do. But now, it seems, I'm the one on the outside.

As the crowd's cheers fall quiet and the chatting resumes, the king nods for the bard to continue. The jovial tune doesn't match the maelstrom forming within me. But I smile and tap along to the beat as thoughts drown out my surroundings. *How could he already have planned this? My new match is already on the way? I have little hope now of returning to the healer's wing.* My thoughts race and realization dawns that there was never a chance Father would let me retire to the healer's ward. I still hold a purpose for him, and until I'm successful, he'll continue pushing onward.

Licia leans against me and whispers, "This night is for you." I take comfort in the solid weight against me but not in her words. She doesn't seem angry with me, but how can she not be? All she's ever wanted was to marry and get out of Merula. But the weight of her against me allows my breathing to slow and the feeling of drowning in a crowd of people slowly subsides. I reach for her hand under the table and she squeezes it in solidarity.

The tune slows and the bard begins another. As he begins, his face is unreadable, stoic even. My mother forgets herself for a moment and moves to embrace this song with a dance, but quickly settles back into her seat with a scowl from my father.

I sit back in my chair, enjoying this new melody. Familiar in a way that a passing smell reminds you of a particular moment from your past, but you just can't put your finger on it.

He sings again of conquest. How original. I almost let my thoughts wander again, but his words pull me under, forgetting the new turmoil within and instead focusing on the bard and his story.

In days of prosper, a tale was told,
Of a treasure hidden, shining gold.
Through valleys deep and mountains high,
Brave souls sought it 'neath the sky.

With hearts of courage, they did roam,
Through forests dark and fields of loam.
Guided only by their hopes and dreams
They journeyed on past peaks and streams.
At last, the treasure came to sight,
A beacon in the darkest night.
They shared its light with all they met,
A gift of hope, no soul to forget.

"Oh that's clever." Licia leans in close. "To paint Merula as a treasure Father has shared with everyone. That's a new one."

I smile, but I can't pull my eyes off the bard. After the last chord, I'm left dazed and exhausted. Even though I haven't left my seat in hours, I feel as if I've just journeyed across the realm and fought an Ancient for my life. That whole song sits awkwardly within me, like a garden bed with uneven rows—knowing that something must be done here but not quite sure how to go about fixing it all.

Oh, he's good. And how many cups of wine have I had? After the big spill, I thought I'd barely touched it throughout the night. But suddenly, my legs are heavy and I can't keep my eyelids open. The bard moves to the side as another takes his place.

It's rather late, and the day has been long. I glance toward Licia, but it looks as if she's taken the opportunity to slip off. Is she truly okay with how the evening panned out, or could she really be cross with me? But the rest of the crowd now sways and taps their feet along with the next musician who takes the floor. I decide no one will miss me if I retire for the evening, rising slowly to keep unwanted attention at bay.

CHAPTER THREE

My body relaxes as the doors close behind me, dampening the sounds from the great hall and instantly putting space between me and everything King Hadeon said this evening.

I pay no attention to the guards lining the doorway as his words replay over and over again. *"...your duty... second chances."* Betrothed again.

I don't even know Lysander Sturdevant. I knew Avicii. And look how that ended.

The familiar feeling itches in my periphery. It comes on faster and frequently now since that day. I've learned it's only worse if I fight it, so I succumb to the anxiety enveloping me once again. Its spindly legs climb out from the darkness and wrap themselves around me, hooking me until I can't breathe. The walls, so wide and tall moments before, close in around me. The sea salt air from the bay tingles my senses with just a hint of frost as I inhale deeply, gasping for breath, trying to regain composure so I cling to it.

The crisp night air calls to me through the rising swell of emotions and I grip onto it like a lifeline. As my breathing continues to come in fits and gasps, I try to keep my attention on my steps. One foot in front of the other.

By the time I make it to the open terrace, I'm frantic for air. My nails dig into the banister. The unforgiving marble pushes back against my efforts, but I persist. I drink down the chilly autumnal air and it becomes the tonic to my thirsty lungs. The stone digs into my hips as I throw myself as far over the edge of the railing as I can, greedily taking in as much air as I can.

"Just breathe," an unfamiliar voice says from just behind me. The distraction jolts me from my head long enough to find a deep breath. Then another.

"There you go. In through your nose, out through your mouth." His melodic voice is soothing but I'm too tired to speak to another person tonight. Between Father's surprise announcement and the long journey here, my patience wears thinner by the moment.

"I know—" I take in another breath of air. "How to breathe," I say, instantly biting my tongue as the words tumble out. "I'm fine—let me be." The response is unlike me, but I'm too focused on finding my breath to worry if I've hurt a courtier's fragile feelings.

"Come now, I can't leave you like this. If you pass out, you'll likely fall over the railing and into the sea so far below. I'm involved now."

"I—" But the words get stuck in my throat. I push against the banister to stand and as gracefully as I can, wipe the wind-swept hair out of my face. His hand lightly presses against the small of my back, steadying me as I pat my hair and my dress back into place. As I look up though, I bite my tongue again, but for a different reason.

Standing in front of me is the bard. I misjudged his appearance.

He's not beautiful.

He's masculinity personified. His looks are completely debilitating. My knees turn to jelly and I grab onto his arm to steady myself. Looking up, I could get lost in the kaleidoscope of his eyes. The way the pale greens merge and sparkle with seafoam blue reminds me of those perfect days when the fields grow knee high with grasses and the wind moves just right, so if movement had a song, that would be it.

I glance around, knowing me conversing with a bard as soon as I return to the castle will have everyone talking. But we're the only ones standing outside the arching doorways, the entire court remains inside, enjoying the generous hospitality of my family.

His eyes show a flicker of surprise as he bows low before me. "Princess." The movement gives me just enough time to gather my own wits about me.

But it's short lived.

Black dots dance across my vision.

Many years in the healer's ward tell me because of my shallow breathing and standing up too quickly, I'm about to do exactly what he fears. I try to voice this, to warn him before I feel myself falling, but my words jumble in my throat and all that comes out is a cry. The vague thought flits through my mind that I'm going over the railing just as he said.

But two muscular arms wrap around me, fixing me here in both mind and body. Instead of fainting, I fall against his chest. Even in my fuzzy state of mind—the hard, chiseled lines that meet my forehead don't go unnoticed and the smell of fresh snow awakens my senses.

I can feel his body stiffen for a moment and then relax when I relax against him. The same arms that kept me from falling tighten around me, safely tucking me in close to his body. Just like Licia's hug upon my arrival, the contact is a feeling I didn't know I needed.

But unlike Licia's hug, the embrace awakens feelings I haven't felt in a long time. Feelings I thought had dissolved into darkness many, many years ago.

Footsteps break the silence between us; the moment we share fades as a demanding yell fills the air. "What's all this?" Two guards stand at the ready, their hands at their sword belts. They look from the man before me and then to me standing in his grasp, taking in the scene. By the matching stunned look on their faces, I can only imagine the state I'm in and what this must look like.

My savior moves to stand between me and the guards, using his body as a shield.

A mistake.

The guards instantly recognize me as this man before me shifts. "Step away from her! It's okay, Princess, you're safe now."

I open my mouth to explain the situation, but the guards draw their swords, causing me and the man before me to put our hands up placatingly.

"There's no cause for swords," the man before me speaks; his voice clear and steady as if he's still on stage in the great hall, not held here at sword point. "I'll go with you willingly." He waits until the guards are satisfied there's no further threat. One of them nods and motions him forward.

I stand there, dumbfounded and unable to say anything. My hands twist in my skirts as I try to find the right words to say or what to do to save him. As they retreat, him leading the death march, his back is stick straight and his shoulders squared in confidence as if there's nowhere else he'd rather be.

My mouth still opens and closes fruitlessly, gaping at what just happened. How did the moment change so quickly? His fate is sealed if those guards voice what they think happened. And there's nothing I can do about it.

"Wait!" I call as if stalling them for a moment longer will provide a solution. But there's nothing. The guards don't even pause.

But just as they turn back into the hallway, the bard turns back to me one last time. I thought when our eyes locked, I would find dread or defeat. Instead, he winks and sends a dazzling smile my way.

CHAPTER FOUR

I n the darkest hours of early morning, I jolt awake, unsure if it's still night or the new day. Surveying the damage, I notice my pillows are flung unceremoniously to the floor and my sheets are tangled around my ankles as well. My dreams, usually tame in their crafting, were confusing and wild all through the night. The dreams had something to do with the bard.

No, that's not quite right, perhaps his songs? It all felt so real. It all felt so dark.

I dreamt as if his songs were about me. Not about my father's conquests and honors, but my own. Which is silly because I never have, and never will have any conquests or adventures to speak of.

But that one song, the one with the slower melody, I can't get out of my head. It continues to wrap me in darkness, creeping in so the light he spoke of can't shine through. But no matter how hard I try to decipher it, it's covered by a thin veil, keeping it dampened and just out of reach.

At the moment, I certainly feel dampened and unseen. And by returning to my family and to court, I feel lost as if my old life is just out of reach.

I hoped returning to the castle would be a new beginning, one where I had a small say in where I spent my time. It seems this is far from the truth. I failed the first time, so of course Father demands I try again. I spend the rest of the night tossing and turning, with dreams of court and the arrival of Lysander Sturdevant from Etos and an opaque veil of darkness covering everything.

CHAPTER FIVE

When morning comes with her beams of sunlight brightening the room, I awake confused. The opulent drapes framing this enormous bed are unlike the small, basic furnished bedroom I shared with Avicii.

And then, unbidden once again, it all hits me like a summer storm—dark clouds roll in and unleash a torrent of emotions drenching my thoughts and leaving me wrecked.

I'm not in my own bed. I'm back at the castle. In my childhood bed.

Avicii is dead. The garden. Our fight. Our final fight. My failure to Avicii, to Father, to my kingdom.

I launch my last pillow over my head in an attempt to stop the memories from bombarding me.

If only feathers and silk could stop them.

A comforting sea of green surrounds me. The scent of tomatoes freshly cut from the vine fills the air as I lift my now full basket to make one last stop at the wildflowers. I'll pick a quick bouquet and then go in. Avicii always brightens when he sees the fresh flowers on the table. "You are the bright

wildflowers of my heart." He used to say each time I placed a jar of fresh cut flowers on the kitchen table.

"Ow!" I bring my finger to my mouth while looking for the cause of my sudden pain. A bee lies in the flower bed, no longer able to sting. No longer a threat. My finger swells and turns red in an instant, but I gently work the stinger out from the center with my dirt-filled fingernail.

"Rowandine?" a familiar voice calls from the stables. And then quieter as if to himself. "Where has that woman gone off to now?" I didn't expect Avicii for another day or two. He helps me up from the ground, his callused hands warm in my own. I grunt with the strain of the full basket of crops I've managed to harvest today. Avicii takes my hand rake, trowel, and pruning shears from my hands, adding them to my basket before he hefts the crops over his shoulder and I gather my bouquet as we begin our way back to the house. He sighs, the exasperation is clear on his face, but not anger. Not yet. "You know you shouldn't be out here all day digging around in the dirt. It's not good for the baby. Just in case. You need to be careful."

And there it is. The same fight we have every month when my courses return. I brace myself for the oncoming storm and he sees the moment when I flinch. His hand drops from my arm, causing me to stumble a moment before I can right myself on my own.

"Again?" he asks, the color rising in his face along with the frustration. I straighten at the familiar tone, preparing myself for what's to come. With my free hand, I press my thumbnail into the throbbing bee sting, an attempt to anchor myself before it all falls apart, again.

"I'm sorry, Avicii. I don't know what's wrong," I mumble with disappointment as thick as molasses in my mouth. Once again, I'm unable to give him the one thing he asks of me. Of what my kingdom asks of me.

"I know what's wrong." I look up at him, confused at the certainty in his voice. But the small glimmer of hope kindling to life deep inside me at his understanding vanishes when I see the familiar rage in his eyes. "What your father gave me is broken. I should've pressed him harder for Licia. Your sister would've at least been able to produce a child."

His words land like a slap across my face. Being compared to Licia is nothing new, we've grown up next to each other all our lives and I've heard the whispers. Our differences have always been apparent, and I know I've always appeared as the weed in her garden, but to hear this—this from my husband. My husband who once loved and cared for me.

But no longer.

Rage overcomes him. His fists clench and unclench. I watch, knowing I'll be fine as long as he—I try to inch myself backward as the rage reaches his arms, shaking and fierce. But this only infuriates him further, fueling the anger now radiating off of him.

"If there is no heir, then—"

"I may be royal, but I am the youngest. My brother is the one who will produce an heir, no one is concerned with what the third child can or can't produce." I try to sound reasonable, but we've had this discussion too many times to count.

"That's not how your father sees it, and you know it."

I cringe, knowing he's spoken to my father about this and he's right. Hadeon sees this as a slight to him personally and a black mark against our family being the fertile bunch he claims. This will shed unwanted light on the fact that Killian has only produced two girls so far and Licia's untried womb.

Light feet pad across the marble floors of the bedroom, pulling me from my nightmare. My memories. I lift the pillow off of my head and slowly look toward the sound.

"Are you asleep?" Licia's voice is low and scratchy with sleep and a hint of something I could probably identify if I'd slept better. "I thought I heard you talking." She looks around the room as if I've hid someone behind the curtains.

I launch the pillow at her, surprised at her assumption. Exhaustion still pulls at me, but I've missed this. "I must've been talking in my sleep." I make space beside me and pull the covers open, knowing Licia will join.

"Bad dream? Have you had a lot of those since—" Her voice trails off, but I know she means since Avicii passed so unexpectedly. Little does she know it's not just the nightmares that keep me up as of late.

"Must've been. Yes and no, it's all a lot to process so suddenly," I answer honestly. Her presence warms the room and chases away the lingering darkness.

"Well, this may help a tiny bit." The smell of clove and cinnamon warm my insides as she wafts a sweet roll under my nose. I'm instantly more awake. My favorite pastry? But that must mean...

"Happy birthday!"

"It's my—our—it's the eleventh already? Oh!" I throw my arms around her. "Happy birthday to you, too! I've completely forgotten. With everything going on, I barely know what day it is."

She hands me the plate, frowning at my pain, and reaches down to grab the pillow I threw at her, fluffing it until she's satisfied and joins me, snuggling down into the covers, just as we used to.

Even in sleep, we were inseparable. Using the last moments of the night and first moments of the morning to share secrets and dreams with each other.

She pulls apart the sweet roll as I pull from the other side. Our motions are rusty, but we easily fall into our birthday morning routine.

"Did you ever think on our thirty-fifth birthday," she begins around a full mouth of sweet, goey goodness, "we'd be sharing a sweet roll in our childhood room? One a maiden and one a widow?" Her big sigh is more telling than her words. She's not the only one disappointed in the way things have turned out.

I can't help but let out a laugh. "There's a maiden in this room?" I make a show of looking all around the room for someone else. "I hadn't realized we had company."

She laughs, elbowing me lightly in the side. "It's rude to mention a lady's indiscretions." She brings her free hand to her chest in mock outrage, her curling bangs falling into her eyes.

"I believe you were the one who brought it up, dear sister," I reply through a laugh that echoes into the high ceiling of the room.

A comfortable silence falls while we both pull another chunk from the roll.

But Licia brings up the inevitable. "You must miss him. You were so happy in your cottage tucked into the hills, far enough away from court to not be bothered," she says dreamily, and I realize it must indeed be a dream for her. She's still here, at the beck and call of our father and his politics. At thirty-five, she's reached a stage in life where societal expectations weigh heavily. I still don't understand why he kept us close all these years, almost too long for anyone to have us.

I choose my words carefully, knowing she's looking forward to her marriage, even though Father refuses every suitor who comes for her. "We were happy together." And that's accurate enough. It's just been so long since that was the case. "What about you? Who's been keeping you happy as of late?" I try to change the subject, the wound still too fresh to poke.

"Father mentioned you two weren't able to bond?" It's almost a whisper, but loud enough for me to hear. She's not looking at me, giving me a way out of the conversation if I want it.

Bonding with a partner isn't something everyone can do, and most humans can't. But it is something expected of royals. Killian and his wife bonded almost instantly. And although it can't be seen, if you know them well enough, there's a change in them both, especially when they're together.

Some people say it's a spark that surrounds the person and gets brighter when they're closer to their mate. Others say it looks like a colorful bubble just on the peripheral surrounding them. Licia always described it as more of a feeling when she was around people. Even when we were little, she would feel the air vibrating a certain way between two people and she just knew. I've never been able to see it, let alone feel it, so I wouldn't be sure what to look for. I was hoping to get my first glimpse with Avicii.

Unable to ignore Licia, I respond. "No. It never happened. I kept waiting for something. We tried everything—finishing each other's sentences, sleeping together under a full moon, feeding each other from a silver spoon. We even mixed our blood with an obsidian dagger." I cringe thinking about the last one, remembering the way my blood bloomed from beneath the steel blade as Avicii slid it across my palm.

Licia laughs outright at my absurd response and I try to mask my thoughts. "Those are all just silly superstitions. If you and he were mates, it just would have happened, with or without you willing it so."

My cheeks redden and I stare straight ahead, avoiding eye contact with her. "We knew that. But hoped there must be some sort of truth in one of them." What I leave unsaid is, I had hoped it would've made it easier to bear his child. Something we were never able to do. Something he reminded me of constantly. It was my fault.

She sits up, propping herself up on her elbow. "You're right. I would've tried everything under the stars as well. I'm sorry your bond never clicked into place. But something has changed within you. You're not yourself since you've been back."

She's right of course. I feel it, too. I can't put my finger on it, but I know it has to do with the last day I saw Avicii. I can't recall all that was said, but when the messenger found me at the cottage and handed me that letter, I couldn't even bring myself to cry. I only felt relief with the news. But I can't let her see my confusion, not when I don't know exactly how I feel or even what happened. So I just shrug at her comment.

"But tell me, there has to be a special someone?" I try again to change the subject. "Or a special *someones*?"

She smiles, hugging her knees into her chest and staring off dreamily. "There is someone. It's too early to tell, but I think it's something more this time. He's my everything, Roe!" She throws an arm across her eyes exaggeratedly, making light of her serious feelings and suggests he really is someone special, and it frightens her.

"I bet he is, if he has you stumbling over yourself." I try to hide my smile but can't help it.

"This is news! I'm so happy for you. Is it someone Father has introduced you to?" Knowing that if it's not, she'll have a hard time moving forward with anything more than the trysts she no doubt finds time for now.

The slow shake of her head and the way her lips curve from a wistful smile to a frown tell me otherwise though. There's no hope there. Her and her secret lover will only ever be that. No matter how her heart feels.

I wrap her hand in my own, our sticky fingers intertwining and the empty plate forgotten. She rests her head on my shoulder and I rest my head on top of hers. We stay there for just a moment. Her grieving for a love she'll never freely have and me trying to forget all that's happened since I thought I found love.

"Don't worry. We'll figure out just what you need and set you right." She pops up, visibly shaking off the mental cobwebs, at least for now.

"Speaking of that, I think what I want to do is spend the morning in the healer's ward." I follow her lead and start climbing out of the cozy nest we've made. "I don't think anyone will miss my absence."

"You know you shouldn't go down there, Roe. Father has made his thoughts very clear about that already."

I shrug her off. This is the one thing I won't bend so easily on. Being in the healer's ward is the only place I've ever felt myself—next to my garden in the hills. "I'll be discreet."

Before I disappear out the door, I look back at her. Her face is unreadable. "I'm sorry about the Etos king."

She looks at me as if her mind has already moved to the next task of the day. Her hand fans the air. "He's no match for me. And I'm not upset with you of all people."

Her reassuring smile carries me all the way to the ward.

Chapter Six

There's a light bounce of anticipation in my step as I turn down the last hallway before the ward. I follow the threadbare, azure carpets toward the small section of the southern wing given to the healers. Few courtiers, and rarely anyone outside of the family save the healers themselves, come all the way to this tower, so my father hasn't seen fit to update any of the furnishings or carpets since he's arrived. Instead of the golden banners of our house draping over what's left, I'm able to view the portraits of all the Fae who came before us.

This end of the castle is exactly as the Fae left it over thirty years ago. The intricate woodwork dances along the walls and the carefully handcrafted quilts hang along the stone walls hinting the Fae weren't as vicious as they're made out to be. But the way they drove apart their world and sectioned the realm off suggests otherwise. I've never been able to reconcile the two, though. Especially when I get to the portraits of the rulers just before Father. Queen Bronwinn and King Azulean were so regal. They look as if they're still watching over us, almost waiting for their moment to return.

My smile falters as Father's proclamation rings again in my head. Why wasn't Etos Licia's match? By all counts, it should've been her. She's older, if only by a few moments. She's more beautiful by everyone's standards.

And she's always been his favorite. She's the clear match to a king of such stature.

It was different with Avicii and me. With us, Father broke propriety because we were so clearly in love—or so I thought—and Avicii was his right-hand man. Since Avicii favored me—or so I thought—how could Father say no?

To overlook Licia twice doesn't make sense. And for her still to be unwed and at the castle, after all these years, something isn't adding up. Although Father makes it difficult to have much of a life inside these castle walls, she's clearly making it work here with her trysts and networks that keep her more than busy.

A faint tune winds its way down the hall, distracting me from my thoughts. The soft strumming is so similar to last night. I try to shake it off as a memory. But as I proceed down the hallway, I peek my head into one of the old libraries.

Amidst the dusty, untouched books and furniture that could be a hundred years old, there he is. My delight he's in one piece and not rotting away in the dungeons is quickly eclipsed by his good looks. He's even more beautiful this morning than he was last night, surrounded by the entire court and all the finery. His thick, dark twists of hair fall into his face as he strums a tune. His all-black attire swallows the light surrounding him. The late morning light streams in through the windows stretching from the floor up to the ceiling, and it catches in the strings along his instrument as he plays, drawing me in closer. My fingertips brush against the tops of velveteen chairs set in front of an empty fireplace as I walk closer to the large window, overlooking the gardens. And closer to him. My breath quickens as if sensing danger.

Before I know it, I'm standing right in front of him. Am I really that bold?

"Good morning, Princess." In one smooth movement, he stands up and places his four-string beside him, closing the distance between us.

I inhale deeply, momentarily distracted by his graceful movements. "Stars above." Escapes from my lips and I can feel my face redden from the lack of control. He's just so gorgeous and the way he plays—

"I'm sorry, Princess?" A look of confusion and perhaps a little smugness plays across his face in the crooked smile and narrowing of his eyes.

He's close. And just like last night, his fresh frost and pine scent wraps around me. He reaches out and his fingers brush my cheek as he pushes a stray curl behind my ear. I catch myself leaning into the feeling, the softness of his touch, the closeness of the gesture.

But instantly, Avicii flashes in my mind—his tall, wiry frame, not unlike the man before me, and the look he used to give me after weeks of being away from home, like I was the first blossom after a long winter.

Just as quickly, a shudder rolls through me as his prone form flashes through my mind. An image of the last time I saw him. His unseeing eyes staring up into the clouds and his body framed with the very garden that kept me company every day he was away.

Noticing the change, the bard takes a step back. Without saying anything, he assesses me trying to find the change. His brow furrows and he puts his hands in his pockets—a hesitance that wasn't there before coloring the moment.

I try to recapture it, grasping at anything.

"Forgive me—" I don't recall if Licia ever said his name last night.

As I wait for him to fill in the blank, I notice his features are the very definition of masculine perfection. His chiseled jawline and high cheekbones give the impression he's been cut from dark stone. His clothing is simple but cut to fit him with precision. At first glance, his shirt is rather plain, but with closer inspection, I notice the intricate embroidery of the same color sewn along the wrists and neckline when he moves. It's as if he's wealthier than he lets on. But that must be my imagination. When I glance at my incredibly simple dress, I can imagine he's probably thinking the opposite about my basic mourning black.

He gives a small bow to introduce himself. As he straightens to his full height, I crane my neck upward to keep eye contact with him.

"Thaddeus. Thaddeus Quicksilver." His lyrical words swirl around me.

"You play—forgive me, bard—Thaddeus, but you play as if gifted by the stars themselves." I recover my blundering rather poetically.

"I'd like to think I am," he says with all the assurance of one who has indeed been gifted by the stars and I can't help but laugh.

Unfortunately, it doesn't come out as a pleasant titter of one whose been trained her entire life here at court, but a loud bark of a laugh from someone whose been hungry for conversation for too long. His lips press together, an attempt to stifle his amusement, which only causes my cheeks to redden further. "But I thank you for the compliment, Princess. It's certainly not all who think so." He gives another small bow as he says this then takes my hand in his own and brushes the tops of my knuckles with a gentle kiss. And with the soft way his lips brush my hand, my thoughts drift to what those lips would feel like brushing their way down my neckline. How with each exhale, his breath would tickle across my skin. And with his gaze still on my own, I can feel the blush rising along said neckline and further into my cheeks.

His cool touch sends a zing from my fingertips to my toes, breaking my revery. He flips my hand over and traces the lines on my palm. As his touch pauses on the twin fresh scars, I have to fight the overwhelming feeling to pull my hand away, knowing that he couldn't possibly guess what the lines are from. But does he pause a moment too long? Or is this my imagination?

I should just thank him and continue down to the healer's ward. I can't take much more of this embarrassment I continue to heap upon myself. With my gaze locked on the space between my knuckles where his kiss lingers, I try to find the simple words I can say and then be on my way.

"Thank you for last night." Easy and straightforward.

Except the gleam returning in his eyes says my words are anything but. And I know Licia's description of him is more than accurate. There's something about him that screams for me to turn and run. But I can't help but bite the inside of my cheek to keep from smiling.

"I couldn't leave once I was involved. I'm involved now."

"I was just tired from a day of travel." I feel the need to defend why I was in such a state.

"Of course, being on the road for any length of time is exhausting. Especially by carriage. The stuffy box gets old when there's little to look at. I'd much rather take it all in by horseback, if I may be so bold." He moves toward the window as he says this, looking out across the expanse of the boxwoods lining the garden and the road beyond that leads out of the gates of Merula and beyond.

I try to imagine riding horseback all that way. It seems daunting, but for other reasons. But could it also be invigorating? Some of the best days at the cottage were when I had crops to share and would spend the day riding around the mountainside to our closest neighbors. The wind dancing through my hair, the rhythmic clomping of Navi, covering ground faster than I can take in—the experience was always uplifting.

"All the golden hues are riveting. And when they start to mix with dusk, it's a veritable treat." His bright smile matches the light in his eyes. I wouldn't have guessed he'd have so much to say about the countryside. It almost makes me feel as if I took the ride back to the castle for granted. But my thoughts on this ride in particular were heavier than the golden rays of autumn.

"I've never seen the countryside through such an artistic lens. The way you speak of shades of gold and dusk is the same way you sing your songs."

"It's just where I'm from, there's not much color."

"You're from the north?" The only place I can think of without color is where it snows relentlessly and the land is covered in layers upon layers of ice. Something I've only seen from afar.

"Yes, I'm originally from Freathia. But, as a bard, I've traveled all over the realm."

"It's never snowed here in Merula," I say as I look out toward the farmers' fields, remembering how brilliant the shades of gold were there as I rode through. A smile tugs at my mouth, perhaps I've a little artist within me as well; I just hadn't realized it before.

"What do you find so amusing?"

"Your artistry is contagious, it appears." I look past him out the window. The colors brilliantly meld together in a way I've never noticed before.

A comfortableness settles between us that wasn't here moments before. Something I haven't felt in so long. But something I shouldn't and can't explore for more reasons than I can count, it seems.

Backing away, I attempt to make my excuses to leave. "I'm sorry for interrupting your practice, I heard your playing and just wanted to thank you. I'm headed down to the healer's ward."

"Are you ill?" A look of concern clouds his sharp features as he looks me up and down, searching for the cause of my ailment.

"I'm fine. I just... helping the healing. I mean—" I can feel my cheeks redden once again; the comfortable feeling dissipating with my stumbling. "I help heal those in the ward. It's been a while, and I was headed there until I heard you playing," I manage to get out, taking a small step back in preparation to exit the room.

"You're a healer then?" he asks, the now familiar uneven smile across his lips growing.

"Yes. I mean, no. I mean, yes, if it was up to me, then I would be. But of course." My arms flail before me, trying to illustrate what I mean, but coming up about as successful as my words. "Of course, I can't."

"Well, I'm sure there's more to you than first meets the eye, Princess." The way he mocks my title is both infuriating and refreshing. I haven't felt like a princess these past years in the mountains. But when he says it, it's as if he means it. He returns to strumming his four-string, watching as I make my exit.

Unsure of a proper response to such a statement, I nod and quickly turn to go. Then, turn once more. "I look forward to hearing you play some more, Thaddeus."

He looks up from his instrument, and his pale green eyes pierce me with their lightness. "And I would play for you anytime, Princess."

My eyes widen and I turn to go before he can see my response. I've never been good at hiding my feelings. Especially when I can feel the blush rise along my cheeks as sure as the sun. Once more, I find myself astonished by the way my body responds to him—a traitorous reaction that stirs something deep within me. It's as if I've been transported back to my youth, where emotions swirl uncontrollably, leaving me both exasperated and exhilarated. This intoxicating blend of feelings is a reminder of the thrill of desire, a sensation that is as maddening as it is invigorating.

I stop just outside the door, taking in slow breaths to regain my composure while he continues to pick haphazardly across the strings in a light and playful way. Stars above, that is—he is—I can't even gather my thoughts quickly enough. I press myself against the wall, letting his light song bring comfort and calm before I step into the bustle of the healer's ward.

Bold is the first word that comes to mind. He's bold in a way I've never experienced. Not like father's take-what-is-mine boldness. Or Killian's grown-up-royal boldness. Not bold in the way Licia knows she's beautiful, nor in the way Avicii knew he was so powerful.

At the thought of Avicii again, I look down at the mourning black of my dress. The embarrassment floods my features all over again. My shameful body. How could it respond in such a way to someone not even weeks after my husband died?

A small, insistent part of my mind reminds me that even with Avicii, my body never responded like it does from the small touches and almost-smiles from Thaddeus. Avicii never looked at me the way Thaddeus does. Like he wants to lay me down in front of a burning fireplace and slowly undress me, watching the way the firelight plays against my skin before he devours me from neck to navel.

Now, my body and my mind defy me. I can't fall for him—the very bard Licia warned against. He's dangerous. He feels dangerous. The very air around him crackles and drips with danger. But, stars help me, that's one of the reasons I'm so drawn to him. Avicii was so safe, and look where that got me. But now is not the time for me to get wrapped up in another man.

I'm a widow in mourning. And apparently promised to the king of Etos. I know what's expected of me. I know my place in this game. Why doesn't my body fall in line?

The memories of Avicii and of Thaddeus' light touch threaten to return so I push against the stone wall separating me and Thaddeus, propelling myself away from the thoughts that haunt me and toward my place of solace.

Soon, the familiar fresh scent of sun-bleached sheets fills my lungs and washes a much-needed calmness over me. The tall windows are thrown open to let in the cool sunlight and the crisp, autumn air.

On my way into the wide open room, I grab an old apron in an attempt to keep my gown clean. The rows of beds along the perimeter of the room are mostly empty this morning, except for a few people still asleep.

Healers move around the room with strident purpose. Between their bustling forms I soon spot a tall frame I know well. She's draped in layers of blue drooping fabric and her silver hair is piled messily on the crown of her head, flopping with each move she makes. Her eyes are a bright, earthy green, a color so rich I always thought they held a whole treasure trove of knowledge. Her small, pointy nose gives her a childish appearance despite her years, starkly contrasting the many wrinkles lining her eyes. She spots me and moves my way. Her arms are laden down with bandages and small jars of herbs, so I grab a few to lighten her load.

"My sweet Rowandine! You're a sight for these old eyes." She wraps her now free hands around me, clasping my face in her hands, and looking me up and down. "Ten years is too long to go without my best apprentice. And the happiest of birthdays, my dear."

I bask in the warmth of her embrace. The familiar smell of cinnamon and herbs wrap around me, lightening my load if for just one moment. "I've missed you so, Thaliya. And I can't thank you enough for the seeds and supplies you sent me with on my wedding day. I would've been completely lost if it wasn't for you. Who knew I'd be up in the hills of Merula for so long?"

She assesses me; her hard gaze speaking volumes. She knew—it would appear—and did not agree with how Avicii whisked me away. At the time I thought it was terribly romantic, but now—I know better.

"Well, thank the blessed stars we have you back in one piece. And you always seem to appear just when I need you," she says, wrapping an arm around my shoulder and turning with me, gesturing toward the bare shelves against the wall. "Take these and restock the shelves, and then you can work alongside me until you find your footing once again."

I carry the handful over toward the shelves but as I walk past the backdoor, I barely miss colliding with a screaming woman who barrels in with a young child in her arms. I'm closest to the door, so the woman shoves the small girl into my arms. The dried herbs and supplies spill everywhere and are instantly forgotten. The woman's frantic screams follow me as I rush toward the closest bed with the weight of the limp child weighing down each hurried step.

CHAPTER SEVEN

While assessing the prone child, I try to focus on the woman's words, most of which are too shrill and incoherent to catch at all. The young girl can't be older than eight and is unconscious. After a quick assessment, I don't see any blood or obvious injuries. Her dark skin has an ashy pallor, which is worrisome, and her tiny hands are cold to the touch.

"What happened before she fell unconscious?" I turn back to the woman, cradling her hand. The contact has a calming effect on her. She looks down at the girl and takes a deep breath, as if realizing her words are the key to saving the small child.

"My Ness—" Tears slide down her cheeks. She blinks them away and tries again. "Nessie, my daughter, was out playing this morning while I was preparing the bread for the day."

Thaliya, sensing a serious problem, has found her way to the mother's side. She pulls her in close while the woman's body wracks with sobs she desperately tries to stifle. "The soldiers came. On one of their raids for food. Usually, they don't bother those of us in Merula, but I've heard tell of them bothering the homes of those who can't stand up to them. I hated to do it, but I had just told Ness of the raids and to be wary. She's still so young, happy, and full of hope—" Her ramblings, the parts I can make out, paint a picture of brutality I can't even fathom. "There must've been at least six of them. With my little Nessie standing her ground, not seeing the danger of turning them away—the child is truly afraid of nothing." She turns into Thaliya, stating the last part as an important aside.

"The king's soldiers?" I ask. Thaliya reprimands me with narrowed eyes at the incredulous tone in my voice. But I can't help it. I can't believe the king's guards would harm a child. The bruises covering the child tell a different story, though. The woman glances at me and then back to Thaliya.

Thaliya soothes her by gently rubbing her arm. "What happened between Nessie and the soldiers?" she asks, bringing the woman back to the issue at hand.

"Words were said. Nessie, ever headstrong, even in the face of grown men, wouldn't let them pass through the gate. She knew they were after our pantry and she wasn't going to let them take all we've stocked up for the winter ahead, knowing they'd take more than their share. They surrounded her. The ring of the first slap, followed by Ness falling to the ground had me running, no longer frozen in place watching this horror unfold. I ran at them with my tea towels flapping in my hands." She gives a small, hysterical laugh. "I guess they didn't want an audience. I think I spooked them, but not before one of them delivered a swift kick to her stomach. They turned as one and walked off."

My mind races with this information, but I try to focus on the parts that will help the child. If the kick hit just so, she could be bleeding from the inside. If this happened this morning, she could've been bleeding for hours before the mother brought her here. I look up and meet Thaliya's gaze and her face hardens into the same facade I've seen before. She sees it, too. There's little we can do for the child now, but we'll try anything to save her.

Another healer guides the mother, now besotted with tears, away so Thaliya and I can work. We both kneel beside the child's bedside and the buzz of the ward falls away until it's just me, Thaliya, and the child.

"There's not much we can do for her now." She clasps the child's hand and shakes her head, a barely perceivable tremble to the strong woman's features.

"We have to try. There has to be something we can do." My hands rest over the girl's abdomen. "I know there's something we can do."

Something changes in the way she looks at me, assessing or weighing how invested I am.

"Yes," she says simply.

"Yes?" Confused, I look around the room and then back at the child, thinking someone will come to save her, someone I haven't yet discerned.

"Okay, we will do this. *You* will do this." She gets up to pull the curtains around this bed and returns, placing herself across from me. She places her hands on top of mine, still resting on the child's stomach. "Remember, Roe, know yourself, know your path." She repeats the phrase I have grown up with. One she would start each lesson with no matter how small. Even after all these years, I use this as my mantra to recenter myself amid all the chaos. The panicking mother behind me fades into the quiet buzz and my breathing slows with the phrase repeating in my mind, *know yourself, know your path.*

I ready myself for her instruction, but nothing comes. I look up from where our hands rest together with question. But I only find she's looking at me expectantly as if I should know what to do.

Time is running out, I can feel the young girl's heartbeat slowing, and her lips are tinged blue around the edges. I don't understand what Thaliya is trying to show me, but there's a tightness growing in my chest and it's getting difficult to ignore.

Her pursed lips and furrowed brow tell me she's waiting for something. I wish she'd clue me in on what it is so I can move forward. This girl's life is in our hands and she's waiting. "What are you waiting for?" I blurt out, trying for a whisper, but the anxiety I feel ratchets it up to more of a whine.

"What are *you* waiting for, Rowandine? Use what you know. Use what you can feel," she says, still patiently awaiting me to figure out her puzzle. She waits a beat longer and evidently takes pity on me. "Close your eyes. Use what you feel to help her."

"I feel as if I should get someone else to help," I say; the frustration rising alongside the panic. Thaliya bats at my hand in reprimand but does not lose focus on the girl.

"Close your eyes. Envision where the bleeding is. Feel how to fix it." She pats my hands again and nods me forward.

I stare at her a moment, replaying her words to make sure I hear her correctly. Deciding she did in fact just say heal this child through feeling, I give a slight shake of my head, unsure of what she's asking me to do. But I close my eyes, trying to figure out how to focus on what I feel.

"Can you feel it?" she prods.

"Yes, yes of course I feel it." At first, I just feel the child's skin beneath my fingertips, cool to the touch. I don't want to let Thaliya down, though.

But then, I try to visualize what's going on within the child. It feels wrong, like there's too much blood in a place it shouldn't be. I can feel her pain and how her little body is fighting to hold on. I grab onto that fighting feeling and wrap it within my desire to heal her.

A warmth begins to grow in my palms. At first, I think I've made it worse and she's bleeding out before us, but no. When I crack my eyes open, there's no blood, just Thaliya's hands on top of my own and a pale white-green light glowing underneath. Startled, I jolt back. But Thaliya holds tight so our connection doesn't break. She murmurs comforting, inaudible sounds and encourages me to continue.

I close my eyes once more, falling back into whatever we've created. With my eyes closed, I use the warmth from the light and try to point it toward the broken and bleeding parts of the child. The light doesn't need more than a small nudge before it knows its path and where to go. In my mind's eye, I can see it mending its way through the child. The way the warmth fills all the cracks and patches and broken spots is too much to comprehend. But the bleeding dissipates and I can even feel her skin start to warm and her breathing even out.

I'm afraid to open my eyes, but Thaliya's hands fall away from my own and she whispers,

"There, there." Tears slip from my closed eyelids because I think she's comforting me for an impossible job with an impossible outcome. But the child's body shifts and when I look to see what's happening, she's trying to twist out of my arms and off the bed, searching for her mother.

Something between a sob and a laugh escapes me as I sit on my heels and watch as Thaliya reaches back and removes the curtains. Instantly, the mother swoops in and swallows her daughter with hugs and kisses.

Thaliya's movements catch my eye. She's busying herself to give the family some space, so I follow suit. As soon as we're out of earshot of anyone else, the question bursts from my lips. "What just happened?"

"You felt it." I notice then that she's practically vibrating with pride.

"You're ready."

"Ready? For what? Wait, Thaliya—"

She moves quickly to the back of the ward where her office is. She motions me into an old chair beside the fire and sits opposite of me in its match. I try once more now that the bustle of the ward has fallen away and only the gentle crackle of the fire before us fills the room. "What just happened?"

She smooths her apron across her dress, busying her hands while she finds the right words. She takes too long, so I begin. "There was a light. A light coming out of my hands." I stare down at the offending appendage, but there's no trace of the glow—the magic—from moments ago. "Thaliya, we fixed the girl. With light." This can't mean that I—there's no way. My father is the one responsible for ending magic's hold on the human race.

"Yes." She smiles. I can see pride and exhaustion in the way her eyes crinkle at the edges. She leans in closer with her elbows on her knees. The firelight dances behind her, bathing the room in comforting warmth.

"But that would mean." I lean in closer and my voice drops low, even though we're completely alone. I swallow hard before managing to get the words out. "That there's magic here."

"There's always been magic here. Merula was home to the Fae first, after all."

"No." I bolt upright as if stung. That can't be. There hasn't been magic in Merula since Father overtook the Fae. He freed the humans from their inferiority in the shadows of the Fae and other magical races before they used their magic to destroy us and wipe humankind off the continent. I shake my head. "No."

Thaliya's lips thin with unease, but she pushes forward. "And you're a part of that magic."

Thrown off by her truths, I look at my hands once again where the pale green light emanated from, but now, they just look the way my hands have always looked—a little callused from my work in the gardens and earth and the two parallel lines of fresh scars, but nothing special.

"You felt it, just now. You felt the power of the earth's magic coursing through your body. So powerful, you were able to heal that little girl, an impossible task." Her voice is gentle and slow as if she's explaining something to a child.

"That can't—I can't—" I look up, but she's nodding as I try to work this out.

"You have something special within you, so special. So special you don't even know how much you can—"

I think about my poultices, and how they work quicker than any other healer's. Even the ones who have continued on with their studies way beyond where I'll ever be. I think about the way if I lay my hands on someone who's wounded or ill, I can always make quick assessments about what should be done.

And what about my gardens? And how any person who came by the cottage always remarked on how exceptional they were. Even Avicii was beyond surprised at my garden. I'll never forget how he looked at me the first time he came home. His response was so excessive, and not with the excitement I felt at the time. I should've known right then—both about Avicii and the magic.

"Can you do this, too?" Raising my hands and spinning them back and forth, trying and failing to completely grasp what *this* is and unable to hear more about myself at the moment.

Her nodding stops and she leans back in her chair. "Yes. The others here don't know I do. Maybe they sense it, but they're unaware they have a Fae with earth magic in their midst." She motions toward me. "Two, in fact."

I blink and go completely still. If what she says is true, then I am not an Aeronwick, I'm entirely something else.

Chapter Eight

"So... what you're saying is, I'm part Fae?"

"Not just part Fae. You're a full-blooded Fae. And royalty. The rightful heir to the Everguard throne." She's speaking more quickly now, like she's held onto these words for a lifetime and can't hold them in a moment longer.

"But that can't be. This doesn't make sense." I try to count the years since I came of age, but it's been too long to count under duress. "Any magic would've shown itself during puberty. Everyone knows this." What I don't say is this is actually when many villagers fall ill and die of mysterious illnesses. The rumors that circled spoke of Fae magic misfiring. Killing those who were burdened with magic, but Thaliya sees the fear before I fully comprehend it. "Am I going to die?"

Everyone knows the Fae have been cursed, the dark magic that flows through their veins twisted them into something unnatural. This is why Father came to Everguard in the first place, to rid the people of such a scourge.

"No, Rowandine. You will not die. You are not sick. In fact, you'll probably long outlive us all." She gathers my hands into her own, and I can feel the love and sincerity flowing from her.

"Everything you know of the Fae has been a lie. Everything you know of

Everguard is skewed to protect your family."

I hear what she doesn't say—that my father rewrote the history of an entire realm.

"Your mother, by birth, knew the obstacles you'd face as you grew up. She bound your magic tightly to your heart, so it would only unfurl if your life was threatened or you loved deeply. I can only imagine the trials you faced at Avicii's hands."

I look up, stunned that she could guess at something I've locked so far within myself, even I can't recall the worst of it.

"But now, your magic has fully awakened, and now it is time."

Fully awakened? Parts of this conversation feel familiar. But how can that be? This is all new. Before this, I was just a woman trading her princess crown for a farmer's trowel and hand rake. A woman who spent time with her husband when he was in between tasks for the king.

Avicii. Did he know?

After all this time, small pieces of that last day I saw him keep trying to wriggle free of the chest I locked them in. Moments I still don't want to remember.

And now, magic pulses beneath my skin.

The garden. I could grow anything in that garden. We always had plenty to share with families around us who needed it. But today, I actually felt the earth sing beneath my skin. The last time I felt this was—I shake that day off, but not before the look on Avicii's face resurfaces from where I buried it.

Buried. Wrong choice of words. A shiver dances up my spine.

The thoughts in my head are a maelstrom. I try to grab onto one that makes sense.

"Time?"

"Time for the Fae to return to their rightful place. For you to return to where you were meant to be. For you to take back your throne."

I reel back in the chair, letting the soft cushions swallow me. I stare at her a moment, replaying what she just said. Thaliya, who I trust more than anyone—who I've never once questioned—sits before me telling me the impossible. This is all too much.

"But if I'm Fae— if my family finds out—" I look up, hoping to find a gentle answer on her face, but she nods, solemnly confirming my fears. I nod along with her, but for a different reason.

"They can't find out. I can't take the throne. I can't do what you ask of me. I'm just a gardener. I'm just a healer. I'm promised to another realm. I have nothing for the people of Everguard. Nothing."

Suddenly, the office that has always been my haven is too small. The hazy warmth of the fire becomes stifling. I open my mouth to say something to Thaliya, but can't decide what should come out. Waiting a moment, I close my mouth once more. She watches, waiting for me to gather my thoughts. I know she wants me to stay and ask questions. Be a part of what she asks, like I've always done before. But this time she's asking too much.

I lurch for the door, tripping and grabbing for the handle as if my life depends on it. I don't even turn back. I don't even respond at all. I leave, rushing out of the healer's ward as fast as I can, not caring if I draw attention to myself on my way out.

I run through the hallway, unconcerned when heads turn, and not stopping until the chatter in the hallway and the storm in my mind is swallowed up by something else. I dive into the first doorway that isn't a blur. Falling onto the chaise in the middle of the room. The velveteen pillows dry my tears as I bury my head in them. Fae? Could I truly be Fae? Royalty is something I've always been, and to no consequence.

Until now it seems.

I didn't even ask about my family. What that means. Just the weight of knowing is too much to bear. But I'm curious. Fae royalty, as in Queen Bronwinn and King Azulean? They were brutal and unforgiving leaders. And they were responsible for separating all the races. The shifters now reside in the west, the Elementals and Conjurs in the east, and the Ancients have all but hidden themselves away in the mountainous north. Could I possibly have this all wrong, though? Has everything been a lie crafted by the very man I thought was my father?

This, as well as the thought of me sitting on the throne, is too much to swallow. I've always just been a part of the background. My only part to play was to marry, which I did, happily at first, and it only ended in disaster.

Now, though, according to Thaliya, I have a bigger part to play.

Warring with this new knowledge is the thought that marriage to Lysander Sturdevant from Etos is what's expected of me. My father has arranged it, my family is proud of the match despite me already being widowed, and the people of Merula expect it of me. I'm expected to do what is right and what is best for Merula and the realm of Everguard.

Despite what Thaliya says, my true path is clear. There is only one path to follow. The one that is best for all involved. My sobs fade into sniffles as I make up my mind.

Only then do the calming, melodious sounds register and I realize I'm not alone here.

Chapter Nine

"Princess," a strong voice says behind me, punctuated by the strums of his four-string. "What could trouble someone such as yourself?" I don't look up from the pillows but can feel him move around the room until he sits beside me on the chaise. His fingers comb through the tangles of my curls, hesitant at first, but when I don't protest, his fingers move as expertly as they strum his strings. I shudder then relax into the contact.

Turning to face him, I know I must look a complete mess. My dress is covered in stains from the healer's ward, my hair has all but discarded the tie holding it back, and I can feel how sticky and tear stained my burning cheeks are.

But something about him relaxes me, just being near him is soothing. And something about his calm demeanor nudges me toward him. It's as if I've known him all my life. Like the silences between Licia and me during our studies. No matter how long quiet fell over us, I could feel her beside me, and even through the silence, we both felt the comfort and solidarity between us.

As soon as I turn toward him, his fingers trace my tears, drying them with the softest touch. He looks at me; his eyes searching for an answer.

"I thought I knew who I was, what my place was here, but it would seem

I know nothing. And it's too much." My words pour out, confiding in a stranger seems safe. Like anything I say will dissolve into the air around us. I lean into him, finding a small amount of strength in the contact.

"But don't you know? When you know nothing is when you're able to learn the most." I tuck my legs beneath me and allow him to pull me in closer. "I believe it's when you think you know everything is when you get yourself into trouble."

"I wish I believed you. But I've known my place my whole life. I've known the plan for Merula and my part in it. The best way for me to be a part of Merula's future is to play that part. And up until now, I had no problem doing so." I speak into the safety of his chest, surprised at how bold I'm acting, and how right this feels. With my hand resting on the pure muscle there it distracts me from the raging thoughts in my mind. I try to recall the last time I found myself in the embrace of a man but nothing comes to mind. Avicii was never one to spend time afterward together, and even though there were others before him, I can't recall feeling so comforted by a man's touch. "But after today, I'm not so sure."

My hand brushes against something hard between us. I lean back out of his embrace. "What's this?"

"Ah, my dagger." He unbuckles it and puts it beside us. "You never know when you'll need one." He shrugs and his bright, playful smile lightens the struggle in my mind. I can't help but laugh.

"There you are," he says, and those simple words make my heart flutter. Something it's been doing a lot lately. Around him.

I trace his smile with my fingertips, unable to pull my gaze away as I think about how kissable it is. How I shouldn't get involved with him. How I shouldn't be attracted to him. How he shouldn't be attracted to a widow.

But how kissable are those lips?

His eyes grow dark as if my thoughts are written across my face. I bite my lip, unsure where this can go, but I can feel his attraction, and this, he is what I want.

And in the midst of this moment, I can feel the difference between myself wanting something and agreeing to something someone I love desires of me. This feeling is different and a little exciting. I lean in, inches away from those kissable lips.

But I can't do this.

I'm recently widowed. I'm promised to another. For my realm. I can't indulge with Thaddeus.

"I can't." I push away so fast I almost fall backward. His quick hands catch me from falling but don't move to pull me in again. He looks from my lips to my eyes to the doorway behind him, trying to decipher what's changed. "I can't do this. I'm sorry."

With his hands on my hips, he guides me to standing. His demeanor is calm, but I can see the confusion in his eyes as he stands as well, giving me the distance I need.

CHAPTER TEN

Blades of grass tickle my elbows and under my knees. The warmth of the late afternoon sun and the crisp autumn scent of dormant leaves fills the garden. The surrounding scent grounds me. From my vantage point laying on the ground, only the highest edges of the garden brush my vision. Otherwise, the late afternoon skies paint a blank canvas across my mind, which is exactly what I need after what Thaliya imparted to me. After what happened with Thaddeus. My mind's still reeling.

But I know what I did was right with Thaddeus. The vast blue slate above me helps me forget everything.

Ever since Thaliya explained my earth magic, I've made the connection to how I've always loved lying sprawled on the ground and how it brings me peace and clarity. I've tried several places around the castle lands, but lately, this spot here, surrounded by the small pond and the gurgling statue of a beautiful woman reaching toward the sky, has been most comforting.

My palms skim back and forth across the blades of grass, the small movement is comforting as I will the sky to whisper the answers, any answers, to me to calm my swimming mind.

Closing my eyes, I sink down into where my newly awakened power sits, humming, waiting. It warms me, from the inside out, and I let it wash over me in gentle waves. The feeling of such warmth, such power, is something

I haven't felt yet, outside the safety of the healer's ward. Outside the safety of Thaliya's instruction.

Now, instead of directing my magic into healing someone, I just sit with it, learning the feel of it. The way it feels like a new limb awakening within, prickling back to life after losing feeling. The power builds and churns within, curling around my senses while looking for a place to go, like vines creeping up a gate post.

The thick, cool blades of grass bring me back into the moment and the feeling within becomes too much to hold onto, to hold inside myself, so I open my eyes.

What I find is startling.

What, moments ago, was brown with the changing of the seasons, is now a lush green. Small red flowers bloom along the pond and weave themselves along the great garden walls. Even the grass around me has become plusher, the blades gently pressing me into a sitting position.

The scene surrounding me is incredible, but it doesn't make any sense. Even the air smells ripe with spring.

Am I dreaming?

No.

This is my doing. I can feel the magic in the earth reaching out toward me, asking, waiting for me. I had no idea my earth magic could be so beautiful and awake—so different from healing, yet so similar.

I hesitate then brush my fingers across the grass, touching one of the pointed, blooming flowers leaning toward me. It's not an illusion. All of this is real, and I created it. I swallow a laugh as I move closer to the small pond, feeling as powerful as the stone warrior woman. She looks so fierce with a stream of water trickling from both her sword and arm outstretched to the sky above. I move closer to the water with a thought to see what happens if I reach my power out toward the pond, but the statue itself holds my attention. I've passed this spot a thousand times. She's one of the Fae statues left over from the royal family.

The Fae female is fierce and beautiful. Her big, arcing wings are pulled in high behind her back. While she stands in a fiery stance, which matches the predatory look in her eyes, along with the massive, long sword outstretched, she is not one I would want to cross.

Her legs are lithe and long and her hair falls to her waist in big, wild curls, and if I look closely, I can see the points of her ears sticking out between the curls. Her flowing dress, blown out behind her, contrasts with the intimidating way her body is positioned, but it gives her an ethereal air.

With each time I've passed through her in the garden, I've wondered who she was in her lifetime. Was she a goddess? A royal? A warrior? She certainly embodies everything a Fae queen would, from the obvious beauty and strength and the power and knowledge from many more years than a human would ever experience.

When I was younger, I liked to pretend I saw my future self in her. Her wild and untamed hair reminds me of my own. At least, sometimes I'd like to think my hair looks like that. Gryphon had always teased me about my ears, saying I must be part fairy because they're all wrong. And now looking at this statue, maybe I'm reaching because of what Thaliya said, but maybe I can see the resemblance, even though my ears look much more human than her own.

I certainly don't have the same fierce beauty she commands. I've never picked up a weapon in my life and I don't have even a hint of the muscles Gryphon so boldly flashes to his many admirers. I enjoy reading and studying, but I can't even fathom the amount of knowledge and life experience one would gather over hundreds of years of an immortal life.

My mind wanders to my mother, Queen Tristana. A woman so unlike this statue before me. A woman who stresses the importance of obedience and submission above all else. Can someone have more of a connection to a marble statue than the living statue I call my mother. It must be so, because now that I know my true lineage, I can hardly look at the husk of a woman.

The Fae demands my attention again. Her stony gaze is ferocious but also knowing and somehow urgent. I ignore the colorful fish coming to the surface in hopes of a sprinkle of crumbs and stand, trying to get as close as I can. I'm momentarily distracted by the way one of my vines has snaked its way up the statue and I trail it all the way up to her fingertips.

Something inside me calls to her, and the closer I get, the stronger the song becomes. At first, just a low whistle, like the rustle of fall leaves left on the trees. I can't help but answer the call. The chill of the murky water sloshes over my boots, and suddenly, I'm filled with a symphony of hushed notes, as if I had my own set of wings and I flew alongside this Fae across the sky.

A glint catches my eye, and I move too quickly toward the back of the statue. I slip and grab her waist to catch my fall. Only able to find my footing again while I see the glint once more. Something is up in her hands, on her pointer finger—outstretched to the sky.

I don't have a clear view so I reach up on my tiptoes and feel around. A small, smooth part meets my fingers that doesn't match the rest of the porous statue. I inspect her hand with my own, reaching even higher on my tiptoes to manage, trying to slip over the wet, moss-covered rock at my feet.

Then I realize there's something around her finger.

I look up toward her Fae face, and she looks as if she's about to burst from her stone entrapment and mistake me for the enemy she's been staring down for millennia. Satisfied that she won't spontaneously burst back into life, I pull the ring off her first finger. The water from the tip of the fountain sprays across my face as I block its path for a brief moment. The ring slides off easier than I expect, and the enthusiasm of my misjudged pull causes me to fly backward into the muck.

Panicking for a quick moment, I search the shallows for where the ring could have landed, only to realize the ring sits on my finger and I am sitting in the grimy pond with water up to my hips. Disregarding the mud oozing into my boots and up my legs, I check the ring. It's magnificent. Despite the mud, the ring is spotless and shining.

The silver metal spins up my pointer finger three times. On the middle spiral, there's a large, pale turquoise stone the size of a large seed gleaming at me. On each of the spiraled ends are thick pearls, which are so milky and iridescent, they reflect the light of the sun onto the leaves surrounding me. The ring sparkles so brightly. How could I be the first to find such a treasure?

Looking back up at the statue, I see another detail for the first time. Something is written down her side, carved underneath her arm. It looks like runes or some ancient language. The language of the Fae?

I quickly glance around; lucky no one has stumbled upon me so far. A sense of a youth long past fills my heart as I hike up the bottom of my dress and use the mud coating my hands to copy the symbols onto my calf.

Glancing down at the mess I'm covered in, then at the ring, and back toward the statue, I wonder if there's enough time remaining in the afternoon to find the answers to the many questions suddenly swimming in my mind.

CHAPTER ELEVEN

I instantly feel I'm not alone when I enter the library. There are small, muffled sounds coming from the far shelves. Who would be in the gardening and herbs sections? I thought only I frequented the back of the library, but apparently not. I move toward the dark stacks where the torches barely reach and the muffled sounds turn to barely audible, urgent whispers.

The sounds summon thoughts of Thaddeus. The way his deft fingers gently stroked my hair and traced my tears. If only I let him continue his trail down to where they'd knot in the small of my back. I imagine how his hands would feel if they wrapped around my back, pulling me closer. The way his kisses would feel across my lips. Him pressed against me, and the strength I'd feel in that moment.

I shake the thoughts from my mind. That is not why I'm here.

Moving slowly with my back against the bookshelves, I find the stack the whispers are coming from. It has to be more than one person, and only some of the words they say sound familiar. I gently pull some books from eye level out of the way to get a better look at whoever is sneaking around the library. Apparently not slowly enough though, because several of the books clatter to the ground beside me, revealing the presence of another.

The whispers abruptly stop. Footsteps move around the stacks back toward the front doors of the library. I press myself against the books, making myself as small as possible. My wet, stained clothes help me blend further into the darkness of the bookstacks.

I can't bear to look as someone blurs by.

"Who's there?" a voice I know well asks the room. I see Gryphon run past where I stand over the fallen books, hastily pulling his shirt back over his head. My hands fly to my mouth, stifling my shock.

I quickly realize how guilty I look. Standing here in the dark instead of following Gryphon back to the front of the room, but for some reason my feet won't respond and I can't find my voice. While I try to coax my legs back into action, another form passes my hiding spot.

"What was it, Gryph?" Shock freezes me once more in place. This voice I also recognize. Although I can't say I've ever heard it so breathy and lilting before.

As she passes by my hiding space, the flush of her cheeks and the way she runs her fingers through her messy blond curls say more than words ever could.

"It was probably just some books falling. No one is here," Gryphon surmises after his footfalls move around the shelves closer to the front of the room.

"I suppose I should start getting ready for the feast, anyway." Licia and Gryphon's voices fade as they exit through the library doors and continue down the hallway.

A huge rush of air leaves my lungs. That was certainly not what I thought I'd find while coming to the library today. I'm so glad they were too preoccupied with each other to notice me creeping through the shelves.

Licia and Gryphon. My two favorite people. Together.

Why wouldn't they tell me? Have I been gone so long that so much has changed? The chasm of me leaving these walls has grown too big for repair. I thought we could go back to how things were between us three, but maybe it's too much.

I'm still the same, though, so what is it that has changed?

Before I get too distracted thinking about all the complications, I move deeper into the library toward the oldest books, which certainly isn't saying much. Most of the books here are fairly new. I've heard whispers it's because my father destroyed all the books from the Fae's library that were here before us.

Moving through the dark, leather-bound books the warm smell of old pages wafts around me. But quickly, I'm disappointed in what's left here. I am not surprised when I find nothing at all about old languages of Everguard or runes. Clearly, Father deemed runes and symbols as "magical nonsense" and felt it did not have a place here.

Sighing, I quickly grab a pen and one of the smaller, older books right at my fingertips to copy down the symbols onto something slightly more permanent. I pocket the small booklet where the runes rest safely and brush off the now dried mud symbols on my leg.

Perhaps this is not where I'll find the answers I need.

Chapter Twelve

"See to the male over in the corner bed. Vicious wound, but I think you can tend to it easily enough." Thaliya barely glances at me as she moves from bed to bed, assessing and checking the patients within. The one look she does give me reminds me not to use my newfound skills unless she's present. We can't have suspicions rising before we're ready.

She's been distant since we spoke in hushed whispers about my past. I can't tell whether she's hurt I didn't take the news more graciously, or if it's because of the upswing of injuries and ailments as of late, or she's giving me space to process everything. Despite the way I left it between us, I can't stay away from the healer's wing.

Perhaps it's because of this place, or perhaps it's because she's my first memory. One that's been muddled over time, but small pieces remain.

Her big smile and strong hands reach toward me, light halos her long silvery hair. Her warm arms wrap around me, calming me as she whispers words I don't understand into my hair.

She drew me out of darkness and brought me to this wide-open space full of light. Ever since then, I've been a permanent fixture here, always helping where I can. I've picked up a thing or two to where Thaliya now depends on me, even with some of her more difficult cases.

"I'll do my best," I say in automatic answer, recalling the many travelers who'd pass through our small cottage farm in need of a stitch or a poultice. Once or twice, I set a bone. Even though we were so out of the way, there were always plenty of passersby needing attention.

I change direction without stopping and head toward the far corner of the room where a dirty, wounded male sits with his eyes closed and his right shoulder bandaged, already seeping with blood through the layers of carefully placed bandages. As I get closer, I can smell the days of travel on him. I try not to wrinkle my nose at the overbearing scent.

"Hello there." I pitch my voice low so as not to startle him, but his eyes remain closed. The lines around his lips and the deeper ones bunched around his eyes tell me he's in a lot of pain. "My name is Roe; I'd like to take a look at your wound if you'll allow it." Unsure if he'll answer me, I reach toward the bandage but suddenly stop as he jerks awake and grabs my left wrist. Startled, I completely freeze.

Every once in a while, the ward receives someone a little touchy or even a little drunk. I've learned from experience the best way to deal with those types is to remain calm and move as little and as slowly as possible.

His body stiffens then he opens his eyes. He looks from my hand, now opening and closing slowly in an attempt to twist out of his grip then back at me. It's hard to tell in this dark corner of the ward, but recognition seems to light his eyes, which is odd because I'm certain I've never seen this man in my life.

He pulls me closer to him and I automatically lean in, thinking he's about to whisper something. Fear rises and I try to twist out of his grasp. With the rest of the ward behind me, I can't even try to catch someone's eye for help. But instead, he inhales deeply and then suddenly releases my wrist.

"You may," he replies as if his behavior is completely normal and nothing odd passed between us.

I turn toward the bandage table set up beside me, attempting to gather my wits and decide if I'm in any danger. My breathing slows, and I look back at the vagabond beside me. Although quite large, incredibly dirty, and a little strange, he doesn't seem to wish me any harm.

I proceed with unwrapping his shoulder with care. The four deep slashes hint at a swipe from a large beast. Seeing it, I almost remark on my surprise he made it here in one piece, and I'm about to say so when he finds his words and I realize he's not the token drunk warrior passing through. "I know it's bad, but you should see the other guy." His bright smile shines through weeks of beard growth. I'm taken aback at how out of place that smile is against his roguish exterior—a diamond in the rough.

He looks up just long enough to see me crack a smile. "Did 'the other guy' happen to have sharp claws and walk on all fours? What was this?" I motion to the wound, trying to place the size and shape but even all my late nights studying large volumes on animals and plants native to Everguard right besides Killian as he studied the latest battle maps from overseas, I can't think of anything that would do this much damage with one blow. Perhaps an overly huge wolf?

Rather than answering my question, he asks, "Roe, you say? That's an odd name. I don't think I've come across a name such as that before." His muscles flex. I catch the blood that oozes out of the undressed wound with a practiced swipe of cloth.

Still wary, I respond succinctly. "Roe is short for Rowandine."

"Rowandine of the..." he lets his question linger.

"Of Merula, of course. Where you find yourself." I wait a moment before continuing for that familiar dawning of recognition that I am of the royal family. But it doesn't come, and I send a quiet "thanks" up to the stars for being able to remain anonymous today.

"Ahh, yes. But of course. Of Merula. Well, I thank you for tending to my wounds, Rowandine of Merula." He gives a slight nod of appreciation in an almost regal way. If I hadn't witnessed his outburst before, and he wasn't so incredibly dirty, I would've decided he was a high noble of some sort.

I leave and return with a poultice I've made myself. It's big enough to cover the entire wound, which is certainly one of the bigger ones I've seen lately. With practiced hands, I affix a fresh bandage back over the wound.

"Igh, what's that?" He grunts and crinkles his nose at the freshly bandaged area.

"I could say the same about you." I bite my tongue, unsure if that was too forward. "Anyway, don't pay mind to the smell. Remove it in the morning when you change the bandage and you'll be well on your way to mended." I pat his shoulder gently as I complete my care instructions, enjoying the look of surprise on his face. The same look I've grown accustomed to throughout my healing career as I find my poultices work well and quickly, which seems to be surprising to most who find themselves in my care.

Now that I think about it, I wonder if I've somehow woven something from the earth into each poultice I've ever made. Surely that would go unnoticed by the rest of the healers, except maybe Thaliya.

"Well, Roe, I would not be so concerned with what's beyond these walls than what's within them," he says by way of thanks.

Odd. But my ears perk up and I respond in kind, "I did notice on my travels into the city walls that the fields weren't as bountiful as they've been in years past, and the streets were quiet. Is this how Merula has been of late?" I ask, unsure how much I should be sharing with this man, but I feel like this much is harmless.

"Oh? So you're just passing through as well?" He looks pointedly at my gown beneath my apron with raised brows and I realize he's probably picked up on more than just my name in these past few minutes, no matter how grimy his brown traveling leathers appear.

"Ah, yes. I arrived just the other day, after a long—" I pause, biting my lip as I search for the right word for where I've been. "Absence."

"Yes," he says, another short answer, but this time I wait patiently and am rewarded when he continues. "You're right in your observations. A lot has changed these past few years, and certainly not for the better. Hadeon—" His gaze slants toward me, and his warm sable eyes meet mine, and starts again. "King Hadeon prefers to look at the bigger picture, and does not spend time worrying himself about trivial things." He tilts his gaze back to me, and I try to wrest the confusion from my face.

I know from my time spent with Killian in the library, that Father spends much of his time with his High Council, which consists of him, Killian, the Head of Guard, Patton Montford, and a few of the wealthiest men in Merula's court. Little of his time is spent with the people themselves of Merula or the surrounding lands. But even if Mother is the one hearing all the concerns of Merula's people, would she share their struggles? And surely Father would work to rebuild what's faltered since his arrival. Since I've arrived, I've only heard brief snippets of his conversations with Killian, but none of it sounded concerning for the people of Merula. In fact, the opposite is true.

"The king does nothing for his people?" I ask, trying to keep any inflection out of my voice that would give away I have anything to do with King Hadeon and the way he spends his time.

"He's already left his homeland, Nefaria, in shambles while he conquered Merula. He has no need for these people any longer. There's nothing left for him here except an old castle that's seen better days. Soon, he'll head north, torching anyone who opposes him. The other races stand no chance against his ruthless ways."

"Even with what's left of their magic?" I can't help but think humans can triumph over magic so easily, but it's happened before.

"And I'll bet my last coin he's already started making nice with the lands to either side." I raise my eyebrows at this. He must've heard about the upcoming nuptials here at the castle.

He pulls a coin out of his pocket and flips it a few times before tossing it my way. My reflexes are quicker than my thoughts, thank goodness. Before I know it, the smooth coin rests in my palm.

"Good work, Rowandine, love." Thaliya comes up behind us and helps the man out of the bed. My hand closes over the coin just before Thaliya pokes her head over my shoulder. "You'll be right as rain before you know it."

As he rises before me, with the help of Thaliya who's stronger than she looks, it does not go unnoticed that he takes up half the room with his size. Under all the cloud of travel, I get a whiff of woodsmoke and cedar. "Thank you, Rowandine of Merula. No doubt I'll be back to my whole self in no time." He only winces a little as he flexes his muscles, trying out the work I've done.

I can't help but watch as he grabs his shirt from the end of the bed and gingerly works it back over his head. The way his muscles flex and move remind me of something Gryphon said recently about a creature lost to us. Was it the wings of a dragon? Or something else he mentioned in passing?

He clears his throat and catches my eye one last time then walks toward the exit with Thaliya striding after him to keep up with his large steps. He stops only to lean over and have a brief conversation before exiting through the back door and I can't help but be left with the thought they know each other.

I'm unsure what transpired between the two, but as I return my supplies to the front of the room, his words echo in my mind, and they sound a lot like Killian's. The night he spoke of rebuilding Glorixia. The love for his people of Merula lost in the sparkle of a new and shining city. I look toward Thaliya, and she's still watching the horizon long after the man's gone.

I pat the coin in my pocket while the blatant anger that man feels for my father pulses around me, slowly dissipating the farther I get from the ward, but his words stay with me all the same. He already has Merula and will be looking north and to the surrounding lands soon. Father said my new match is coming from over the Caldertasi Sea? Are his moves really that transparent? Or is that man more than a vagabond passing through?

CHAPTER THIRTEEN

"R owandine, there you are, child," the king booms, jarring me from my thoughts. I take a deep breath, trying to calm the maelstrom within. As I do, Father takes several steps away from me, wincing as if my messy appearance has a mind of its own and will jump to him if he remains too close. The word 'child' drips from his lips with hints of disdain. I bow my head, instantly feeling like a young child getting caught rather than the woman I am now.

"Good afternoon, Father, Mother," I say, with a small bob to each, inwardly kicking myself for sounding all of three inches tall.

"Walk with us, Rowandine, we've been meaning to speak with you since you've arrived home," the king says, continuing his stroll onward, leaving me to fall into step or fall behind.

I give a small smile I do not feel and fall into step with them. Father seems to suck the light from the hallway with his large frame and constant scowl. Mother trails a step behind him, always the wilting flower starved of sunlight because of the shadow he casts. He pointedly looks at my attire once again and begins. "Rowandine, perhaps you've forgotten due to your absence, but the healer's wing is not a place fit for a princess." The word princess seems to stick in his mouth unpleasantly, but he manages to push through. "Especially a princess about to be married off to King

Lysander Sturdevant, King of Etos. What will your betrothed think if you're constantly running around healing those who can't take care of themselves?"

He sweeps a hand toward my soiled skirts. His voice shakes as he tries to control his anger. Avicii's stinging words from the past echo within Father's admonishments, and I shrink with the weight of disappointment closing in again. "You, as a royal princess, only need to marry and strengthen our line by having children, and obey the head of household. How is it I've set you up for all three and you've failed so miserably?"

The way he so easily throws this in my face causes me to lose my balance. "I tried, Father," is all I can manage to get out before tears threaten to fall, which of course will only make this meeting worse. While I blink back the tears, the past comes flooding back and I feel all of ten-years-old, the disappointment thick in the air as his anger unfurls around us.

My mother steps out from behind him and her frail hands feel strong as she supports my forearms until I find my footing again.

"Hadeon," her voice begins as a whisper, but as she continues she also seems to find her footing. She touches his elbow gently, attempting to steer a warhorse with a ribbon. "She's lost her husband of no small amount of time and has just returned home. We can stand to give her a modicum of time and comfort before we ship her off once more, no?" The way she pats my arm reminds me of how she used to comfort us when we were small. What happened to that woman? The statue flashes in my mind and I wonder if my mother has a different kind of strength. One that has waned these past years but may still be lurking somewhere in there.

"She needs no time. She needs no comfort!" As Father's words ring through the hall, Mother shrinks back into his shadow, nodding even as she disappears to nothing. The woman I had a glimpse of moments ago is now gone.

I bow my head in apology, attempting to hide the anger rising in my cheeks. Perhaps there's more truth to the wounded man's words than I first thought. I've always looked at my time healing with Thaliya as a way to give back to our village, not something that makes me weak. But obviously Father does not see it like that. "You're right, Father, I'm sorry. Of course, I should spend my time more wisely. I'll make my choices with the good of the kingdom in the forefront of my mind from now on." My words are sincere. Although, there's an unfamiliar knot taking shape in my stomach.

Working in the ward this morning, I was happy and alive. And now, I feel as if my happiness has been dumped and scattered across the hall like a broken pot of soil. And now, with Father, I want to make him happy, make a proud match. But at the same time, I feel as if I am being pulled in the wrong direction.

The king nods in satisfaction at my obedience. "We will see you this evening at dinner. Make sure you're prepared. Clearly you were not last night. All of court will be there." His features pinch together one last time as he glances at me. He turns toward my mother and then continues striding down the hallway. My mother is left to scurry off behind him.

I watch as they barrel down the middle of the hallway, causing servants to rush out of their way with trays and piles of freshly laundered clothes trailing behind them. The king and queen oblivious to all the destruction left in their wake.

Coming down the hallway from the opposite direction, Gryphon bows low to the king and queen. After they pass, he nods subtly at me in mock formality. It takes every ounce of my self-control not to revert to my thirteen-year-old self and throw myself at him with the hugs I've missed these past years. Instead, in a movement appropriate for a grown woman, I link my arm in his and continue along with him in the direction he's moving.

"You look as if Licia just turned over all your newly propagated seeds," he says as we continue down the hallway, servants buzzing around us.

"She would never! And I've missed you, too," I say simply rather than spewing out everything that's happened in the last few moments, not to mention the last several years. Instead, I keep it in, simply happy to have him in my presence at the moment.

"It's been too long," Gryphon agrees. "I'm sure you have some tales to tell, oh you must've seen so much while traveling the entire realm with Avicii." He practically swoons, reminding me of when we'd always dream up ways our parents would allow us to go off into the world to experience all the different ways of life. We'd spend days at a time planning how we'd meet with different races and what we could trade and learn from them. Gryphon was the innovative one. He had so many ideas or plans that would benefit the different villages along the way. But I was just so eager to learn more from them. More about the plants they used in healing and how I could bring it all back to Thaliya and to Merula.

But that was never written in the stars for us. Human royals would stay amongst the human royals, never traveling further than these walls and us too busy with lessons only covering the basics we would ever need to know about the surrounding people. Even then, Father never saw fit to go into the village or hear from his people, let alone the surrounding villages.

Gryphon looks down at me, waiting for me to begin a tale, but his face falls when he sees my reaction. "He never even took you, did he?" He bangs his fist into the wall beside us. "No wonder you look so miserable." He tightens his grip on my elbow and pats my arm. "Not because you lost your husband, but because he was never the husband he promised to be, the one you needed him to be."

I melt into Gryphon's side. Stars—he's good. I've missed him. Although I'm just slightly younger, he and I have shared cradles and wet nurses and used to wreak havoc together around the court every chance we got. When I'm with him, I'm someone totally different from the person I'm expected to be at court.

I'm not sure why the queen's sister hasn't yet married him off, but without him by my side here at court, I would likely drown in the endless sea of expectations and rules I've returned to.

And if I could, I'd thank her everyday for allowing him to stay by my side in all our lessons, rather than sending him to waste his time sword fighting with Killian and the other men. Gryphon is no warrior, and he never will be.

Sometimes I wonder just where I'd be without his friendship to level me out here at the castle. And other times I fantasize that Jonaraja, his mother, has a bigger plan for his future. One she's held close all this time until she's ready to unleash it.

Gryphon already has every eye at court—of all the women and the men. I'm convinced it's the way he never takes anything too seriously unlike many of the other available bachelors flitting about. His sense of humor mixes perfectly with his big heart, and that's what gets everyone. I can easily see why Licia's drawn to him.

He's always been good looking in a gangly-as-a-newborn-calf way. But since I've been gone, he's grown into his height and filled out his slim frame. Lean where he was once too thin, and now his large eyes almost fit with his narrow face and high cheekbones. "We'll have to get you out of here one night." He tilts his head to the side in thought. "The Moon Festival is later this week. I hear something is happening down at the shore." His hushed voice tells me this is highly confidential information, so I match my face to his no-nonsense tone.

"What would you know about how the villagers celebrate anything? And anyways, I don't think you'd want an old widow tagging along with you." I look down at my dress; the morose color a flagrant reminder I should be in mourning.

"Don't give me that, Roe. I know you're ready for some fun. It's been too long indeed. Leave it all up to me." And with that, he pats my hand once and gives it a squeeze before elegantly twirling me out of his clutch and sending me on my way.

CHAPTER FOURTEEN

Before meeting Licia to get ready for another evening of King Hadeon parading his family in front of court, I decide I have enough time to check the library once more. Those runes keep appearing in dreams along with a darkness so dense, I can't breathe. If I can figure out what they mean, maybe I'll be closer to figuring out more about my past. There's one more section I think to check, one that may just be untouched by Hadeon and his magic-fearing hands.

The last time I was here, Licia and Gryphon had occupied the garden and herbs section, so I couldn't check it. But since everyone else seems busy preparing for the evening, I have the library to myself.

I've been thinking, the statue itself is in the garden. It's a stretch, but maybe there's a log or journal of some sort that would list different flora and fauna in the castle garden along with the garden sculptures and their locations.

This time, the library is completely empty. The silence is a stark contrast to the buzz of the healer's ward and a welcome comfort after the run in with Hadeon and Tristana.

In the stacks, the selection is overwhelming. I run my fingers along the spines of the books, looking for something to catch my eye. I stop at a particularly dusty book, pulling it off the shelf before I even read the title.

A Study of Ornaments, Whispers from Stone. The spine reads in looping gold letters, almost too faded to make out.

The illustrations are intricate and specific. My heart beats quickly knowing that if the statue is in here, it would surely have a detailed description of what the runes mean. But the feeling fades quickly as I realize this tomb must be too old to have something about that particular statue in it. There are runes, though, on a few other pages, so I pull the book to my chest, thinking tonight I'll have more time to slowly work through it.

A breeze lifts my loose curls off my neck and I spin to see what the disruption could be. There were no footsteps to announce someone, at least none that caught my attention. A deep laugh sounds behind me, between me and the stacks I was just facing. I jump at the close proximity of it and his hands find my hips. I look down to calloused fingers running up and down just below my ribcage.

"It's you." Knowingly, I rest my hands on his. The last time we were together, I relished the way his lips felt against my own but refused him because it was the right thing to do, but it wasn't what I wanted. He's mysterious and alluring in a way that moves me to action, moves me closer to him. And this time, rather than fight it, I lean against him, my back finding satisfaction in each muscle and curve I can feel flexing as I lean closer. And this time, I won't run.

Thaddeus takes the opportunity to give me a flourishing twirl deeper into the row of books. I smile, feeling lighter than I have in years. Lighter, and so many other emotions I don't yet have a name for. But I like it. I like the strength I feel when my decisions are my own.

In the middle of the bookstacks, Thaddeus gives me a playful grin and his eyes are full of heat. He brings my hand to his lips, kissing each finger, starting with my pinky and ending at my pointer finger. Then, he directs it into his mouth and sucks a long, slow pull from my knuckle all the way to my fingertip. An involuntary intake of breath at the brazen act leaves my mouth at the same moment my thighs tighten.

He smiles again, this one softer.

My gaze flicks from his lips to his eyes, and what I see completely undoes me.

Thaddeus' hungry gaze locks on my lips. Pure desire in his eyes.

I lean in, strength pouring through me, giving me more confidence than I've ever felt. The moment our lips meet, a groan of satisfaction leaves his lips and I'm undone.

Any reserve or hesitation I felt before is completely gone. My hands find the evening scruff across his face and wrap around his neck while his hands pull me closer into him, where I instantly feel his arousal against me.

I'm no stranger to kissing, and I was a married woman, but this—there's more desire in this moment than I've ever felt with any other lover. My hunger for his kiss—his touch—grows with every moment.

He guides me backward, not breaking from our closeness and presses me up against the darkest section of the stack. My body arches up to his while my chest rises and falls against his own with anticipation.

The mix of old book smell and his fresh frost scent makes me dizzy and I lose myself in his hungry kisses. His lips crash into mine, demanding attention just as the bulge in his pants presses hard against my thigh.

My hands trace the muscles in his back, up his shoulders, and up into his hair with the tips of each twist brushing my fingers. He pulls my leg up, wrapping it around his hips as I try desperately to find more friction and relief. He obligingly catches my thigh and pulls me closer until only my toes touch the ground. The feel of him against me, even with all these layers, is sure to bring me to a quick release.

My mind drifts for just a moment, reminding me that just weeks ago, I was content on my own. My small cottage was enough and my moat of a garden wrapped me safely inside my own world. Even my husband left me for months at a time, leaving me lonely but content. And now—

"Come back to me," Thaddeus breathes against my lips. The shock of a soft nibble against my lower lip pulls me right back to where I'm supposed to be. I return the heat of his kiss; my tongue tracing his lips and then delving into his mouth, deepening the kiss, leaving no question that my mind is elsewhere.

Then, he falls to his knees in front of me, pushing my skirts up and up as I gather them in my hands. He kisses his way up my thigh, but all pretense is gone. His hands find my undergarments and guide them down my legs, placing kisses everywhere the clothing touches on its way to my ankles. He guides each foot out and surprises me by putting them in his pocket.

His eyes meet mine in a silent demand to stay quiet. The way he looks down on his knees staring up at me makes me feel so many things. I feel powerful and strong, and soft and languid all at the same time.

Above him, I feel powerful and in charge. Something I've never felt before except in the healer's ward. But this is different.

The energy flows through me, pooling at my core.

His kisses find my warm center and I melt into the books behind me. His moan of satisfaction is muffled by my skirts, but mine—mine is not.

As his tongue licks and sucks between my legs, my pleasure continues to mount. I pull my skirts even higher, so they're up around my hips, giving him more room to work, but I crave more contact.

With one hand, my fingers run along the twists in his hair that have broken free of the band holding them back. My pleasure continues to grow and my body is in an upward spiral toward release. Just when I think I'm about to go over the edge, he pushes two fingers inside of me to match his rhythm. My body answers him and I ride his face harder, rocking back and forth.

He adds another finger inside of me, finding the spot deep inside me, the one that makes me come undone in a way I've never before. Is this how it's supposed to feel?

A string of inaudible words pass my lips as his motions quicken. While his tongue and fingers are busy, his thumb finds that perfect bundle of nerves, rubbing and circling it until I can no longer hold on. My hands fly up to the shelves behind me—searching for something to grab onto—as I lose all control. I don't even hear the books fall to the ground beside me as I cover my mouth before the entire library knows just what's happening in this stack of books. I ride my pleasure for what seems like hours, and Thaddeus obliges; his movements never waning, bringing me over the edge again and again.

I can't take it any longer and I pull him up to me. Our lips crash together and I can taste myself on his lips. He exhales a frustrated huff as his fingers blindly fumble with the laces on his pants. But just before his cock springs free, voices and booted footsteps enter the library, gathering around the map table from what we can hear.

With a raised eyebrow, Thaddeus looks to me for his cue. I shake my head, knowing that if I get caught with him, his life would yet again be on the line. He reluctantly loosens his grip, holding my hips and giving me a moment to find my balance once more before he straightens and adjusts his pants. My skirts fall around me and I busy myself by fluffing and straightening them.

His cool touch brushes a strand of hair away from my face and he kisses me tenderly, sending my sensitive nerves tightening and sparking once again. The sensation sends a thrill through me knowing my undergarments are in his pocket.

"You undo me completely." His quiet voice is hoarse from misuse so he clears his throat. "Until I don't know who I am anymore."

I nod, agreement at the tip of my tongue, but then I realize it's the opposite—I know myself better than ever before. And he's been part of the unlocking.

CHAPTER FIFTEEN

"If it's a widowed princess they want..." I look down at my dress as Marlys affixes the last black pearl to my hair. *Then that's exactly what they'll get.* After an afternoon of trying to puzzle out everything Thaliya laid out to me, another reminder of *my place* from my father, and then my fully eye-opening yet incredibly selfish tryst with Thaddeus, this has led me to see what I must do. Thaliya asks too much of me, but she's right on one account—the people of Merula, the entire realm of Everguard, need to be taken care of. I realize the best action I can take is to be the princess our people want to see—happily married off and sent across the sea. I must be the bargaining chip so the people of Everguard remain at peace.

Know yourself, know your path. Thaliya's words ring in my mind with a tinge of a question. I know myself. I know what I have to do. Her words are a taunting storm cloud above my head. My time in the healer's ward ticks by. Reconnecting with Licia and Gryphon will only make it more difficult to leave them a second time, and this time, probably for good. And each moment with Thaddeus is a stolen one. Moments I will put in a box and forever hold dear.

So, this evening, the layers of black taffeta and tulle stand for more than what people can see on the outside. The small glimmer of hope for what

I saw myself doing has been extinguished. And I'll learn to be okay with it because this is who I must become. I see now this has always been my path forward.

"Stars fuck me sideways." I'm pulled rudely from my reverie and self-pity by Licia, who's fanning herself. "Now, *that's* a dress."

And she's right, the way the dress fits snugly against my curves while the tulle spills out along the floor like unruly zucchini vines late into summer, is very modest yet—

"Stunning. Absolutely stunning," she says, frowning at her own reflection, which is beyond words beautiful. On anyone else, the daring cut outs across the front of her dress would look scandalous, but on her, with her petite frame and voluminous hair, somehow she makes it look sophisticated.

"I don't understand how you're still here." My hands circle around the room while Marlys tsks at me to stay put.

"Honestly, I can't either." She pouts prettily while her gaze sweeps across our vast chambers.

"But it's not all bad." Her frown turns wicked. "A girl has to keep herself busy in such a big, lonely castle."

And despite my gasp at the admission, I know she doesn't just mean physically and don't doubt her words for a moment. I think back to the day in the library and am sure she has plenty of ways to keep busy here. She's been fighting her own battles here and she's doing just fine.

CHAPTER SIXTEEN

"Gryphon, I can't leave. This whole evening is for me. All of these people are here to see me, after all this time I've been gone. I need to be here for them, do as I'm expected. And I'm expected to dance with and entertain everyone here. Not go on an adventure to a late night party with you." I respond in an almost shrill, definitely exasperated tone while swinging my arms around like I've lost all control. I steal a glance toward Father, who's celebrating tonight and is too busy in his cups for once to pay me any mind at the moment.

Gryphon looks back at me, nonplussed. "Well? Have you danced?" He tilts his head in question.

"Yes..." My exasperation mounting even further.

"And have you spoken to guests?" His voice remains level as his eyebrows raise.

"Of course, but..."

"Roe, now is the perfect time. The night is young. You've done all that's expected of you and the king and queen are otherwise engaged. And Sturdevant has yet to arrive." His voice trails off as I follow his gaze. The king and queen are indeed otherwise engaged. Both with large wine goblets loosely swirling around in their hands and both in conversation with a visiting high lord or lady. "I told Baylor we'd meet him at the Moon

Festival," he presses. "We have only heard stories of such a night!"

"You told Baylor what!" I throw him a scathing look. "Wait, who's Baylor?" But just as I ask, I wonder why tonight of all nights, after all these years, the villagers are actually celebrating the Moon Festival. The idea of being able to experience such a celebration thrills me more than I thought it would.

"You remember Baylor, the stable master?" He shrugs off my question as if he's common knowledge. "It's perfect, really. The entire court is busy here. Extra guards have all been called to the castle rather than enjoying themselves in the tavern. Everyone is here, Roe. So if we want to take a chance, now's the time. Let's be twenty-two again! Tonight, our only limitations are the ones we set upon ourselves. When else will we ever have this opportunity?" He's positively humming with hope at this point. If I don't cave, he might explode with all of this vibrating energy.

"Okay, let's go. I'll meet you in the tunnels. I'll have to change out of this gown into something less noticeable."

The tunnels? Stars, I haven't been to those since we were, well, way over ten years ago, anyway.

The tunnels are the one place Gryphon and I would go to escape from court life and the pressing matters of turning from adolescents into adults too soon. I laugh a little to myself thinking we're returning to the same place, only this time desperately trying to escape adulthood. "This is ridiculous," I say under my breath. "Should I find Licia?"

"That we're grown adults who still have to sneak around like teenagers? Or that I've actually convinced you to go?" He laughs and then turns without waiting for a response, quickly weaving through the crowd and out of the ballroom. "And she'll find us." He waves a farewell over his shoulder, dancing with anyone along his path as he leaves the room.

I take in the room one more time while I let the current of dancers carry me toward the door. The dancing is in full swing and the band of instruments continues to progress into more lively songs. Offhandedly, my thoughts drift to Thaddeus. I suppose this wouldn't be the type of event he plays at but I do a quick sweep of the room to ensure I haven't missed him. Instead, I spot Licia spinning in quick circles and laughing without abandon with one twin from Greymoria—the realm to the south of Merula—across the Caldertasi Sea. Both their skirts twirl in frilly petals of purple and gold. I can't tell which twin, though. Unlike Licia and me, they look exactly alike and even dress in matching gowns of lilac with shimmering pink cut outs.

While passing the refreshments table, I realize I'll be no good to anyone at the Moon Festival unless I grab a quick bite. Gryphon can wait just a moment longer.

I move with purposeful strides toward the pies and bite-sized cakes along the far end of the table. The mountains of mini chocolate cakes drizzled carefully with sweet caramel sauce draw me in closer.

As I reach for one of the cakes dusted with salt, my hand brushes someone else's, reaching toward a pumpkin cake topped high with whipped cream.

"I wouldn't waste time on those," I say without looking up and stuffing the small cake into my mouth. Chocolate clearly being the superior choice.

"And why's that?" I'm caught off guard by a familiar voice that sounds like dark honey folding over itself. I attempt to compose myself quickly before looking up, patting my lips to make sure there's no crumbs. Some good that does me because as I look up, I melt all over again. My eyes trail up the broad, muscular chest the honeyed voice came from. His dark brown hair is coiled in the same thick twists and held back with a tight band. His brown skin deepens with the flickers of candlelight surrounding us. Sharp, high cheekbones frame his vibrant pale green eyes, which meet mine and darken when he smirks as if he can feel how his voice alone has unraveled me.

I drink in the bard, Thaddeus, and inhale sharply as I take in his proximity. Ts so different from all the other people here. My cheeks heat with the memory of our last meeting. A man of few words, but many talents. Exactly what I need right now. Danger and adventure swirl around him as he waits for me to speak. A small part of my mind notes to tell Licia later that yes, the rumors about the bard are true, all of them.

I swallow, trying to find my voice again and manage to croak out around a mouthful of sweetness. "I'd suggest the chocolate cakes, Thaddeus, if that's your idea of a treat." His name on my lips sounds dangerous spoken aloud.

"Is chocolate caramel your idea of a treat, Princess?" His eyes briefly drop to my lips, trailing down to my neck, and back up as his large hand switches direction and grabs a tiny chocolate cake instead. His fingers gently brush against my arm and a delicious chill swims through me.

I stare at him awkwardly with another bite-sized dessert halfway to my mouth. He pops his cake into his mouth without a second thought. "Tastes like a bite of the heavens." With the way he looks at me while he says this, then licks his fingers, warmth blossoms below my belly and my toes curl in my shoes and I know he's not just talking about the cakes anymore.

I move to take a step back, but he bows and motions as if he'd like the next dance. I know I shouldn't, for so many reasons, one of which will kill me if I keep him waiting too long. But the playful look in Thaddeus' eyes draws me back in and I discard the uneaten cake on the table and take his hand.

He quickly pulls me close and whisks me back toward the dance floor. My eyes close and I can't help but inhale the fresh, snowy scent that rolls off him. His steps are sure and fluid. I feel light in his arms as if we're floating on air rather than across this tiled ballroom floor. I've danced with others this evening, but this is the first time I feel completely weightless amidst the court and all its guests.

"I'm surprised you get an evening off." He's dressed as if he's a duke this evening, trading his more basic black on black for trousers and a waistcoat tailored just for him and trimmed in silver swirls.

"I have many jobs here at the castle." I look back up at him and he smiles knowingly. His hand rests on the small of my back and trails lower, dancing across my skin. The same half smile that's found its way into my thoughts at all hours of the day lights his face. I can't help but smile back. "Princess, if I didn't know any better, I'd think you're enjoying yourself."

He plucks the thoughts right from my mind. "It's turned into quite the party, hasn't it?" I answer quickly, still watching his face, although there are no clues written there. He's so beautiful; he looks like he could be carved from dark stone. Perhaps one of the statues of the old gods out in the gardens. A small piece left of the royal Fae from years before.

We continue to float effortlessly around the room without comment. I can't help but notice no one is watching us. It's as if there's a curtain surrounding us, a veil hiding us from the rest of the room. I look back and forth between his eyes and his chest in front of me, not sure how I can feel so comfortable yet unsure of myself at the same time. He feels so familiar;

his closeness reassuring. The song ends once again, I bow to the bard, and he bows lower to me. His eyes linger on mine, then once again slowly drift down my neckline and back up.

His implication is clear, emboldening me to say my next words. "I look forward to our next meeting, Thaddeus."

"It may be sooner than you think, Princess." He turns and I can't help but note the way his broad shoulders flex through his fitted waistcoat before he's swallowed by the crowd.

Gryphon! Oh, stars! Gryphon! He's going to be so mad. With Gryphon in mind, I turn and go, weaving through the crowd of dancers and revelers as quickly as possible without drawing attention to myself.

The moment I pass through the oversized doors, I fill my lungs with fresh air. While dancing with Thaddeus, I forgot how stuffy the great hall is. The music fades as I walk down the hall until all I can hear is the quiet click of my silk slippers against the tiled hallway.

The grand hallway that connects the ballroom to the front entrance is a beautiful mosaic of blues and greens swirling together. The patterns and colors are soothing against all the flaming yellows my father has draped throughout the castle. I've heard discussions of renovating the entire hallway and ballroom; however, castle decor is low on his list of priorities. And for this one small thing, I'm grateful he's busy doing other things. These floors, just like the statues in the garden, are small reminders of the Fae who once walked these corridors. Growing up, I often imagined their tall, lithe forms gliding down these halls or dancing through the gardens. These floors, and the statues are some of the very few things left of the entire powerful race. That my father, the king, took down such a grand people both confuses me and makes me deeply sad.

As I wind my way back up the eastern tower, I think back on the little I know of the Fae race. Until very recently, I was taught they were a vicious people and my father had to cross the seas of Caldertasi into these lands where he valiantly defended the other races from the wrath of the Fae. I'd also been taught that the Fae fell quickly to my father—despite their superhuman strength and centuries old power—because my father had studied them carefully for years, and he and his council devised a lethal plan to quickly conquer them, saving not only the humans, but all the races from the Fae.

I had also believed that since my father has risen to power, our kingdom remains peaceful and all the other races live peacefully somewhere within the realm. Although, in all of my thirty-five years, I've only come in contact with humans within the castle walls. It sickens me I have not questioned any of this until now.

The vine-like carvings twist under my fingers as I climb the winding staircase up to my tower. The multi-colored tiles accompany my climb. The small pieces look like sea glass fitted together in the most careful fashion. I look at the staircase and wonder what else a race like that accomplished in other areas of life if they've taken such pains to create such beautiful things out of something as mundane as a staircase.

I reach my chambers and twist and yank until my gown pulls over my head and I can breathe again. The fine cloth falls in a heap on the ground as I search for something more fitting for a village celebration. Of course, I've no idea what that might be as we've never seen a village celebration in all my time. I settle on a gray tunic with small silver stitching. My leggings are a deep, autumnal plum in recognition of the full moon festivities. I pull on my comfortable boots and lace them all the way up my calves.

Quickly moving toward the door, I pull pins and pearls out of my hair as I go. I shake my hair out and curls fall heavily around my face. No time to waste glancing in a mirror as I know Gryphon will scold me no matter how quickly I move.

I fly down the dark passageways on wings of freedom. My fingers graze the cool stone along the walls as I get closer to where Gryphon must be waiting. His silhouette stands in the small open space where we used to always meet. The high stone arches always made us think it was once used as a place of worship. Last time we were here though, it was only used by us as a place to meet and store important items we wouldn't want others to find.

I laugh with abandon and jump into his waiting arms. He swings me around in circles in our dark, secret place. In this moment, ten years suddenly fade away and all my most recent troubles dissolve into the darkness surrounding our torch light.

Our banter carries us the last long distance under the castle before we stop at a worn wooden door. The invigorating night air waiting for us on the other side seeps through as we throw our weight against the old door and it slowly creaks open, only enough for us to slide through one at a time.

We step around the door to find vines and hanging moss covering our entry to the edge of the village. The door creaks closed and Gryphon takes a hesitant step forward to make sure the coast is clear.

As we step out from behind the vines, Gryphon hands me a thick bundle. I unwind the two silk ribbons and open the fabric to a mask. I look closer and study the animalistic features around the eye holes and covering the nose.

The white crackled shell of the mask reaches up the forehead and out past my ears in sharp, curving points. The area around the eyes are lined in gold and made to curve up in a reptilian manner. Because of the eyes and the way the white shell crackles, it's as if it's made of large scales. The nosepiece is small and curved and ends in a rounded, golden triangle. The entire mask is encrusted in glass crystals.

"A white dragon?" I ask Gryphon in awe of the mask's elegant beauty.

"Seems fitting. From what I remember, you used to run around breathing fire all through the halls," he responds, smiling.

I hold the mask up to my face.

"I hear the villagers have been working for weeks on their masks. They say wearing a mask is a symbol for looking inward, as the Fall Equinox is a time of inward reflection, a time to allow our pasts and futures to come together. Just as the Moon Maiden and the Moon Mother blend together with the present. Bringing us all together with the stars above."

"That's beautiful," I respond, feeling the echo of all I've been going through. Where's this been all our lives? "Well, if I'm a dragon, what does that make you?"

He shrugs and pulls on a mask of silver with large ears flopping out on either side. The nose piece is long and rounded and extremely floppy. A laugh bubbles up from deep within me and comes out louder than it should in the silence that surrounds us. "An elephant?" I laugh, trying to get out in between fits. "I'm surprised you didn't keep the dragon for yourself."

He looks down his long elephant nose at me with mock seriousness. "You know, elephants are incredibly wise creatures and they remember everything." I can't help but burst at the seams. The emotionally immature man beside me always keeps me guessing. And he's the only person I know who'd be able to confidently pull off wearing an elephant mask to any kind of celebration.

My mood sobers to match his as I tie the golden ribbon around my head. The mask itself is light enough, and I'm sure I'll get used to looking through these holes quickly. We lock arms and wind our way through the forest. By the time the forest thins, our feet have found the sandy shoreline.

CHAPTER SEVENTEEN

T he night is dark, but the moon hangs full and low in the sky, lighting our path. The stars above twinkle in time with the drumming in the distance and the bay beyond shimmers with a reflection of the moon and stars above. We leave our boots propped next to a tree to mark our entrance back into the woods and move down the sand toward the rhythmic drumming. I adjust my dragon mask one last time as the salty smell of the sea makes me giddy with anticipation as we move toward a huge bonfire.

The celebration is in full swing with people whirling and gyrating around the massive fire pit. Several drummers and a woman with a flute sit on the outskirts of the firelight, keeping a fast beat. Their music is magic, weaving its spell over all the people here. It's clear they've been playing for some time this evening as their faces glisten with sweat even on such a chilly night, but they don't appear to tire.

Tables are piled with small treats, breads, and fruits. Huge casks sit at the end of the tables, where people freely refill their mugs. Blankets are placed just out of reach of the gentle rolling of the waves and, judging by the shadows moving around, many people have retreated toward these darker, more intimate spots. The salty, cool night scent mixes pleasantly with the smell of charring logs from the fire.

I send a side glance toward Gryphon to watch how he takes it all in. His eyes are as large as ripened tomatoes. The fire dances in his eyes and a slow, small smile plays on one side of his lips. Both of us are too entranced to use words.

We soundlessly move closer to the growing music of drums and flutes that wind their notes around us and pull us closer to those dancing around the flames. The rhythm of the drums begins to hold my hips in thrall and my body quickly becomes one with the surrounding music. I wink at Gryphon and disappear deeper into the middle of the crowd.

I can feel the deep *boom, techa, tech, boom, techa, tech* of the drums from my toes all the way up through my fingertips, which sway back and forth above my head. The beat fills me and my hips swirl in wide motions. The smoke from the fire fills my lungs with warmth and wraps around me as I twirl. I dance like the dragon my mask claims me to be, strong and fluid. My feet match each strike of the drums and are soon lost to the rhythms around me.

Dancing like this is not something I've ever done, but the way the music fills me and moves my body is intoxicating. My tunic feels tight and restrictive against my heaving chest as my breathing becomes quicker and deeper. My body feels strong and right, and for once, it feels like my own. I can't drink up the lightness in my heart quick enough.

I open my eyes again to the world surrounding me. The people around me continue to spin closer and then away again. The rich blues, maroons, and creams of the village people run together in a happy swirl. Some villagers—female and male—and some less obvious, dress in bright colors to celebrate the Moon Mother in maiden form, which represents her vitality and bright future. Swirls and sparkles of paint mask those around me as well, which celebrates the Mother within us all. The low, dipping necklines and bare chests shine with sweat and pay homage to the Mother, reminding us all that we are young only once.

The beat picks up and the cool breeze blows my hair out of my face. Suddenly, I find strong hands on my hips, instantly reminding me of the library. I can't tell if it's the strong hands or the music, but there's a pull to the figure behind me. I whirl around, expecting Gryphon. However, this is definitely not Gryphon. Instead, I stare into a strong, male chest. My gaze travels over flexing muscles up and up until my breath catches when his pale, playful eyes slant slightly upward and his mouth slowly curves into an almost smirk. His white wolf mask guards his other features, but those eyes pierce through me, giving him away.

Quickly trying to recover, my mouth opens then closes again as his hands guide my hips to find the music once again. Lost in his mischievous gaze, I match his rhythm.

No words are spoken aloud, our bodies do the talking. Maybe dancing is where language becomes physical because I swear I understand exactly what he's telling me. His eyes lock on mine. The other dancers and blazing fire I'd been so closely observing moments before are now a sparkling blur around us.

My hands, which until now had been stretched awkwardly halfway above my head, come to rest on his bare chest. As soon as I touch him, my body hums with something. Anticipation? Desire? Recognition? Watching as my fingers slide along his dark, flexing muscles—I'm completely mesmerized. I can feel it in his chest before I hear it as a throaty chuckle rolls out of those now grinning lips.

"Dance with me?" His question rumbles out, asking for my consent.

"Yes." My voice is breathier than I intend it to be.

His smirk widens into a smile, but he continues dancing while his hands trail down my sides and return to lightly rest on my hips, following my swaying movements with his body pressed close. His thick thighs straddle my own and our movements together have a warmth waking inside, growing and blossoming until parts of me I've completely written off are humming anew.

With this new feeling of bravery awakening inside, my hands move from his muscled chest down his flexing abs and back up, resting on his shoulders. I go from looking into his chest to flinging my head back in a spray of curls.

He answers, boldly crashing his lips into my own. My body dissolves against his, and every muscle of his presses into all my softer places. I open to him, pressing myself closer and allowing him to deepen the kiss. His hands on the small of my back pull me closer.

The solidness of him beneath my fingertips, the heavy beat of the drumming, and his fingers pressing into me are all that matter at this moment. I'm consumed by my senses as he moves from my lips to the small of where my ear meets my neck. A place I wasn't even aware of until now. His trailing kisses go from demanding to softer and then he whispers in my ear, "You're dancing as if all of this is yours." His lips, still so close to my ear I can feel his breath against my neck. "You own the night. And it looks good on you, Princess."

"All of what?" I look around, suddenly self-conscious of how I'm dancing.

"The people, the castle, and the stars themselves." He gestures wide to encompass everything surrounding us.

"That's ridiculous. None of this is mine, could ever be mine." But even as I say the words, I wonder what that would look like. Even growing up royalty, and technically in line for the throne after my siblings, it never occurred to me what that would be like. But suddenly I know, it would look like this, the whole night surrounding us. Pure joy, people coming together, and a hint of whatever feeling this is in my chest. I look back up to reply, but he's vanished.

"There you are, Roe." I feel someone grab onto my wrist. Twisting around, my eyes find Gryphon's bright, blue eyes and wide smile grinning at me. His smile falls as he takes in what has to be a thoroughly confused expression on my face.

"What is it?" Gryphon leads me away from the bonfire to the quieter and cooler surroundings. He peeks around me in search of what has me spooked. I give my head a little shake before looking back up at him.

"I'm fine. I just bumped into someone." I let my voice trail off, unsure how to answer.

Gryphon gives me a quizzical glance, but leaves it at that. He shrugs and his eyes travel the crowd, trying to get a glimpse of what has made me jumpy. My gaze travels over the crowd as well, but there's no sign of the tall, dark, and handsome male who was in my arms just moments ago.

Still trying to find Thaddeus somewhere in the crowd, I ask, "Where'd you wander off to?" I still wasn't sure what just happened. Or what exactly he had meant by that. And what was that pull? That silent humming I sensed once again when his skin was beneath my touch?

"I was catching up with a friend." He does his Gryphon-shrug, leaving me to wonder who he ran into to make him smile so wide and I wonder if Licia might've made it down as well. He turns his attention back to me, smiling widely at my disheveled state before taking my hand as we trail into the darkness.

CHAPTER EIGHTEEN

Judging by how low the full moon hangs in the sky, the hour must be late when I return to my chamber. My body is still buzzing from the evening. So, rather than wasting time trying to fall asleep, I decide to head to the library for a book. And maybe Killian will be there, just as he always used to be.

Licia is still not in, so I change quickly from my tunic and leggings, now damp with sweat and smelling of fire smoke, into a simple gown. And then head to the south wing with the light of the full moon guiding my path. The late hour enhances the ghostly feeling I always get. While walking these halls, once again I'm struck at the faded beauty here. It seems traitorous, but I wonder what these walls looked like when the Fae lived here. These now faded paintings and tapestries must've been brilliant and inviting to all who passed. I wind my way down our tower and straight to the library.

Despite the late hour, Killian is exactly where I expect him to be. Even years later, and late into the night, he's in the library among the war strategies section. But he's not alone, another man stands beside him, looking grim and puzzling over what Killian suggested. The map laid out in front of them is covered with markers shaped like towers and horses.

Some things never change. "Isn't it a bit late to be pouring over war maps, brother?" I say as my fingers tap lightly along the edges. He looks up and smiles, the same smile he used to give me when I'd appear by his side, only now, more lines crease his princely face.

"Princess Rowandine. If I may be so bold to say, we are blessed by the stars to have you back," the older man says. He's built like a warrior, and his head of gray hair and scarred features suggests he's seen many battles and made it out alive.

"That is kind, Sir–" He's familiar, but I don't recall his name.

"Sir Patton Montford. At your service." He bows low and then returns his attention to Killian, whose ignored our brief introduction and continues to stare at the map before him.

Ah, so this is the head of guard.

"But if we attack from that angle, they'll see us coming." He looks up at the guard, still too lost in thought to acknowledge me. I take in their map and all the pieces scattered about.

Suddenly, the answer is obvious.

"And if they see you coming, they'll move to higher ground. But if you use the Periserrat Peaks, they're as good as dead," I say, assessing the markers laying before us.

Killian looks up, noticing me for the first time. "Not if they have the higher ground, sister. That would be the advantage," he says, placating me as if this is obvious.

I look hard at him and Sir Patton looks between us. "Yes, the obvious advantage, brother. Which is why it would work." I point to the peaks, the very space they're discussing. The blush of victory rises in my cheeks as they look between one another, not seeing what I see so plainly.

"Why would that work?" He looks at Patton for the answer. But Patton continues to look at me, waiting but already nodding along in agreement.

"If the enemy is driven up the peaks, yes they have the higher point advantage, but they have nowhere to go," I say, watching the map as I continue. I can feel Killian's stare on me. "What if we could weaken the peaks? Dig out from underneath them in some way? Then, they'd have nowhere to go and they'd crumble." But even as the words leave my mouth, I'm wondering why he'd need to do something like this. And how something like this would affect my newly discovered earth magic.

"Brilliant! Yes!" Killian is nodding along with Patton by the time I finish. "Where did you learn war strategy?" He studies me as if he's never seen me before. And to be fair, it *has* been a long time since I've curled up in his lap as he read to me from thick volumes of the most notorious battles.

"I had a good teacher. Or do you forget?" I gesture to the chair that still sits beside the fireplace, only now it sags in the middle from years of use.

"How could I forget?" He smiles brightly at the compliment.

"Well, I'd say Princess Rowandine has given us plenty to think over. I'll retire for the evening, or should I say morning?" He glances out the small window across the table where hints of the waking sun peak in. He bows to Killian, then me, and is gone.

"You're going to aid one of the villages in the east? Who would attack from over the Periserrat Peaks? Surely that'll be more hassle than it is worth?" I study the map, realizing as I ask that from the cluster of gold troops and how he's placed them, they're ready to attack, not defend.

"The villagers of Blagdenbeck, in the valley of the peaks, have been mining Eldorite. We plan to claim the village as our own, then use the crystal they've collected to harness and amplify magical energies to fuel and drive our rebuilding of Glorixia," he says, placing his hands on his hips and puffing out his chest.

"What would we do with Eldorite, though? We have no powers to harness. Everything magical has left the area." I gulp. Killian's desire to use raw power and the fact I just learned I'm one of few who still live and have raw power is a dangerous thought.

"We have sources that believe the necessary powers still remain here in Everguard. Hidden from us, but out there, just waiting to be harnessed." Killian brings his fist down on the map, causing the closest figures to go flying.

I don't like where this is going. Who's this man standing in front of me? Surely not my brother. "But if they've been mining it all this time, wouldn't it be more effective to trade something they may need? Surely we have a surplus of digging tools, or lanterns, or something?"

Killian shakes his head, frustration apparent in the way he's scrunched all his features up.

"That's beside the point, Rowandine. Blagdenbeck is the closest town to the last recorded site of Glorixia." He looks pointedly at me as if I should've seen why this was beneficial right away. When he realizes I haven't grasped this significance, he continues. "Being closer will allow us to rebuild more quickly once we locate the remains of the lost city."

"But I thought Glorixia was lost to the Wastelands?" I ask, pointing to the large sand colored part in the center of the map.

"We have many scholars working to find the exact location, it'll be any day now." He taps two of his fingers in the center of the Wasteland desert for emphasis. "Who knows, perhaps before we know it, Father will set himself up in the old capital of Everguard, at the heart of our realm. That will leave me to rule Merula. Perhaps he'll send Licia somewhere close, and gift her something smaller like Blagdenbeck or Cindra to look after. And you, well, you'll be across the sea, sitting on a throne of your own." I stare at him.

"What? Why do you look upset? If we all held seats in the major parts of Everguard and its surrounding realms, think of the possibilities." He sweeps his hand further north, toward the large and reclusive city of Freathia. The hunger in his eyes makes me take a step back. "What? Like you wouldn't want your very own village? The power that comes with it?" He looks hard at me, brow furrowed, as if this is incomprehensible to him. A hunger I've never seen before dances in his eyes, and I can't help but think it's not unlike the look Father gets when he recounts battles.

"Well, no. If you must know. I'd never want to rule over any part of Everguard. I much prefer helping the people. That's why I spend so much time in the healer's ward, I think." I offer up a small truth, but in doing so, I find another. What if ruling could be helping? If someone was in such a powerful position, couldn't they use it for creating more trade opportunities, or uniting the people in other ways? Father rules with an iron fist, often scaring or killing others for his own gain. But couldn't even more be built under a united front? Wouldn't we all be safer and stronger for it? "Why, what would you do as ruler of Merula? And later on the whole of Everguard?"

"I'll continue as Father has. He's almost tripled his lands since crossing the seas and setting out from Nefaria. And he's not slowing down anytime soon."

"And the people?" I ask, recalling how vacant the roads were on my way into the castle and my conversation with the vagrant.

"What about the people? They can stay. Someone has to do the heavy lifting around here." He cocks his head to the side, clarifying that it certainly won't be him doing said lifting.

I choose my next words carefully, not wanting to upset him, and knowing if I say too much, surely Father will hear about it. "On my way in, I noticed—the fields seemed sparse, and the homes looked barely more than piles of wood."

He squints at me. "Well, you're right, they'll have to work harder to keep up with our growing needs. But for now, we've just finished raiding some smaller villages to the west. They had plenty."

My head reels at his blatant disregard for his own people.

We've been raiding the surrounding villages? That's our solution? I take a deep breath and look down to the map, blinking quickly and knowing tears will only further agitate Killian.

Clearly my time away from the castle has changed the way I see things. Where would I be if my surrounding neighbors didn't check in on me while Avicii was away? I would've had to live on only the crops I grew if not for the many travelers willing to trade fabrics, rare herbs, and even farming equipment I've never seen before. Not to mention the many who stopped for several days to help around the farm in exchange for a few hot meals and a soft pillow at the end of a long day. If I was left alone up there while Avicii was gone weeks at a time, I don't think I would've made it on my own.

"But, if his people are unable to grow enough to feed their families or are afraid for their families' safety because of these raids, what'll happen?" I wonder, not sure that I can handle the answer. Perhaps from Father, but not from my brother, who I've always looked up to so fondly. What happened to him while I was gone? He's always enjoyed studying wars and battles, but I just thought it was part of his education toward being the next in line for the throne. I never thought he'd grow into an exact copy of the way Father does things.

"Nothing will happen. His people are scared of him. Fear and power go a long way, Roe." He muses on this as if he'd like to hang this thought in a gilded frame.

As he says this, I realize fear is easy to root. Love and respect take more time. And time is not something King Hadeon is fond of.

I exaggerate a yawn, planning to feign exhaustion, but Killian's already turned back to his map, weary of the direction of our conversation. Rather than asking more questions, I hurry from the room, my heart sinking while my thoughts play tug-of-war with these newly realized truths and Thaliya's words from earlier.

CHAPTER NINETEEN

At first, I think the rustling at the curtains is Licia coming to wake me. But when I crack my eyes open at the sound, they're still met with darkness. It's not Licia then. My heart races as my mind conjures all the possibilities of what awaits me at the trellis.

The ghost of Avicii come to exact revenge? Rather than laughing at the thought, a chill runs down my spine. Gryphon would come through the passages, but at this hour? We're up too high, there aren't very many other options. I try to calm my breathing in order to hear over my impossibly loud heart trying to escape my chest.

"It's me." There's a whisper followed by a shuffling of feet. I try to place the voice, but a whisper isn't much to go on. I try to adjust my eyes to the darkness surrounding me, but it's useless. Instead, I ready a pillow to launch as soon as the voice has a body. "Princess, put the pillow down."

"Thaddeus." I throw the pillow anyway but my body sings in realization that it's him.

And he's come to me. In my bedroom.

I bite my lip in anticipation, knowing where this will lead.

"Don't do that." He steps out of the darkness and the moonlight highlights every curve of muscle up his arms and down his thighs. His high cheekbones glimmer along with the glint in his eyes. He waits, though, not coming a step closer until invited.

I beckon him forward, hesitantly at first but when he rewards me with his bright smile, I can't help but answer him in kind. Moving the covers aside, I make room for him. When I do, he pauses, taking in my thin white nightgown. I watch him watching me. My eyes travel over the way his shirt grips at his chest and arms. Suddenly, I want him to be as he was only hours ago, when he was shirtless and those muscular arms were wrapped around my hips, moving with my own in a dance under the stars.

He leans down, kissing me as he fits his body over my own, kneeling over me as if in prayer and I am his deity. He leans back on his calves, reaching out to trace under my nightgown and pull it up. He traces his thumbs along my curves as he pulls it over my hips and my breasts. I lift my arms as he pulls it over my head and drops it over the side of the bed. His intake of breath at my nakedness brings a smile to my lips, which he kisses in answer. In response, I pull his shirt over his head and instantly, I crave his muscles to flex at my touch the same way they answered the rhythm of the drums.

I trace a fingertip around the curves of muscles, each chiseled muscle responding to my light touch.

"Tell me you want this, Princess." His chest muscles tense and relax as he waits for my answer.

"Yes," is all I can manage, watching the way his body responds to mine.

"Yes what?" His palms rub up and down my thighs.

"Yes. I want this. Me. You. Now." The statement is so bold, so freeing, and I know for certain that it's the truth.

He kisses his way down my jawline and my throat. His kisses turn into nibbles then into bites. I groan at the sweet mixture of desire and pain that moves through me. He takes this as encouragement and continues his journey, sucking each nipple into his mouth and then cupping each breast as his kisses continue their trail down my belly and then continues between my thighs.

He licks at my center, gradually increasing the pressure of his tongue as my hips match his pace. It doesn't take long. I spare a small thought to Avicii and the partners who came before him, none with the talent this man has. No one knows my body like the man between my legs does. The thought alone brings me closer to release. I can feel the heat rising from my core, filling me, bringing me to the edge. At the last minute I have the mind to throw a pillow over my mouth because the satisfaction leaving my lips would surely rouse Licia. I ride the pleasure until my body is spent.

He only resurfaces once my limbs go limp and my grip on his hair loosens. He rises to his knees and slowly unties his breeches. I wrap my legs around his hips, silently begging for more. My impatience gets the best of me and I move to help but he brushes me off, unceremoniously casting his dagger to the edge of the bed before continuing the slow unwrapping of his length.

I throw the pillow over my head again, but this time in frustration. I hear his low laugh and clothing drop to the floor before he lifts the pillow off my face. "Impatient, are we?"

In answer, I pull him down by his shoulders, wanting his body close to mine. He laughs again and positions himself right over me, pausing just a moment. "Is this what you want?" he asks as he pumps his erection. The way he continuously checks in with me heightens everything. He wants this to be good for me, too. He wants me to be a part of this, too.

I can't keep my eyes off the motion of his hand and the impressive length resting just above my entrance. "Yes, Thaddeus. This is what I want." He's the only thought in my mind as he leans down again and enters me in one long push. I cry out, surprised at the tinge of pain mixed with the delicious feeling of being filled.

I shudder when his whole body presses into mine. Each of his muscles flex and strain as he pauses to allow me to adjust to his size. But his attentiveness only pushes me further toward the edge. His eyes meet mine, his desire burning bright and laid bare. I raise my hips, and that's all the invitation he needs. He answers—thrusting into me over and over again. His eyes don't leave mine, focused on my response, watching for my release. His pace quickens, and I can't help but lose myself in him. I stretch my hand out, searching for the pillow, but instead, he clamps his hand over my mouth; the fire in his eyes ignites as I scream my release against his fingers. In response, he pumps once, twice, three times and my walls clench around him, greedy for as much of him as he'll give me.

He rolls over, out of breath and exhausted. He motions me closer and I snuggle into the crook of his elbow. As we settle, he gently strokes my hair as my thoughts drift.

This is unlike me. Everything about Thaddeus is unlike me, but especially tonight.

And I love it.

Could this be love? Or just a really good time? I suppose it can't be love as most of our interactions have been solely physical, but the connection I have to him, the way I feel so connected to him, makes me think this could be something more if I were able to give it time to propagate.

"Will you be here long?" The question breaks our comfortable silence.

"No. Unfortunately, I have some pressing matters I must attend to back home. A friend is ill, the cure is here in Merula. I'm here as long as it takes me to procure it." His words weigh heavily on my healer self.

"What sickness is it? What do you need? I'm sure I can obtain it for you." Between my status as a princess and Thaliya's knowledge of the lands, I'm sure we can locate whatever he needs in no time.

"I promised discretion. But if I wear out my resources, I'll let you know. Thank you, it means the world that you want to help."

CHAPTER TWENTY

The morning comes too soon. I try to pull the sheets over my head, but my muscles scream with the effort. Am I too old for a night of dancing? Everything hurts, including muscles I didn't even know I had. My thighs burn and my neck and shoulders are in an invisible vice.

I reach out beside me but my hand only finds the cool sheets, not what I'm searching for. *Was last night a dream?* But the sweet ache between my legs tells me he was very real.

"Good morning. I thought I heard you moving, finally." In surprise, I quickly launch a pillow toward Licia's sing-song voice and vibrant footsteps, only for my shoulders to go stiff and my throw lands three steps in front of her. As she throws it back at me, I remember just where that pillow has been.

"What's with you this morning?" There's a lot more bounce to her already buoyant steps. "You're practically floating." I notice as she crosses the room to spread the curtains open wide.

"I know I'm not the only one who had a great night. You didn't find your bed until late, I'm told." She raises her eyebrows suggestively. "I saw you dancing with the bard. He can certainly make his way around the dance floor." Was she at the moon festival? Or is she just talking about the ball beforehand?

"I didn't see you at the shore last night." I sit up, wondering who else would've noticed.

"Oh, you wouldn't have, I'm sure. Too busy staring into those seafoam eyes." Her mocking tone does not escape me. "I'd be careful with that one, though." She shakes out the curtains and looks at me over her shoulder. A second warning from her about him. And she's the one who lives for the thrill, the one who always returns to our room in last night's gown.

I pull the warm sheets up around me, remembering the feel of Thaddeus' hands all over, pulling me close, the way his large hands splayed across the small of my back, grounding me.

"It was just dancing. Don't forget, I'm recently widowed. I must act as such." I lift my chin, but the memory of those hands, the warmth of his breath against my skin, and the heat between my legs makes me unsure of my status and how long I'll want to hold onto it.

"And soon to be married once again." The way she looks at me, and my reaction, tells me she knows Sturdevant has already left my mind.

"Have your fun. It's clear Avicii showed you none." Her words hit hard and low, the fact that she sees the truth so deeply.

"Is it all truths you see so readily? Or just those of the heart?" The question comes out before I realize how much depth it could actually have.

"I may appear flippant and shallow, but there's more going on here than meets the eye." She flips her hair at me and exaggerates her hips as she walks from the curtains and seats herself on the edge of the bed. The sun streams in, illuminating her from behind. Her comment comes off with her usual suggestive tone but I look at my sister differently for the first time. While I've been gone, she's done more growing up than I have.

This, for some reason, brings flashes of her reaction at our first dinner together—when Father announced it would be me not her marrying, for a second time. I wince at the daggers she shot me that night, but now she's the picture of happiness.

"You don't really want to leave the castle." I narrow my eyes, trying to figure out where she stands. She leans back on her arms across from me, like a barn cat caught with a mouse in her paws; her morning hair framing her face and cascading down her back like sunshine.

She waits a moment to answer, assessing me in the same way. "No. I do not. I wouldn't have minded a bit of adventure for once, don't get me wrong, but I'm more useful here, where all my birds sing to me. And although it would be something to have someone with information all the way in Etos, your letters didn't come half as often as I'd hoped when you were off in the mountains. So either we'll have to work on those skills of yours or we'll have to find an alternative." She pats my leg and sashays out of the room, leaving me to wonder how much her and her birds really know.

Chapter Twenty-One

A few weeks have passed and although I was skeptical at first, I've settled into a nice routine. Hadeon has left me to my own devices, at least until he gets word of my betrothed's arrival. It's allowed me to catch up with Licia, spend countless hours alongside Thaliya in the healer's ward, and even steal moments alone with Thaddeus.

Which is exactly where I'm headed. He's been busy in the evenings and late into the nights, so he sleeps well into the morning. This works in my favor as I'll spend all morning with Thaliya while the majority of the court sleeps into the afternoon. That, along with the way the halls to the healer's ward are often abandoned, makes the small office where I first spotted Thaddeus practicing alone, the perfect place to meet.

His usual playful melody isn't filling the hallway as I approach. I take a seat in the high-backed chair looking out the wall-to-ceiling windows. The windows overlook the entrance of the castle but today all is quiet. The temperatures fell in the night and a slight frost like I've never seen covers the grounds, invoking a sense of peace as nothing moves outside except the occasional guard switching duty or making a round. The peaceful scene settles over me as well, but just as quickly, Thaddeus comes into the room shattering the newfound peace.

He hurries into the room and closes the distance between us in three wide strides. I move to wrap my arms around him, but I can tell something is off. His eyes burn with something. Love? Determination?

Oh.

He kneels on one knee beside my chair and grasps both my hands in his. Is he going to propose? I didn't think we were here yet, but if he wants to save me from an Etos king, who am I to say no?

Seeing Thaddeus on his knees before me warms me from within. But there's something else, something different. His eyes are wide and his body hums with a frantic energy.

"Thaddeus?" I place my hands gently on either side of his face, trying to send some of the peace I felt moments before into him.

"I'm sorry, Princess. Things are moving much too quickly." I'm taken aback by his statement.

He's the one down on one knee, right?

I thought we were just enjoying each other's company. Not love, just two bodies becoming one for a time and then going about their business. And maybe some other feelings, but love?

Seeing my reaction, he moves to clarify. "Things between us? I've enjoyed every second, but I—"

He bends forward gently brushing his lips against my own. I've yet to see him at a loss for words. I keep my hands on either side of his face and try to prolong the moment, knowing whatever he's about to say will change this perfect bubble I've wrapped us in.

"I didn't want to tell you so soon, but things are moving swiftly. I've word that your betrothed made it across the Caldertasi Sea as if the stars themselves directed the winds. Between this and—other reasons—we're out of time." He looks from my eyes to my lips as if trying to decide if his important news can wait just a moment—or ten.

With a wince he presses on. "I have something I must share with you. And I don't think you're going to like it."

The urgency of his words and the wild look in his eyes causes me to falter. "What could you possibly say to upset me? And how do you know my betrothed is so close?"

He stands and paces back and forth between the window and me. The bright frost-filled scene behind him back lights his silhouette causing him to look blessed by the stars. Tension radiates from his body and his muscles flex through his fitted black shirt and even tighter black leather pants. He ruffles his twisted hair atop his head and comes back toward me, this time sitting in the seat across from me.

"Roe, I need you to hear me when I tell you this. I know we've only known each other a few weeks, but this is important. I care about you." He looks at me with his hand still in his hair, waiting for my response.

Is he really going to propose? I can see us riding off into the night, going from village to village listening to his moving songs each night and spending each morning in his arms. I have to say, we haven't known each other that long and haven't done too much in the way of talking, but it'd be quite an adventure. To disappear, with his instrument on his back and me in his arms paints a thrilling picture. And certainly, a better option than being shipped across the sea to Etos, where I understand they've taken a page out of Father's book and spend their days raiding and killing.

"Roe, focus." He snaps his fingers in front of my face in urgency. "I need you to stay with me."

"I'm listening." I sit up a bit taller, trying but failing to match his energy. But something's off. Instead, I wipe the nervous sweat from my hands onto my dress. My heart blooms with my feelings for him and I try to keep him from noticing the shake in my hands. I wait, thrilled to hear his next words.

"Rowandine Aeronwick."

The way he says my name rather than calling me 'Princess' has me lean into his next words, a smile growing on my lips. He worries his bottom lip between his teeth for a moment, forming his next words. I notice the creases in his forehead. He doesn't look like a man worried about a proposal.

And then he surprises me completely.

CHAPTER TWENTY-TWO

"**Y**ou *are* of royal descent, but not in the way you think." He pauses, looking up to catch my reaction.

I don't move. Thaliya's words echo in my ears. He knows, and Thaliya knows. My two small worlds colliding over secrets older than I am. My only response is a slight narrowing of my eyes.

I'm still waiting for different words to come from his mouth.

But he waits, his body thrums with a tangible energy. He's still as he waits for me to process his words. He gives me time and studies me, waiting for an outburst or tears, but neither come. "You know."

I give a slight nod, but nothing more.

His body relaxes. He ignores the chair completely and crumples to the ground, bringing me with him. My skirts fill with air as we whoosh to the ground and settle like a cloud around us.

"This will make it easier. Since you know. You and Thaliya must be working on something. This is so much easier." Relief settles across his face. He looks at me for signs of acceptance, but I don't give him anything except my attention.

So, this is not a proposal in the heat of the moment. And he's not planning to whisk me away so we can travel the realm healing villagers with his song and my hands.

Not quite able to make the switch between what I thought was going to happen and what he just said, I stand and walk to the frosty windows. My forehead resting against the glass, and the cold, smoothness grounding me enough to try to figure out where he's going with all of this. I turn back toward him, but keep my palms pressed against the cold, allowing the sting to calm my racing thoughts.

Thaddeus nods, seeing understanding dawn on my face. Encouraged, he continues. "Your parents, your birth parents, were King Azulian and Queen Bronwinn."

For a moment, his words float around me, their meaning as elusive as a whisper on the wind.

"That makes no sense, they were—" They were what? Here before us? Killed by my father? Rulers who lived in this very castle? There are too many ways to end that sentence.

Suddenly dizzy, I move to the chair opposite of Thaddeus. He moves to help me toward the chair but I throw out my arm. The action strengthens something in me, and I'm able to lower myself into the chair and straighten my spine, squaring my shoulders toward Thaddeus, ready for whatever comes. "But Queen Bronwinn died in childbirth, isn't that what the history books of Merula say?" I ask, still not understanding how I fit in all of this.

"Yes." Thaddeus takes a deep breath, his shoulders relaxing just a bit, grateful I'm keeping up. "She died giving birth to you. And your sister."

"Licia?" That doesn't make sense. Why would Father—King Hadeon—I mean, keep Queen Bronwinn's children?

"Not Licia." He pauses, once again gauging my reaction. Whatever he finds satisfies him enough to continue.

"Your birth twin's name is Ombretta. She lives amongst the Ancients, in the north."

"Oh. Ombretta." I nod, but his words are still not making sense. I could've sworn he just told me my sister's name was Ombretta, but it's Licia. My sister's name is Licia and he was supposed to propose when he went down on one knee.

Ombretta? Why would I be here, in Merula and she there, in... "Did you say the north?" Why would King Hadeon let royals, let alone Fae royals, live after killing their parents? "Does Father know?" His words weigh heavily on my shoulders, a weight I wasn't ready to bear.

Thaddeus takes two slow steps in my direction, pausing to see if I welcome his advances. Slowly, he wraps an arm around me, pulling me closer; his strong arms a necessary support. "No, as far as I know, he knows nothing of your origins. His wife was giving birth at the same time, and the Fae somehow got you there in time to pass as her own. You'll have to ask Thaliya, she would know—"

I stiffen at his words. A feeling rising within me I haven't felt since that last day with Avicii. I push back against Thaddeus' chest so he can tell me to my face that both he and Thaliya, the two people closest to my heart, somehow knew all this about my past and haven't felt the need to bring it up until now.

"How would a bard like *you* know what Thaliya knows?" I ground out the words, not recognizing the deep, throaty sound they make passing through my lips.

Hurt flashes in Thaddeus' eyes. I can see the exact moment when he realizes I'm not who he thought I was. And it stings, but this—what he's done to me—stings more. His eyes flick to the sky behind me as if trying to gather enough resolve to finish what he started. "I wish I could tell you everything."

"I can't believe you." I push him away from me with such force he stumbles a step backward toward the window. My voice rises and my hands are trembling. "You wait until now to tell me this? Who are you?" Confusion rockets out of me. I know talking isn't what we do best, but I didn't think—I don't know what to think. But I thought I knew him better than this.

That feeling continues to rise from the pit of my stomach. Something between rage and disbelief cloaked in resentment. I fist my hands, remembering a piece of what happened with Avicii. No matter what I'm feeling now, I can't let the same thing happen to Thaddeus, no matter how upset I am with him at the moment.

I glance out the window behind me. Even though clouds are gathering in the distance, the area below is still calm. Yet, I realize if he's going to live, I need to get out of here. I push past him, making sure to keep my hands well away from him. This throws me off balance, causing me to shoulder him out of the way before I run from the room.

Days go by. Ever since Thaddeus shared what he knew about my past, I've taken sick to my bed, now covered in the oldest books from the library. My collection has grown while I hide from the world. Not even Licia or Gryphon have braved a visit.

The book *A Study of Ornaments, Whispers from Stone* held nothing helpful, but this one, *Rulers of Everguard: A Unique Perspective* has had several interesting passages. According to what I've read so far, the realm had never been more united or more prosperous until King Azulien and Queen Bronwinn, my birth parents. A strange pride swells through me, knowing they're a part of me and they were here for their people, yet I'm still not ready to accept everything Thaddeus has told me of my past.

I turn back to the book, there's nothing on runes, but I can tell I'm getting closer. I look back at the runes I copied down weeks ago in the small leather book. I wish there was something in here I could decipher, but the book is written in a completely different language, one I've never seen.

While I wrap myself in a cocoon of safety, there have been no visitors, thankfully, other than my books, the only other thing I do is sleep. I've spent so much time sleeping, my dreams have turned strange. Most of my dreams are about a dizzying darkness where the only feeling I recognize are twin pinpricks against my skin. This darkness wraps around me like a blanket, both comforting and smothering at the same time. Whispers dance on the periphery of my hearing, inaudible, but I can feel how important the words are.

In my more lucid moments, I attempt to piece together what Thaliya and Thaddeus have said.

Yes, a princess.

But now a Fae princess?

And Licia, the person I've grown up with my whole life, isn't really my sister?

And I didn't even let Thaddeus finish.

There's more.

"Ombretta," I whisper the name, trying it out to myself, picturing the woman who goes along with such a strong name. I picture a mirror image of myself. I wonder if she's a healer, like me? Or if she has a family. Does she have any children running around? Does she have someone she's close to? Or, perhaps, I could be that person.

And then I think of that person for me—Thaliya.

My heart sinks as I think of her part in all of this. How long has she known this significant detail about my life? She never thought any of this important enough to share? Even while I think about this, my hands ball into fists. I can feel the tension all the way to my toes.

Even though I struggle to believe any of Thaddeus' words, there's a tug in my heart that I can't ignore. And after days of lying in bed trying to ignore it, I decide its time I find Thaliya for the answers I need.

CHAPTER TWENTY-THREE

"I am Thaliya Anyassa, head healer of Chessardolian, the Court of the Fae." Her spine straightens and she sits up taller at this proclamation, which is challenging because we've stuffed ourselves in the same broom closet she found me in many, many years ago. I suppose even some things aren't safe whispered in her office.

But even in the dim light leaking through the cracks, I see it. The way her skin glows. Even here amidst a closet full of medicinal supplies and cobwebs. The slight point of her ears, which suddenly becomes more apparent, like she's called it forward. Small truths fall into place, like a painting I've finally stepped back far enough to discover the whole picture.

My eyes go wide with incredulity as a small nudge deep within me whispers, "Truth."

"I'm here on behalf of Queen Bronwinn. I tended her during the birth of her children and the war against the humans of Nefaria. I was there when she gave birth to her two babies." She continues on before I can ask a question as if she can sense my tangled thoughts.

"She gave birth as the walls around her were breached by the enemy. She bravely held herself together so the healers and aides tending to her would not collapse with fright before both babes were born."

I twist the damp cloth in my hand as if I'm trying to release every drop of water.

"One of those babes was you." When those words spill from her lips it causes me to drop it completely. The white linen left forgotten on the dusty floor.

Her hands reach out to calm my own. "And from the moment I held you in my arms, I knew you were special."

I continue to stare at her with wide, unbelieving eyes. "I'm sorry," I breathe in and out to steady myself, but the amount of air I'm able to get in is insufficient. "I don't understand." My desire to agree with her out of politeness, or even deference toward the most meaningful teacher in my life, wars with everything inside me. My stomach sinks as I shake my head, denying Thaliya's words and her soft smile. Even as I do, Thaddeus' words echo in my head, a mirror to Thaliya's. It's just as he said.

"You, Rowandine Aeronwick of Merula, Princess of Everguard. You are indeed a princess. But perhaps not in the way you've always thought." I shudder, an echo of Thaddeus' words surrounding me. "You were born of a great people. A wise and strong people. They were destroyed in one fell swoop by King Hadeon Aeronwick of Nefaria."

She pauses again and checks her many folds of fabric she wraps around her like armor, searching for something. She triumphantly pulls out a slim flask which she then uncorks and hands to me. "Drink," she commands.

Without hesitation, I take a large gulp, and then one more; the liquid warming and burning down my throat at the same time. The terror growing inside me subsides slightly in an instant.

So, it's just as Thaddeus said. Ever so slowly, the reality of everything sinks into my skin, just like a poultice, cold and stinging at first, but then sure enough, healing.

I hand the flask back to Thaliya, motioning that I can handle the rest and she might as well go on.

"Once your true father, the Fae King Azulien, realized the castle was falling to the humans, he and his councilors took precautions in the event he and the queen did not see the sun rise the next morning. He took great risk, and decided he must get his own child, for at the time he was only planning for one, to safety."

"He and his council decided they'd get the child as far away from Merula as possible. Freathia in the north was the logical choice, as at this point, King Azulien had many allies there. Along with his northern councilman, he'd send one of his most trusted warriors to carry the babe across the realm to their own territory, where the child could be raised in secret among the Ancients, knowing they'd one day aid her in reclaiming her kingdom."

"So, it's as Thaddeus said? I really do have a twin? I mean, Licia of course, but..." I trail off, unsure what that makes Licia, trying to make space for both of them in my thoughts and in my heart.

Thaliya nods, encouraging me on.

"And this other sister, she was the one sent north?" I ask hesitantly.

"Exactly. By the time your father realized his wife gifted him with not one but two daughters was about the same time one of his scouts brought news that Queen Tristana, Hadeon's wife, was also in labor—with her second child, tucked away in their own war tents, several miles northwest of the castle, on the coastal side of Merula. So they plotted quickly, deciding that if they worked fast enough, they could pull it off."

"Pull what off, exactly?" I ask, trying to make sense of the story she's unraveling right in front of me.

"A switch of sorts." I can see her shoulders shrug in the dim light.

"So I'm some type of changeling?" Suddenly, dark, liquid fear begins to solidify into a hard rock of worry in my stomach that my own survival came at the peril of another.

"Well, yes, that was the plan. But Zeke, your father's most trusted warrior, had a change of heart. When he arrived at Queen Tristana's tent with you, she had just given birth to her babe. The nurses were getting ready for the afterbirth. However, that's when Zeke's wife stepped in. She has strong connections to the human royals, so there were no questions when she took over the ministrations."

"While the others tended to baby Licia, his wife snuck you into the room, claiming you came along with the afterbirth. Before the healers attending to Queen Tristana could question this statement, Zeke gave a gentle caress of all minds present, allowing them to accept this new truth."

"So, the Fae can actually control people's minds? There's truth in those stories?" I ask in awe.

"Very few. Only the most powerful Fae can do so, especially to large groups and without detection. Zeke was sent for a reason. Your father, King Azulian, knew what may be necessary. So, Zeke did what his wife asked of him. He found a way for both babes to live." Thaliya seems to be winding down her tale, which really isn't a tale at all, but the story of my past. My birth. My beginnings.

Know yourself, know your path.

Needing more time to process, I motion for her to pass back her flask and I gracefully finish off what remains. I wince as the liquid burns its way down my throat. The alcohol sloshing around my empty stomach reminds me I haven't eaten in days. But this pain is slightly preferable to whatever the name of this new feeling I'm experiencing is.

I wipe my mouth with my sleeve and look back at Thaliya. My protector. The one, without my knowledge, whose been standing guard in a sense over me this whole time. She's watched over me patiently with a look that tells me she'd wait a lifetime for me to understand. Perhaps she already has.

The last of the Fae royal line. I have a sister. I've been raised by a family of humans who are the very ones who are, in fact, my enemy.

Where does one go from here?

I'm about to be married off and sent alone into the world as a human, as a woman, as a bride who knows her place. When apparently, in fact, I'm none of these things. Another thought strikes me with the force of a final blow. My marriage to Avicii, our inability to bond, let alone have a child—no wonder. I don't think a Fae has ever successfully bonded with a human. It just wouldn't work.

All of this. Every bit of pain and confusion could have been better if I'd known. If Thaliya, my *protector*, had told me about my past. Instead, I learned of it from a traveling bard, albeit an absolutely gorgeous one who's talented in many ways. One who knows more about my past than I myself do.

My world continues to spin upside down. Just when I think my feet are on solid ground, the ground shifts again and I'm left tumbling into darkness.

Thaliya is still patiently sitting, hands clasped in her lap, and seated on one of the many crates stuffed into this closet. I can't tell what she's thinking as these truths swarm through my mind. But I realize I'm so upset that even her calm demeanor puts me further on edge.

So, I do the only thing I can do at this moment. My anger and confusion bubbles up and over my limit I've been holding in these past few days.

"All this time, you knew about me, all this time?" Fat tears fall from my eyes as soon as I let the words out. "What am I supposed to do with this information now? I'm thirty-five now! I've lived half my life! It's too late to change." My words tumble over each other, each question coming before I'm able to form it. Thaliya, to her credit, sits still and attentive, waiting with the same calm look on her face as it all comes out.

This does nothing to quell the anger still rising within. And now, it mixes with fear. I can't lose control. *Avicii.* My mind races; my breathing begins to come in quick gasps between sobs. I've lost complete control in a moment it's paramount I do not.

Just breathe. Thaliya's voice is clear and low. But my head snaps up to her as I realize her voice sounded in my mind. She rests a palm firmly on my back, rubbing slowly between my shoulder blades. The movement is soothing, and before I know it, my breathing comes more smoothly and the tears, although still falling, have slowed.

"You're upset. That is fair. This isn't how we wanted you to find out. But what's done is done, and perhaps it's time."

A knock interrupts our conversation. "There you are. Sorry to interrupt. There's been another raid, the victims are flooding in. We need all hands on deck."

Both Thaliya and I rise as one to address the world outside our walls.

CHAPTER TWENTY-FOUR

"So, does this mean you have wings?" I can hear the humor in Gryphon's voice as we gaze up into the night's sky. The sounds louder out here close to the woods.

"You know, I didn't even think to ask Thaliya before she was called away." That's why I knew I could tell Gryphon. He didn't even miss a beat. Just asked about wings after the whole messy tale spills out. "Do all Fae have wings?" I ask, realizing I know little about the race, my race.

"I think their power manifests in different ways. My mother used to tell me stories about all the races. Some Fae could fly, some could heal, change sizes, influence others—the list goes on. But those weren't my favorite stories."

"Oh? What could be better than that?"

"Shifters. You know there used to be dragon shifters? They've all died out of course, hunted from every corner of the kingdom, but how cool would that be to actually meet one?" I can feel him shift beside me, sliding his arms behind himself to find a more comfortable position on the hard rock below us.

"And I suppose she also spoke of all the Conjur and their spells and Elementals and Ancients as well? I'm afraid those days are just about over, at least for Everguard. If Hadeon has anything to do with it." I sigh, realizing that his goal of eradicating magic from the land is not only harmful to so many of the people and families who've lived here for so much longer than us, but now I'm directly involved. He means to eradicate me too, even if he doesn't realize it yet.

"Even them. And I don't know. I think Hadeon's picked a bigger battle than he thinks. I wouldn't be surprised if fairies have been hiding under rocks and Ancients have been holed up north in the snow-crested peaks of Freathia, this whole time, just biding their time."

"Thaddeus did say Ombretta was up north. I wonder if she's with the Ancients." I feel better now that I've shared this weight with Gryphon, but there's still so much I don't understand. Every question seems to create five bigger ones.

"Will you go to her?" Gryphon asks, his voice carrying a lightness to it that the question does not.

I weigh the question before answering. Of course I want to meet her, see what she's like, if she looks like me or our parents. But I'm way past my adventuring age, how could I possibly travel that far? Although I'd like to think I'd get there easily enough in one piece, I know what goes on while traveling those dirt roads, what types of people and creatures lurk in the Dread Forest. I know I'm not the invincible teenager I once was, untouchable from danger and harm. "I'd like to." I offer up to the stars.

"Then let's go," Gryphon replies as if I mentioned I'd like to have fresh tomatoes and cucumbers for dinner this evening and it only requires a quick trip to the gardens.

But as soon as he says it, the thought takes root and begins to bloom within my mind.

"I'm glad to hear it," a voice comes from the darkness surrounding us and both Gryphon and I jump at the sudden intrusion. Realizing it's Thaddeus, my heart races at the same time my anger rises, but he presses on, "Because she needs you."

Gryphon looks between Thaddeus and me. "Should I—" He makes a motion with his thumbs that maybe he should leave us alone. I lace my fingers into his and pull him back down to the ground.

"I'm sorry," Thaddeus says, searching my face. He remains standing as if waiting for forgiveness—or an invitation.

His pause reminds me of that night in my bedroom. Again, he's waiting for me to decide. My heart aches looking at him. I miss what we had. The simplicity of it all. But his other words, *when you know nothing, you stand to gain so much*, remind me there's more here to learn. And perhaps more here to do. Maybe we won't ride off into the sunset together, singing to villages and healing others. But maybe I don't have to settle for an arranged marriage either. Maybe there's more. I don't forgive him completely, but I do want to hear what he has to say—the rest will take some time.

"What do you mean? How could I possibly be any help?" I make a motion for him to sit beside us, making space for one more. I settle back onto the thick blanket Gryphon and I've been sharing to cushion the rocks below us because whatever Thaddeus is about to say, it'll take some time.

Thaddeus sits as well, placing his dagger in the grass before facing both Gryphon and me. His eyes narrow as he takes in our hands clasped and for a brief moment, I want to smile at the thought of him being jealous. Of Gryphon. But as soon as Thaddeus begins, I forget all silly thoughts immediately.

"I'm assuming you've spoken to Thaliya. And she's confirmed everything?"

I nod and inwardly shudder at the few things I've managed to stomach. It's all too much and not enough at the same time.

"Your sister, Ombretta, was taken north at birth." He waits for my acknowledgement before he goes on.

"She was taken north to be kept safe until an age to return to the crown. Her and I were to rule the realm together," I repeat Thaliya's words.

"Yes, that was the understanding. However, some of the Ancients realized by drinking her blood—not only Fae, but royalty—makes them stronger in more ways than one."

I know that the Ancients rely on blood to live, just as humans do food and water, but it takes a moment to connect this with what Thaddeus is saying.

Thankfully, Gryphon is quicker on the uptake. "You mean they're using her as some kind of blood cask?"

I shoot him a look. His crass words always get him into trouble, and just the image that his words paint, I gag at the thought. He catches my gaze and shrugs, agreeing in the brashness of it.

"Ah. Yes." Thaddeus wrinkles his nose at Gryphon's comment, but continues. "But it's been going on too long. She's not long for this world."

"She's dying? I thought Fae were immortal." I look up at Thaddeus, my eyes filling with tears for someone I've never even met. The idea that I have a sister and she'll be taken away just as quickly as I found out about her, hurts too much. "But what can I do?" I don't see how I'd be able to help from the opposite side of the continent all the while I'm getting ready to be shipped across the sea.

"Everyone thinks you're dead. You—the Fae heir apparent—If you show up demanding her and your rightful crown, they'd have to acquiesce."

"And how do you know all of this?" I ask the bard before us.

He shifts in his seat as if making space for the truth before us.

"You're not a bard," I say, looking at him. His fine clothes and the way he sits like he's never spent a moment on the ground in all his life. I don't know why I didn't see it before.

"I am not a bard. I'm the Duke of Freathia." One of his shoulders shrugs as if just hit with a physical blow.

"You're one of them," Gryphon says beside me; his voice equal parts awe and fear.

I look between Gryphon and Thaddeus, ready to laugh off the outrageous accusation, but the way Thaddeus' other shoulder drops tells me there's truth to Gryphon's words. He takes a deep breath, waiting for my judgment to fall.

"I am what he says I am," he says, his gaze dropping to the blanket before us. Ready for me to land the final blow.

If he's one of the Ancients... my mind races with all this means.

Silence fills the space around us, the air thick with uncertainty and expectation.

I lace my fingers through Thaddeus' with my free hand.

"Okay." Resolve growing as I look between Gryphon and Thaddeus.

"Okay?" Thaddeus raises his head, hope alight in his eyes.

"Okay?" Gryphon says, disbelief and excitement written across his features.

"You said it yourself, Gryphon, we'll go to her. And she needs us more than ever if she's dying. We must save her. There's no other option."

"Okay. We'll leave soon, I've been gone too long, and I haven't had any updates as of late." Thaddeus stands and brushes off his knees, as if it's all decided. And I suppose it is.

CHAPTER TWENTY-FIVE

As Gryphon and I enter the castle, we're met by an uncharacteristically jovial King Hadeon with my mother trailing close behind. His happiness has me worried, but the look on Tristana's face seals it for me. Whatever Hadeon is about to say, it won't be good.

"Just the daughter I've been searching for." His bear claw hands dig into my shoulders. "We've just had word from the coast. Your betrothed has made brilliant time and will be here in a matter of days, rather than weeks. Soon, you'll be married and off to Etos with the great Lysander Sturdevant, and our two kingdoms will be united against any upheavals that may come our way."

Gryphon hides his widening eyes by sketching a quick bow and hastening on his way. Coward. I search deep within myself to find a smile and beam at Father, replying, "That is the best news, Father. I look forward to meeting the King of Etos." He's taken aback by my happy response. But he takes it in stride and carries on down the hallway, no doubt to meet with Killian and the rest of the council to discuss the 'upheavals' he has in mind. Mother stops for just a moment in front of me. Silently and awkwardly as if trying to remember exactly how to comfort someone, she pats my shoulders. As she does so, her smile feels off, even for her. And her eyes seem to be sending a warning my way. Whatever this marriage brings, it will not be good for me or this kingdom.

I make haste to the healer's wing, the hallways are dark, but I know my way as if it's written on the back of my hand. Knowing that our last conversation ended abruptly, I search out Thaliya. There's too much I've yet to learn.

By the time I walk through the wide doorway into the low lit room, I've convinced myself that I'll be able to successfully rescue my birth sister. With the aid of Thaliya, Gryphon, and Thaddeus, we'll have no problem making our way north to the city of Freathia, home to the Ancients. I'll have just enough time to pack my things and load a carriage, say my goodbyes to Licia and Killian, and leave before my betrothed arrives.

Healer's move with efficiency through the beds, tending to the sick and sleeping. Fires burn high at both ends of the room, warding off the chill of the winter night. Out of the corner of my eye I see quick movement and see Thaliya has spotted me and is waving me over. She waits patiently for me to approach, and then without saying anything, turns and walks with quick steps down the narrow hallway leading to her small office.

As I stare at her rigid shoulders, I hope she's not upset with me for leaving the way I did, surely she knows I just needed a little time to process such news. I begin to say something but she shushes me and pushes open the door, hustles me through, and closes it quickly and quietly behind me.

There are four other sets of eyes staring back at me as Thaliya closes the door behind me. Thaddeus rests with his feet up, taking up much of the small space. I only question for a moment how Gryphon knew I'd be here, but then get distracted by the other two familiar men in the room. But I can't place them.

Thaliya doesn't waste time with introductions, though. "If we are to get you to the north, we have to move quickly. As I understand it, your betrothed is within a day's travel." I balk at her news, and the fact that it's so much more specific than Hadeon's.

"But that would mean—" I begin, trying to figure out how long it would take to pack a trunk. Hours. It would take hours to pack all the clothing and books, not to mention extras of everything because we'll be traveling north in the middle of winter.

"We'll leave just before the wedding," Thaddeus states plainly. "That way, you have time to train. You need to at least know the basics." He looks to Thaliya and then the older man in the room.

The reality of the situation hits me. Once I leave these walls, Hadeon will be furious. And the impact my leaving will have with his treaty with the west, I can't even imagine. I can't help but laugh. A loud, nervous laugh escapes from me, one that's too big for this small space, and several of those around us wince. But I can't help it because the seriousness of the situation is bubbling up into something else entirely.

"You laugh, Princess, but the truth is, if you are to leave Merula, your window of opportunity closes in mere days."

"Yes, of course." I look to Thaliya. "And you'll be able to ready yourself and put the ward to right before then?"

Her eyes widen at my misunderstanding. "Oh, my sweet Rowandine, I wish I could go along with you."

"What?" I ask, incredulity causing the word to come out louder than I meant it to. Everyone else in the room ducks their heads and makes shushing motions to me as I repeat myself in a harsh whisper. "What?"

"I can't go north with you, Rowandine. My duties are here, to the people of Merula." Her words are gentle, but they cut like a knife anyway.

"But I thought—" I thought her duties were to me. I thought she'd always be by my side. I thought she'd be able to tell me more about my parents. But now, there will be no time for that. Suddenly, tears threaten at the corners of my eyes and I become very aware of the other two men in the room—one is an older man, sitting stick straight at attention. He has many daggers strapped across his belt and two on a strap right beside him that must go on his back. The younger man I know I've seen before but I've been away too long. Both men busy themselves looking anywhere else but at me.

"I have the next best thing." Thaliya smiles warmly and presents the younger man to me.

"Baylor?" Gryphon says, laughter playing at the corner of his mouth as he tries to put the pieces together.

"The stable master?" I look to Gryphon for confirmation, recalling mention of him but unable to place him.

"Well, yes. Princess Rowandine, this is my son, Baylor. Baylor will lead you north, along with Thaddeus and Gryphon. I think that will make for a sound quest."

With that proclamation, Baylor's eyes go wide and he looks at his mother. At first I think it's because she's sending him away, but then I recognize his curly blond hair and boyishly blue eyes. His appearance, along with the mention of him being the stable master, allows me to place how I know him.

Rather intimately actually. If I remember correctly, there was a time when he spent most of his afternoons up in the hay lofts rather than working with the horses. I wonder how he ever got promoted to stable *master*?

"She's the one? But you never mentioned she was of the Aeronwick household?" His voice rising with each word, quickly reaching a dangerously high pitch for a grown man. "Mother! You could have at least—"

She waves him off. "You know my reasons, we were charged with watching and waiting. There was no reason for you to know anyway, the more who knew the easier it would be to get out. Why would it matter?" She looks suddenly at Baylor and then at me, her eyes widening in horror.

With this, Gryphon loses all control and his laughter permeates the room. He grabs his knees as his laughter comes out in uncontrollable fits. So much so that he falls to the floor, and I can't tell if it's for show or he's really that affected.

If possible, the older man sits up even straighter, looking terribly uncomfortable at the situation he's found himself in. And Thaddeus, his eyes narrow imperceptibly at the stable master and he folds his arms across his chest.

Horror stricken, Thaliya turns to me. "I'm so sorry, Princess. I never would have—it never occurred to me—" She turns back to her son. "Baylor! How could you! She's the princess!" She swats at him and he ducks just out of her way.

With splotches of red blooming up my chest and into my cheeks, I attempt to put an end to this line of conversation. "It was many years ago. Let's put it all behind us now."

After that small bump, it only takes minutes to decide on a plan. I'll work with the older man, Patton, in the mornings on swordsmanship. Then in the afternoons, I'll explore my newfound ability to heal with Thaliya. We'll do this up until the wedding, which should give us plenty of time as Father and the council come to an agreement with Etos.

I'll be the first to admit, with all the new information swimming through my mind, I only focus on where I need to be and when.

I jump when Thaliya's hands rest on my shoulders and I realize everyone else in the room has left. I've just been standing still, rooted in place by the door frame. "It's a lot, I know. But you're ready. You were meant for this." Her eyes are full of unshed tears as she hugs me. As I sink into her warm embrace, all I can think is how unready I am for this. But if she believes in me, then I won't waste time. I'll prepare myself.

CHAPTER TWENTY-SIX

H is hands are on me as soon as I step out of the healer's ward. My mind is a whirl-wind and I'm completely caught off guard but the frosty scent wraps around me and I let him devour me with kisses.

"I knew there was a reason I couldn't stand that stable hand." He pulls me toward him into the dark. "It's faint, but I can still smell him on you." I crash into his chest, aligning our bodies so I can touch the most parts of him at once. His jealous response is dizzying. It's hard to surface from this heady feeling as I try to match his hunger.

In my lust-filled haze, that comment reminds me of the night when he told Gryphon and me who he really was. Something I still haven't had time to process with everything else piling on top. A deep hum of satisfaction leaves him and he moves to trail kisses from below my ear, farther down, hesitating just a moment at the pulse in my neck. I can feel his teeth lightly brushing across that spot, and my pulse jumps in answer.

His deep hum turns into a predatory growl. This is the first time we've been together since he shared that he's an Ancient. Suddenly, a tingle runs down my spine.

I wonder if he's going to bite me.

And to my surprise, the thought doesn't terrify me. It's the opposite, actually I find my blood heats with the thought. My blood, spilling across his lips and into him. These thoughts turn me on even more and urge me to arch into him, grind into him, unapologetically searching for the friction that will nudge me closer to release, all the while exploring this new world.

"You can have me. You can have my blood. I know you want it." Each sentence comes out in short breaths and I feel a shudder run through him as my fingertips run up and down his chest. He pulls away from me, searching my eyes. He pauses, his body going still as if he's struggling with himself on this. "I can't. You don't know what that means. I won't do that to you." The look in his eyes tells me he's fighting demons to say those words.

I grind against him, tempting to sway him to do my bidding.

"We'd be connected forever. With your blood in my veins, you'd always be a part of me. Even the smallest of drops. You don't understand what that means. It's too much."

I lean back, trying to get a read on him. The strain on his face tells me he's serious. There's no going there.

At least for now.

Instead, I palm his hardness. Rubbing and teasing him, wanting him on me and in me, everywhere all at once. In response, he takes my lower lip in his teeth, tugging and groaning, asking for more.

If he won't have me in that way, I'll take him into me.

I kneel, tugging on his pants to free him to me. The way he springs out of his pants, ready and firm, makes my mouth water. With one hand wrapped around him, I guide him into my mouth, licking and sucking all the way down his shaft and back up. Slowly taking him in, inch by inch, until he hits the back of my throat.

I hum, welcoming him in and he instantly hardens further while his fingers play in my hair. He relaxes into the wall behind him as I move. While

I take him in and out, I squeeze my thighs together, searching for just a little bit of friction to release the tension building in my core, making it impossible to be still as I suck.

With his pressure on the crown of my head encouraging me, I suck harder until my cheeks cave in and he's filling me. His hands fist in my hair and I know he's close.

My movements become faster as I pump my hand in rhythm with him entering me. His entire body stiffens as he comes. He fills me, the sticky warmth sliding so easily down my throat as I swallow every last drop down.

Before I can lick my lips, he pulls me onto my feet and spins me, pressing me against the wall, his hands still in my hair. He wrenches my skirts up just enough so he can slip into me from behind. He drives hard, still slick enough from his come to enter me fully in one thrust.

He pauses. I have just enough time to register that he's taking me in the small alcove just outside the healer's ward. I send a silent prayer up to the stars above that no one finds us here, just as he pulls out and thrusts again.

He teases me, slowly moving in and out while holding my wrists above my head. My elbows anchor me against each thrust as I try to match his moves, encouraging him to move faster. Grabbing my hips and pulling me toward him, he matches my rhythm. Faster, faster, and faster. The sound of skin on skin fills the empty hallway, and I release myself completely to his movements.

Remembering others are close, I bite my bicep, stifling the pleasure lighting me up from the inside out. He rides me until my body goes limp and then falls against me, crushing me against the wall—emptying himself into me a second time.

Chapter Twenty-Seven

Since we decided to leave just before the wedding, things may get a little tricky, and I've heard too many conflicting thoughts about Lysander Sturdevant for anything to be reliable. So I'm still not sure what I'm walking into. Or away from.

That will give us a few days for me to learn the basics from Patton and Thaliya. Patton has agreed to teach me as much as he can about sword fighting and hand to hand combat before we leave. I hope at least something will stick seeing as he's the head of guard. Thaliya is confident she'll be able to progress my studies quicker now that I know what I am and my magic has awakened.

They refuse to leave any sooner, demanding I need to learn at least the essentials before we set off.

We're lucky here in the south we don't feel the bite of winter. We'll have plenty of time to progress up the continent and arrive in the north after the worst of winter has passed. Of course, up there, winter is never-ending.

Now, I have just a few days to soak in as much as I can about self-defense, healing, and anything else they throw at me. Thank the stars I can already hold my own on horseback, or else I'd be out of luck. Baylor's blond curls flash through my mind and I absentmindedly wonder if he's as talented teaching one how to ride a horse as he was with other things so many years ago.

"What're you grinning at? You look like you just watched Baylor falling over backwards into a water trough." Gryphon rudely awakens me from said daydream with a crooked grin, reminding me that he now knows I've slept with the stable master. Maybe I should even the playing field, let him know I know about him and Licia. That'll wipe the grin off his face.

"Yeah, Baylor something..." is all I can manage to get out as we stalk down the tunnels to where Patton is waiting to instruct me on basic combat techniques. Thank the stars for the darkness down here, or I'm sure my blazing cheeks would give me away even more. "Why are you coming to our lessons, anyway? Just to give me a hard time?"

"But of course. How're you going to learn anything without my commentary?" Gryphon smiles broadly and playfully pushes my shoulder. Except he forgets he has at least three stones on me, so I fly into the dirt wall on the other side of the narrow pathway. I grab my shoulder and yelp while he cringes at his accidental show of force.

"What do you do in your free time? Carry barrels across the gardens? Move horses across the fields?" I continue rubbing my shoulder while chastising him.

"My free time is spent with you, Roe. There's no one else." He puts his arm around me, mocking my interest.

I shrug him off and mumble, "You sure about that?"

"What's that supposed to mean?" He looks at me sideways, incredulous I could sleuth something out of him or Licia.

"Not a thing, dear Gryphon. Why? Should it mean something?" I bait him, but he doesn't bite. We arrive at the domed underground room and find Patton standing stiffly along the wall, ensuring he has a clear vantage point of the only two entrances to this underground room.

"You sound like new recruits, squabbling over the last wooden sword. It's a wonder no one else has found this passage with the way you two carry on," he scolds as he passes us our wooden training sword. "Let's begin."

Never having wielded one before, the weapon feels long and awkward in my hand. Gryphon instantly begins swinging his around in exaggerated figure eights. He doesn't look like he knows what he's doing either. He looks as ridiculous as I feel. I know Jonaraja kept him close, but I guess I always assumed he knew at least the basics of sword fighting. Clearly, my assumption is wrong.

"What?" he asks defensively and promptly stops swinging his sword around. "I've always wanted to do that." He shrugs and looks to Patton for instruction, avoiding my gaze as his cheeks bloom with color.

Patton works us hard all morning. We learn how to hold the sword and the basic stances as well as the proper way to hold and grip a sword. Who knew there's an art to hand position to ensure balance and maximize control?

Patton also finds great pleasure in relentlessly running us through the basic cut and strike moves until I can no longer hold my arm up. Only after Patton is satisfied we've learned something does he finally gesture for us to take a break.

Gryphon is a little less worse for wear, as he already has at least some of the necessary muscles. As we rest our swords against the closest pillar, he puffs his chest out like a proud peacock. Clearly happy with his progress.

"Confidence will only get you so far, Gryphon. Remember this." Patton holds one finger up in warning; his warrior frame filling the archways in our subterranean training room. "Sword fighting is an art. One that takes skill, power, and speed. Don't mistake any of those for swagger or foolishness. Both, I understand, are unfortunate tendencies of yours."

Thoroughly scolded, Gryphon wilts like a hydrangea cut for a vase.

"Understood, Sir Patton," Gryphon mumbles, the pomp finally deflates from him. I knock my shoulder with his to show my solidarity, and then wince because all my muscles already hurt.

To announce the end of our break, Patton asks, "Look around us. What do you see?"

I look around the underground room. The same one we've been standing in all morning. Nothing's changed. "I see stone walls? Dirt?" I venture a guess at what Patton is focusing on.

"Wrong. Look again. An effective sword maiden always first assesses her environment. Decide what will help you play to your strengths. Rowandine, you are both shorter and lighter than the average swordsman. Tight places and being light on your feet will go a long way to benefiting you. Gryphon, play on your mischievous side. That, in addition to all the strategy meetings you've attended, will help you stay ahead of your opponent. So try again. What do you see?" He sweeps his arm out wide, presenting the room to us in a new light.

"The statues and pillars are natural barriers I could use to help block," I suggest to Patton.

"Good. More."

"The corners. If we drive our opponents into the corners, they won't be able to escape easily." Gryphon folds his arms in front of his chest to drive home his answer, but then thinks better of it and uncrosses them once more, clearly treading on uncertain territory.

"Right, yes. Never back yourself into a corner. It will be the death of you."

Gryphon and I exchange looks; my fear reflects in his features as well.

"Yes. Good. Enough for today. I'll see you an hour earlier tomorrow." And with that, Patton strolls down the dark passageway from which he came.

Gryphon and I turn down the opposite path, our silence speaking volumes of our exhaustion. I flex my back, feeling the ache of muscles I didn't even know I had.

"So, this'll be a busy couple of days, huh?" I was under no illusion that preparing to save Ombretta from the grasp of blood sucking Ancients would be easy, but I had no idea it would be this exhausting. "At least you seem to understand what in the stars Patton is talking about." Gryphon seemed to get the basic movements of the sword and where his feet should be as soon as Patton showed us. And Patton was right. Gryphon's ability to anticipate his opponent's movements allowed him an instant advantage.

"Yeah, it's trickier than it looks. No wonder all the guards walk around like they own the place; I feel like a total savage wielding that sword with both hands." Gryphon practices some swings with an invisible sword.

"You're right. Your flimsy, wooden sword is incredibly intimidating," I muster up enough energy to laugh at him, but then my abs hurt. And my back hurts. And my shoulders as well. If I could double over in pain, I would. Instead, I stand very still, trying to slow my breathing enough so my entire body doesn't ache.

Chapter Twenty-Eight

All of my muscles scream at me with each step I take, but I promised Thaliya I'd stop by the ward after training. I hope she'll take it easier on me than Patton, who clearly expects more of me at my very first lesson. I'll have to practice before I go to practice at this rate.

I enter the quiet ward where the smells of late autumnal sunshine and spearmint greet me. I wash my hands as Thaliya has taught me, scrubbing each finger and nail, then moving to the insides of each palm. I take time to scrub the outside as well and then up my arms. Thaliya has always stressed the importance of cleanliness, especially around the sick.

I find her tending to a young boy who's firing questions off while she finishes tying his arm into a sling. She reminds him to keep off it and then looks to his companion, who must've accompanied him here, and repeats the instructions. They promise to return in several days to have the healing assessed.

Thaliya gives them one last look as they sprint across the room toward the back entrance then are gone. Most of the people she tends to come in from that door, rather than through the castle itself. The people of the village depend on Thaliya and her staff to see them through simple colds and mend them when they've broken bones as well. She and her team are the most skilled in the surrounding villages and care deeply about the villagers' welfare.

The king keeps a blind eye, either because he knows and agrees with what Thaliya does or he has more important things to worry about than what the healing staff does in their free time—I'm not sure which.

Before we begin our lessons for the day, she cups my face between her palms, her gaze softening. "Oh child. You've grown into such a strong woman." I look at her questioningly, not only are her actions out of character, but I usually feel anything but strong. For the most part, I'm still treated like a small child here. "You'll see, just trust yourself." She presses a kiss to my forehead and stands back. Her hands find my shoulders and squeeze my arms all the way down to grip my hands in hers, as if she's seeing me for the first time and the last time all at once.

I suppose that's how it is. I now know everything and she can be herself around me, fully. I smile back at her, and in this small moment, try to get across how much she means to me. Everything she's done for me and everything she's taught me has molded me into the woman I am today.

She leads me toward a sleeping child in a cot. His arms are bandaged from elbows to fingertips. He's asleep, but the grimace on his small face tells me even in sleep he feels the pain. He has a thin layer of sweat along his brow, creating a halo across the pillow.

"He's the smithy's boy. An accident with the flames. He's burned his hands. When he's conscious, he worries he won't be able to help his father in the forge and cries because his father can't keep up with the king's incessant demands."

"That's a lot of weight on such slight shoulders," I respond.

She looks at me expectantly, as if there's something I could do to help this poor boy. I unwrap his bandages to check the damage. His poor tiny hands. Big, angry blisters cover every inch of his palms, all the way up to his elbows. And that's the best of it. In some spots, it looks as if his skin has melted away completely, giving way only to muscle and bone. The damage is so severe, he clearly won't be able to help his father any longer, at least not in the way he's used to. "Should I change his bandages?" I ask, even though his bandages look like they've just been tended to.

"I wonder if there's something more you might do." She nods, encouraging me. "Go ahead, rest your hands upon his chest, see what you can feel." She motions toward the sleeping boy.

My eyebrows raise at her request, although now that I think about it, she always begins her examinations like this as well. I'd just assumed this was her way of comforting her patients before checking them over.

This is just like the young girl. My mind goes back to how that felt and I try to replicate it. She's right, I'm able to begin by using my hands to read what was wrong on the inside.

I rub my hands together to create a little warmth before placing my hands on his chest. I watch him for a moment, silently asking permission before I begin. In his sleep he winces once more, so I move closer, sitting beside him on the cot.

I open the ties of his undershirt so I can access his chest. At first, only the warmth of his skin presses against my hands. Despite his injury, his heart thumps are strong under my fingertips.

I look at Thaliya for some guidance, but she nods for me to continue.

I close my eyes to help guide my focus. At first, nothing happens. Then a small hum begins deep down within my gut. The hum rises within my body and then swiftly moves down to my palms. A warmth washes over me, through my palms, and toward his chest as if I've become a cresting wave within the sea. The warmth is still within me, but it's also coursing through him and searching as well. Slowly, I realize I can guide this power moving through me, so I nudge it, urging it closer to his arms.

I gasp with surprise as my arms suddenly burn with all the pain he must be feeling. I push my focus past the fierce pain to keep from letting go. As the pain intensifies, I picture my arms and his own. How they looked when they were whole and unmarred. I picture his skin now blemish free. How his arms must've looked before the fire.

Ever so slowly, the burning recedes from my arms. The energy flows back up my body in a swirling wave from my center down to my feet. From there, it dissipates completely.

I open my eyes, hesitant to look at my hands. I'm unsure what to expect after that searing pain. My hands still rest on the boy's chest. I flip my palms up, back and forth, but there is no more pain and my hands appear fine.

I then find the boy's hands, still resting on top of the loosened bandages. The blisters are gone. His hands are pink, but no longer angry with blisters. I flip his hands over as well, tracing along the lines of his palms, just to be sure. The skin is slightly scarred, but whole.

I look to Thaliya for confirmation of what I just achieved. Her eyes are wide with surprise.

The room begins to spin around her wide eyes and I feel a lightness within me. Darkness swallows the spinning room, and then it swallows me as well.

I awake in a cot with Thaliya sitting by my side and gently tapping against my cheeks. "Wake up, Dear, sweet Rowandine, wake up!" she repeats until my eyes flutter open.

Relieved, she slumps against the back of her chair and grabs my hand to squeeze it tight. "You fainted. You did well, but you fainted. That'll pass. It's clearer than ever. You have such a deep strength within you. We'll continue to grow it and you will do the most impressive things. You just wait." Her face relaxes with warmth and glows with excitement.

A strength within me? No one's ever said anything like this to me. The words warm me like thick wool socks on a cold winter night. And suddenly, I feel the humming stirring deep within me again and hope she's right.

"You're exhausted. You'll need to eat more now that you're training. You must keep your strength up so you can continue to grow, or all will be for naught." She shoves an apple at me and waits until I take a bite.

Remembering the boy, I sit up quickly and glance around the room. The cot he had previously occupied to my right is now empty. My eyes keep searching the room, expecting to find him somewhere else.

"He's gone. He went home. He awoke shortly after you healed him and ran back to his father to share his good news. You have saved him as well as his family."

I fall back into the bed, still lightheaded but relieved he's okay. He's more than okay. He's healed. And I healed him. How in all the stars in the sky was I able to do that?

"He will be just fine, thanks to you. It's you I'm more worried about. I didn't think you'd jump all the way in with no direction. You clearly have more natural ability than even I detected. Which will make this both easier and more challenging. You have all the power within you, and from the looks of it, you're also able to draw power from the earth as well. Now we must learn to harness it all." She pokes and prods me, moving my limbs and making sure my reflexes are in working order.

Despite my efforts, my eyes close once more. No matter how hard I try to fight it, the curtain of sleep falls silently across my eyes. I drift down into a deep slumber.

The strange dreams return.

I feel the ground beneath me pulsing with a primeval energy, taking the pain I sent back into it and churning it to create something new. It redistributes the energy to find balance. I fall deeper into the earth and my dreams swerve and swirl into a new scene. A moment that seems more like a memory. The edges are sharp and clear rather than blurred like the images before.

I dream. Deeply. Of a small group of women. The power radiating off them like the sun's rays on a cloudless day. They're all huddled around a book, planning and laughing together. I see the importance of whatever they're discussing in the set of their brows and worried glances, but they also seem to enjoy each other's company. There's a heaviness lurking unseen but clearly felt in the darkness surrounding them, pressing in from all sides. Suddenly, a warm glow burns from the middle of the circle. It's their hands. Looking closer, on each of their index fingers sits a ring. The glow becomes brighter and brighter.

I wake suddenly, sitting straight up in the cot Thaliya left me on and looking toward my left hand where the three-stoned ring still sits. Without a moment to waste, I discard the blankets wrapped snugly around me and take off back to my rooms.

I limp back to my chambers, cursing my legs for not being able to move faster. I feel as if I've spent the day being dragged behind a horse, rather than sleeping the afternoon away in the quiet ward. My muscles ache from being used in a way they've never been used. My mind and entire being is exhausted and wrung dry from exerting all my energies on healing that young boy.

And although I can barely stand up straight, I regret no part of today. For the first time since I was a child running through the gardens with Gryphon and Licia at my heels, I feel as if my day was spent exactly as I'd like.

This feeling of making decisions based upon what I desire is something completely foreign to me. I've spent my life being shuffled from one point to another, being told how to act, and what to say. I often find my mind has been changed. Not because of my own thoughts, but because someone has told me what to think instead of listening to myself to decide.

Maybe though, just because those thoughts are inside of me, doesn't mean they are necessarily my own. The realization is foreign but the weight of the truth sits heavy upon me.

Today, I woke up knowing I wanted to learn to defend myself. I woke up knowing it was important to explore the part of me that enjoys healing. Today, I realize these things have been dreams of mine before I even knew to dream. I smile to myself, knowing although today was grueling and painful, the hurt echoes in all the right places. I guess I had to lose myself completely to those around me before I could begin to find myself.

I've come so far in just one day. I can't imagine what I'll feel like days or a week from now. I try to picture my life after I leave the castle. Riding all day out in the fresh, almost-winter sun, sleeping under the stars, Gryphon and me finding our way north like explorers. It sounds like a dream. But I can't pretend it'll be all butterflies and flowers. I know what we're up against. I know it's the real world we're entering. And it sounds like anyone we meet will have a grudge against the king and anyone related to him. We'll have to be careful; we'll have to be ready.

I fling myself onto my bed, reaching under the mattress to pull out my small leather book. I flip through it, searching the pages. The dream reminding me of a page I've seen before. It's one of the first few pages. There, carefully illustrated, is a circle of women. Here, on the page, they're dancing rather than talking as they were in my dream. But the mood is somehow the same. I can just make out the lines of rings on their fingers.

I could kick myself for not being able to read all the hand-written notes around the picture. I can feel the importance of it. Does this mean there's others with rings like this? Does my ring belong to someone else? Or is it somehow meant for me?

CHAPTER TWENTY-NINE

S played out across our nest of blankets, I bask in the glow of warmth the fire before us projects as Thaddeus trails his fingertips across my bare belly, as if he's playing a light, playful tune. His fingers move quickly and deftly, something I've been privileged in experiencing many ways as of late.

"What's she like?" I ask, as he absent-mindedly traces circles across my bare back.

He looks up, a question on his lips, but then he sees the answer in my eyes. "Ombretta?" At my hum of assurance, he continues. "She's strong. Like really solid. In her resolve, in her beliefs, and in her strength, too. Like no one I know, and that's saying a lot because I've been around for a while. And loyal. I don't know a soul more loyal. She's been by my side for a long time." He smiles and his canines flash.

I wonder what he means by loyal, if they have more of a history than he's letting on, but her strength is also fascinating.

"But if she's as strong as you say, why hasn't she figured out a way to escape?" A silly question to ask, but I wonder nonetheless.

"It's complicated." His gentle caresses along my back suddenly shift, and I'm on my back underneath him. "And I don't need complicated right now. I need you."

Our stolen moments are few and far between as of late. Between training with Baylor and working with Thaliya, my windows of free time have shrunk. But in the past days, we've made time for each other. The fire behind us just caught again on a fresh log, sparking to life and bathing us in hues of reds and oranges.

We've made this small, forgotten space ours for now, and frequent it as much as we can. "You are my muse. I must have you in every way possible before we leave this place."

His fingertips are refreshing, painting a cooling path over my love-warmed stomach. "I'd not object to more right now, but I fear we will be missed."

"But until then, you are mine." He rises over me. His erection growing, readying for another round. His body presses against mine, all his hard parts fitting perfectly against all of my soft parts.

"He's here! The king has arrived!" The hushed voices travel from down the hall to where Thaddeus and I steal a moment together.

I still underneath him, afraid of what this could mean. For me—for us—for this time we've carved away for ourselves. This will be the end of it, for certain. He groans and rolls off me, our love-making forgotten for now. I rise, gathering blankets around me even though I know no one will find us here, those voices are too close for comfort and they've broken my small measure of peace.

I stride to the window so I can see what all the commotion is about, my warm palms steaming the cold glass beneath. There's much movement below where the gardens meet the formal entrance to the castle, but I still as a figure dismounts his horse. The stiff figure, mostly just a dark riding cloak from this distance, lands to the ground as if in slow motion. As I get my first glimpse of my betrothed, Thaddeus' big hands come around my hips, warding off any threat as he joins me to watch the King of Etos arrive. Although his modesty is a clear afterthought as he stands beside me in all his glory, his full erection saluting the Etos king from high above.

The figure far below turns as if he feels eyes on him. He finds us immediately, and his dark stare bores into me, traveling from my sex-mussed hair down to my bare toes in the ceiling-to-floor windows. With his gaze locked on mine, even from this distance, I'm certain he knows me at first glance as his betrothed, and does not appreciate what he finds.

I try to remain still, holding my chin high, and relying on Thaddeus to keep me upright. Leaning on him for strength, I hold Sturdenvat's gaze for one more moment, and then turn away back to the warmth of the fireplace.

But the fire, that blazed hot and full a moment ago, has drafted once again into small embers, and our nest of blankets no longer looks as inviting.

CHAPTER THIRTY

"I can't do this." I storm into our chambers, not caring when the doors slam open with force and then shut right behind me. I enter the room as Licia prepares for the evening. Her gown tonight is intended to make the newly arrived King of Etos jealous of the slimmer, courtlier sister, for sure. She sparkles from head to toe in an emerald velvet—Marlys' small effort to ward off the hint of southern chill. She drips with diamonds and pearls and her shining blond hair piles in curls upon her head.

"You can, and you will." She spins, heavy velvet swirls licking her heels. After seeing my reflection, she shrugs and continues. "Or you won't. Have you seen him, though? He's tall, dark, and mysterious for sure." She licks her lips as she recounts her first impressions. Apparently, they were much closer and positive than my own.

"It's too soon." I'm almost frantic, but not because my betrothed has just arrived. Or perhaps that's exactly why. I can't envision what's next. His arrival sets things into motion I can't even fathom, could not have even imagined until days ago.

"Your sex hair would beg to differ, dear sister." Licia moves away from the mirrors as Marlys huffs behind her to lounge on the small sofa. She sinks neatly into the pile of pillows, like a perfect, pink lily among lily pads. "I don't think it's too soon; I think you've become too attached to the bard—"

"Thaddeus—"

"Like I said." She shoots a pointed look my way. "Too attached for your own good." She closes her eyes as if I'm too much to bother with, but I know she loves this scandal—this is what she lives for.

"I have. Grown attached I mean, but that's beside the point."

"Is it, though? Weren't you hoping the bard would whisk you off to the most romantic parts of what's left of our magical realm?"

That hits a little too close to home. My skin heats, remembering days ago when I so naively thought he was preparing to do just that.

"You did!" She sits up at this, her voice echoing off the tall ceiling. "He's a bard!" I watch her features, wondering if she believes what she says or if her flitting birds have told her otherwise by now. I know Thaddeus has kept his identity close and I have no idea how connected Licia is to what goes on outside of the family. "You'll do better than a bard, and I'm not saying the King of Etos has to be the one, but there's more out there than him."

"I don't understand what *your* problem with Thaddeus is. So, he can play the four-string, I think it's attractive." A blush warms its way up my collar bone, when I think of all the other benefits of taking a musician to bed. But I turn my attention back to Marlys' ministrations, frustrated with the way Licia keeps picking at who I choose to spend my time with. We're both adults here.

Marlys claps her hands to stop our bickering, but also to signal she's done and I may move freely now. She's certainly done it again. Gone is the sex hair and reddened skin from where Thaddeus' clean-shaven skin roughened my own. In its place, is someone fit for the throne. Now, my eyes are lined heavily with kohl giving the impression I have a secret. My hair, like Licia's, is piled high with curls, but she's carefully woven a few braids throughout. I feel like a shifter warrior with the way the sides are braided close and the curls rise high, giving me an extra inch at least.

I can tell she's taken careful consideration with the dress. It still has hints of mourning black, but the dress itself is silver. Simply cut, the intricacy is in the layers, which curl and float all around me cascading to the floor. Mixed in with the silver, is the mourner's black but also a bold blue, which is the color on Etos' banners. "It's beautiful, Marlys."

"You're beautiful, your grace." She bows, and leaves me with Licia, who's sat up enough to see over the sofa's back and is now fanning herself.

"Well. That's an improvement. You ready for yet another night of dancing?"

"Never one to honey-coat it." I roll my eyes at her; my frustration momentarily lifted, and in its place, uncertainty weighs heavily.

CHAPTER THIRTY-ONE

Nearing the great hall, the typical sounds of loud music and even more loud conversations don't greet us. There's no sign of anyone moving in and out of the great space.

"I thought we were running late. Where is everyone?" I look at Licia, but she's as confused as I am.

"Late is a given with you, but I don't—" She's cut off as our brother storms toward us.

"We're in the dining room." Killian strides across the hall; his exasperation evident. "Didn't you get the message? And yes, you're both late." And if he's already this frustrated, I'm not looking forward to Father's reaction. "King Sturdevant wanted a more intimate meeting with you, so naturally we rearranged some things." With this explanation, he hurries us back toward the room he just exited. Licia's surprise mirrors mine, and I try to get it under control before we walk through the double doors.

If Lysander Sturdevant requested a smaller audience and Father acquiesced, then there must be something more at play here. Before I can list the options, Licia and I are through the door with everyone turning our way. As we enter, everyone rises and Sturdevant moves to my chair, pulling it out for me and motioning me to sit beside him. His movements are practiced and graceful. He's taller than he appeared from afar, and I have to tilt my head upward as I get closer. I give a small bow and smile in thanks but I can't help but feel hurt when his tight smile matches the steel in his eyes. I know our first sighting of each other leaves much to be desired, but I hope we can mend the tear before it grows irreparable. Even if it is only for the next few days.

Quite the gentleman, which isn't what I expected after our distant encounter, I sit and he smoothly pushes my chair in and returns to his seat. Licia, smirking, waits beside her chair until Gryphon reluctantly does the same for her. He makes a big show of the inconvenience until his mother, Jonaraja, coughs pointedly and he returns to his seat, quietly as if a young boy scolded. Licia beams and looks at her nails until the servants place steaming dishes of fish from the bay beyond the castle and vegetable stews and meat pies on the table.

"We are gathered here this evening to celebrate a great union of realms." Father's booming voice is too much for this small space. "Everguard and Etos, united in goals and power, will be unstoppable moving forward." Father raises his glass to King Sturdevant, who sits beside him, majestic in his seat, and returns the motion.

After glasses clink in cheers, I watch as Gryphon not so subtly sizes Sturdevant up as he spoons large quantities from each of the plates around him onto his own. To his credit, Sturdevant pays him no mind. He focuses on the task at hand, cutting his meat into small and even sizes.

Father's eye catches mine, a reminder I'm to be more prepared for this evening as my previous performance proved a failure. So, before Father and Killian can rope Sturdevant into conversations about lands and politics, I rake my mind for something—anything to begin.

Just as I open my mouth, a four-string strums from the other side of the room. I cough, suddenly choking on the food in my mouth. In between gasps, I follow the sound and I don't know how I missed the musician set up right beside the entrance to the room, just over Gryphon and Licia's shoulders. Thaddeus looks amused as he lazily strums chords to set the ambience for the evening meal.

His eyebrows raise slightly and he tilts his head in invitation to continue whatever I was about to say to the king beside me. But any conversation I could dream up dissolves on my tongue.

The tension growing between Sturdevant and me now has a name. And a very, very beautiful face. I can't help but stare at the ease in which Thaddeus continues playing, uncaring of the scene unfolding before him as if his station is above us rather than the bard he plays at.

If he's the very picture of ease, I'm the opposite. The room feels too small as I imagine the rest of the meal trying to get to know the king beside me while all I really want to do is get lost in the dreamy eyes and musical prowess of the man across the room.

I can feel Sturdevant's gaze on me. I stare at my plate rather than meet his eyes. This dinner can't get any worse.

Gryphon and Licia's whispers from across the table only add to the weight of the room closing in. They speak so easily with one another, a language I once knew.

I take a deep breath, trying to calm my nerves and everything else swirling inside of me, and open my mouth, hoping something comes out.

"How do you find our mild winters, your grace? I would imagine it's a nice reprieve from further north." The weather? I couldn't do better than the weather? I take a large sip of the wine in front of me.

"The weather." He looks at me, amused at my choice in topic. I can see his calculating effort as he traces his gaze from Thaddeus back to me. His amusement grows as I try not to shift in my seat at the discomfort. "Is a welcome change from Etos. However, I had hoped it would be warmer upon my arrival."

I may have been living a married but solitary life up in the mountains; however, his meaning comes off plan and clear. I can't decide which upsets me more—the fact I was caught with Thaddeus or his already tarnished image of me. But strangely, hurt blossoms in my chest. I do care what this man before me thinks of me, even if I have no intention of ever marrying him.

"My sister tells me you share her love of maps." Licia presses her napkin delicately to her lips as she directs her comment toward King Sturdevant. I shoot daggers at her, but try to calm my features just as quickly. I haven't even spoken to Sturdevant yet, how would I know something like this? How does *she* know something like this? I don't know why I'm surprised, though. The way her birds flit about the castle, seeing and reporting all to her before much of the castle has heard even a whisper.

"Oh really?" Sturdevant turns toward me, his smile genuine and warm; my first impression not completely smudging his interest in me.

Killian joins in, which is uncharacteristic of him, but I suppose where maps are concerned, anything goes. "Yes. Rowandine and I would spend hours poring over maps of Everguard mostly, but sometimes the surrounding lands."

"The library has a vast collection, your grace. I could show you sometime?" I venture, angling my body toward him, not only to show interest, but also so I don't have to watch Thaddeus' steady gaze as I attempt to win favor from this man who is a king, yet so unlike my father.

"What draws your attention, if I may ask?" Sturdevant goes back and forth between Killian and me.

"It's a wonder someone has traveled so far and wide. Trekking over streams and mountains in order to track the topography. I fear I'm a little jealous of the adventure of it all." A blush fills my cheek. Am I being too honest?

But his smile broadens as he replies, "I not only can appreciate your answer, I have to admit, I've had the same thought once or twice. We actually bring a mapmaker on all our excursions. Her skills are invaluable to our party. I'll have to introduce you at some point."

I tilt my head, thrown by how warm and kind he is. Everything he says is sincere.

"She's being modest, your grace." Killian, still excited to be conversing about one of his favorite topics, inserts his thoughts into the conversation. "She could practically chart terrain in her sleep. The way she plots routes, even for whole armies, is second to none."

Pride gleams in his eyes as he says this as if he raised me himself. Which, in this case with our love of studying and charting terrain, he did. "Killian taught me everything he knows." I nod in his direction, giving credit where credit is due.

After Licia's brilliant parley, the conversation flows smoothly the entire evening. She effortlessly weaves Lysander Sturdevant and me together, masterfully painting me as an incredibly talented, incredibly desirable princess.

And for the evening, I almost forgot about the bard cooly staring daggers at me all throughout the meal. Almost.

∞

"I think you made a good first impression," Licia remarks as we make our way back to our end of the castle.

"I hope you're right." I don't mention to her that it wasn't in fact our first sighting of each other. But as far as conversation goes, it couldn't have gone better. "How do you do that?"

"What?" She looks around trying to guess at what I mean.

"How do you make conversation so easily? You just glide right through it, like a skiff on water.""Oh it's just one of those things I've had to get good at along the way."

"But you've always known how to talk to people. You always know the right thing to say."

She shrugs as if it's not a big deal. "I guess I use what I learn about the people around me. Draw them in with all the things I know about them, hang on their every word until they show me their whole world." She gives me a knowing smile.

"You've made it into an artform." I shake my head, knowing I'll never come close to her ability to draw people in with conversation. I marvel at her gift and the way she's able to spin her words into a web that catches every tiny detail.

We arrive at the staircase that takes us up to our rooms. I move to follow Licia's ascent, but a shadow shifts across the open window. I pause, straining my eyes to make out why the light changed. Just as I decide I'm seeing things, someone grabs my wrist, pulling me toward the window in the alcove.

My thoughts are still on the kingly Sturdevant, but the touch is too familiar, too charged to be someone who's so intentional.

"I couldn't stand it." His breath is warm across my neck as he nuzzles the sensitive part beneath my ear.

"Couldn't stand what?" I ask, matching his breathiness, although I know exactly what he's referring to.

"From where I stood, the king had you hanging on his every word. It did things to me that twisted my insides." Thaddeus pushes me into the wall, landing kisses down to my shoulder. "I wanted to jump onto the table and proclaim that you're mine. And then splay you across the table and devour you, as everyone looked on."

I stiffen in his grip. *You are mine* are words Avicii would say to me. A chill runs through me, and not in a good way.

He steps back, but leaves his hands resting on my hips. "I wouldn't do it. If that's what you're thinking. I know the king would have my head on a spike before I even finished my sentence for something like that."

Before I can respond, Licia's light steps backtrack down the stairs. "Roe? Did I lose you?"

A rustle beside my ear has me turning back to Thaddeus, but somehow he's no longer beside me. I take a quick glance at the window before heading after Licia.

CHAPTER THIRTY-TWO

D ark red once again seeps across the floor of Thaliya's office.

"Do you see how if you hold the thought in your mind you can feel the power within your body respond here?" Thaliya draws a circle with her unwounded hand around her own abdomen as we practice pulling power.

Even though we're in the healing ward, we both agreed patrons and healers alike would catch on too quickly if magic was involved. Which has left us in Thaliya's small, cozy office with her holding a dagger and me trying not to faint each time she drags it across her forearm. "Your power is of the earth, so you must be grounded in order to pull from it."

This being the case, we're sitting on the cool stone floor with the carpet rolled back. Sitting cross-legged gives me the most contact with the ground, allowing the most access to my magic.

"Is it different for others? Are there others?" She hasn't said much of this since her first explanation. I suppose I don't blame her; I'd be wary of someone who was expected to save the entire realm but runs from the first mention of it and refuses to believe in her magical gifts, even as they unfold in front of her.

"It's different for others. My gifts are earth based as well, since I'm a healer. I can always feel it trickling in around my ankles at first, and then it slowly rises up toward my center, and then out of my fingertips. But those who call from water, air, or fire have different experiences with their elemental power." As she explains her experience, I can feel my magic rising within me, but instead of a small trickle, it feels more like a wave cresting within, warm and knowing as it moves from my seat and thighs touching the stone to my core. A small tempest brews within as the magic feels around, searching for an outlet.

"And there are others. Not as many as we'd like, but the Fae are here."

"Here? In Merula?" I can't imagine remaining here after what Hadeon did. The cruelty. The ruthlessness. The hatred. All so apparent in his first step onto Everguard, and it has only grown in the past ten years.

"A small number are here. Most reside in Chessardolian, our homelands to the east. There, they are safe enough to rebuild our people." Her gaze is distant, and I wonder how long Thaliya has been in Merula, and at what cost. "This has healed up nicely." There's not even a scar. Her skin looks just the way it did before. "I'd say you're beyond me now, unless I'm willing for Patton to impale me on his sword, which I am not," she says emphatically, nodding and rising out of her seat to return to the ward, ending both our conversation and our practice.

I know I should remain in the ward to help, but suddenly I'm very done with blood for the day. I close Thaliya's office door behind me and follow the small hallway back into the ward and out the doors.

"Princess Rowandine, they said I might find you here."

CHAPTER THIRTY-THREE

I look up, startled, still wiping my hands on my dress. Thankfully, it's reasonably clean.

"Your Grace." No one has ever come to call for me down here. I stand still, unsure of how to respond, but oddly flattered that he's sought me, especially after his standoffish demeanor at dinner.

"May I accompany you back?" He offers his arm.

I look around, still surprised he's here. It takes me a moment to catch up, but just as a look of unguarded disappointment crosses his face, I double check that my hands are clean and gently, hesitantly rest my hand on his bicep, which I absentmindedly note is thicker than Thaddeus.'

"You come down here often then?" His tone is neutral and light. The answer is straightforward enough, but I find it difficult to get out. I've forgotten how to do this. With Avicii, there was so much excitement. I couldn't wait to leave these walls and travel the realm with my love. Little did I know, I'd neither travel the realm nor remain in love.

And with Thaddeus, everything happened so fast. And there's less talking and more of everything else. I smile, my mind wandering to last night, where he made use of those long, talented fingers.

"My question amuses you?" He looks at me, unsure of himself for a moment.

"I'm sorry, King Sturdevant," I stumble over my words before recovering. "I'm just surprised. No one ventures out this way, least of all for me."

He watches my face, searching for sincerity. He's trying, I realize. He's searched me out to create a relationship with me before we leave for Etos. Instantly, I feel terrible knowing that I'll leave, no matter if we build a relationship or not.

He's not my future, but he thinks I'm his.

Knowing this, I'm not sure how much to share with him. How much of myself to give.

"You may call me Lysander." His smile is warm and the edges of his eyes wrinkle with the lines of someone who smiles often.

"I do, yes, Lysander. I like spending time in the ward, I try to help where I can." Hesitantly, I look up to see his reaction. He's still smiling warmly at me; his steely eyes continue to melt.

"That's a valiant way to spend your time." He pats my hand with his own as we make our way down the hallway, passing the small office room, forgotten to everyone but Thaddeus and me. "I'm sure the king appreciates the good you do for your people."

"Something like that." He tilts his head in inquiry and for some reason, perhaps because he seems like the exact opposite type of ruler than my father, and I feel like I can, and perhaps he'd even understand. "He doesn't like me down here. He's actually asked me not to come."

Taken aback, he recovers quickly. "Then your work is even more commendable."

His words melt my heart. The smile I give him is true. And he returns it, his confidence returning in full force.

I like him. He's kind and he sees me and I like him.

I can't.

I'll leave him at the altar, there's no room to like him. As the coldness of this realization creeps up my spine, he must see the change in my face.

"Is this where I should leave you?" He mistakes my sudden realization for my having to leave. I look around, barely aware of my surroundings. Thankfully, we've stopped in front of the library. The wooden double doors call to me and I let them.

"Yes, I was going to spend some time in the library today after the ward. I hope you don't mind." I try lamely.

"Then this is where I leave you." He makes a quick bow and kisses my hand. "I look forward to when you have a moment to show me those maps you and Killian spoke of."

"Of course, your grace." I don't move to turn into the library, and he waits patiently until I startle from my thoughts. I turn to the library and back to him as if this choice will guide my path from here on out. He smiles down at me and prepares to say something.

I don't want to know what he's about to say. I give a quick curtsey and without another look up, I excuse myself to the library. I move more quickly than necessary, so of course I trip over my dress just as I cross the threshold.

I hear Lysander behind me, moving to catch my fall. But I land in another's arms.

CHAPTER THIRTY-FOUR

T haddeus catches me with one arm and pulls me into him. The muscles in his arm wrap me close so my back presses against his chest, his nose snuggling in the small part of my neck right under my ear. I look up, smiling my thanks to him and see amusement and something else dancing there.

A cough reminds me of Etos, who is still standing an arm's length away. The ease and confidence from a moment before is replaced with an anger so bright I can feel it. I watch, tension clouding the room as the men stare each other down.

It's a strange feeling, both men in front of me, vying for my attention. Just weeks ago, my husband would leave me for months at a time on my own, not caring how I fared or what I did with my time, the loneliness eating me up. But now, whatever this is, feels the same. I've enjoyed my stolen moments with Thaddeus, but now that Etos has arrived this can no longer continue.

At the same time, even though I'm promised to Etos, little does he know, I'll be long gone before our marriage words are exchanged between us, so there's little point in spending the time to get to know him.

Unsure what to do, I let Thaddeus lead me deeper into the library with my hand in his as he pulls me along the stacks. I look back just once, Etos still watching; his fists clenched by his side and tension radiating off his strong shoulders.

Just out of sight, I drop his hand. Thaddeus turns toward me at the sudden change.

"I know you're still processing everything—"

"Just *processing* everything? You mean, just processing that just now, you and the king of Etos were practically snarling over me like I was a piece of fresh meat? Or maybe I'm just processing the reality that I'm promised to said king but I'm about to leave him and the life I know to go trekking into the snow-filled mountain tops? Or maybe I'm processing the fact that despite how well we've gotten to know each other as of late, you didn't feel it was necessary until days ago to bring up that you knew I had a sister. A sister in peril, at the hand of your people?" Disgusted with everything and not sure where this rage is bubbling up from, I try to move away, but there's only so much room between the stacks of books on either side of us. "Not to mention that you're one of them. A bloodthirsty Ancient, just like them."

"Eh, yes." He steps closer, bravely closing the space between us once again. "I thought between Sturdevant and me, I'd be the lesser evil." He smiles, but I can tell by the way he doesn't fully close the distance between us, he's not confident this will end in his favor.

My body sings at his proximity, but the wound of his omissions are still too raw. "I can't keep doing this. It should be easy to end this. There's nothing but lust between us," but as I motion at the space between us, I can't help but recall the overwhelming pull I feel each time he's close to me, what of that?

"There's more here than just the fire between our bodies. I know you feel it, too." He reaches toward me, but I press myself against the stacks. A flash of last time he was pressed against me here sears my mind, but the feeling isn't the same and I quickly shake it off.

"That's the problem. I can't be with you. I thought I could trust myself with you. I thought this would be easy. I thought we would work. I thought I could trust you. The feelings between us are too much, I can't keep track of what's real and what you mean to me. And what's just my reaction to your pretty words." I inhale and wait. I watch as he goes from hopeful to something else.

"I need you, Roe." The sound of my name on his lips undoes something in me. But he can't be a part of my life while I figure this out. I'm just beginning to understand who I am and what it means to listen to myself. And even though every part of me is screaming he's a part of this recent unlocking, and I should fall into his arms, I know it's not the place for me.

His face crumbles as my resolve hardens. I can see the wall go up between us, and even though I know it's the right thing, it hurts to see him on the other side.

CHAPTER THIRTY-FIVE

"Yes. Good. You're shaping up to be quite the natural sword maiden, just as your mother was." Patton looks at me with a bright smile and his head canting to the side, seemingly recalling moments from the past. "The flow of these movements suit you. I commend you for your light and fluid stance. You've certainly come a long way these past few days. Usually this combination is harder to master." He then looks toward Gryphon, whose stomps could take down the whole tunnel system. He no longer enjoys the practice sword in his hand.

Patton thinks I fight like my mother. Was she a Fae warrior as well? The statue from the garden flashes in my mind and I know without a doubt my mother has been here, watching over me this whole time as well in the quiet alcove in the garden.

He must've known her, trained her even. He's the best of the best after all. Even Hadeon recognizes Patton's power and now he's training me. The realization that Patton, Thaliya, and Baylor all knew my parents and now have waited all this time for me to rise up and stand for everything my parents stood for stokes the small flames of bravery kindling deep within me, just starting to make themselves known.

"Remember though, most of the fighters you come up against will be bigger and stronger than you. Use this to your advantage. You have the power, flexibility, and mobility to strike hard and fast." He moves to the middle of the stone floor. "Always start your moves from out of range, sliding toward your opponent when you strike, making sure to stay out of close range of your opponent, like this." His words are booming and succinct and I wonder if those above us can feel the vibration of his words. It's as if he's addressing an entire army, not just me. And while it's intimidating for sure, it's also refreshing to be spoken to in this way, like he knows I understand and will be better for it. Like he knows I'm not a delicate flower that will blow over in the wind.

I nod and continue my slow technique work. The repetition of each striking movement is a soothing part of being down here. Patton has stressed the importance of finding our rhythm within our flow. I've yet to master this, but with each strike I practice, I feel my muscles molding to the memory of where they belong with each movement.

Patton turns to where Gryphon continues to stomp and strike. "You're thinking too hard. Get out of your head, boy." Patton's frustration is clear. Gryphon, who held such promise on day one of practice, has fallen significantly behind. He wants it so badly that he's getting in his own way. "Stay light on your feet. Shorten your stance and for star's sake stop stomping. It's more of a roll as you place your foot down. Light. On the balls of your feet."

Gryphon turns toward the stone pillar in frustration and begins unloading his anger on it. His strikes are halted and heavy. Unfortunately, only proving Patton correct.

"Mother's locked me up in this castle all my life. I'm no better than a spoiled princess." He turns to me, a small moment breaking through his frustration. "No offense," he shoots my way with a shrug of his shoulders before he returns to land blow after blow.

"None taken. We've got this, together. We have plenty of time to practice along the way. We'll be safe for a while yet, right?" I turn toward Patton, who looks slightly less confident than I feel.

"This is important. I need to keep us safe." Gryphon looks pleadingly at his sword and throws it across the room in disgust. The wooden sword clattering loudly across the stone floor and echoing through the tunnels before us.

"I can manage for myself, thank you," I reply primly, just as a spoiled princess would.

Despite my spoiled princess upbringing and how hard these past few days have been, all of this feels like exactly where I'm supposed to be. Each step of progress I make with the sword in my hand or healing and treating the sick, is my own. I am no longer paying attention to the treks already laid out before me, but creating my own path.

"That's enough for today, take a break while I grab something." For someone his size, he gracefully moves to the dark corners of this room.

At Patton's declaration, Gryphon and I grab our knees, dropping my wooden practice sword to the ground with exhaustion. Patton takes this moment to stride across the room, returning with two long pieces wrapped in cloth. "I thought there would be more ceremony here, but there's little time for that now."

Despite his words, he hands each of us one of the cloth wrapped pieces with reverence. "Here are your swords. May they strike swift and true."

Patton hands each of us a sheathed sword. I draw mine out of the scabbard, watching in awe as the blade sparkles, even in the dim light of our underground training room.

"It's beautiful," I say with awe, turning it in my hands and trailing my fingers across the intricate details etched into the blade curling all the way down to the tip like a vine.

Patton nods in agreement as I take in the majesty of my sword. My own sword. I never imagined I would see the day, but here it is.

"It's lighter than I thought it would be," I say, swiping it through the air back and forth to get the feel of it.

"That doesn't make it any less deadly," Gryphon snorts and eagerly does the same with his own.

"Keep up your training. Several times a day. And don't forget, a true swordsman always names his sword." Patton stands tall and looks at us as a proud father looks upon his child.

"What should we name them?" I ask, completely taken aback. Who knew swords had names?

"You'll know. Now, off you go. I'll see you later tonight." And with unshed tears shining in his eyes, he turns on his heels. The sentiment is so unlike him, and it moves me to tears as well.

As we step into the hallway energized from our early morning training, a shadow meets us.

Killian strides toward us, clear determination set in his shoulders and a look of frustration burning in his eyes. I exchange a look with Gryphon, communicating both my thanks he suggested we leave our new treasures in the tunnels and a plea for him not to leave me to Killian's wrath.

"Where have you been? Lysander has been asking after you and no one could find you anywhere." He sizes up Gryphon, clearly getting the wrong idea. Gryphon grins down at him, but the look Killian gives in return has Gryphon bowing and walking away quickly, mumbling something about the stars and a hornets nest.

"I—" I begin, but he cuts me off before I can even formulate the rest of my sentence.

"I know what you're doing. And it's not going to work."

I trip over my own feet while my brain goes into overdrive, trying to figure out how Killian could have figured anything out. And if he's figured it all out, why is he talking to me about it rather than driving a knife through my heart? How much does he know? I look around, making sure there aren't an excessive amount of guards lurking in the alcoves we pass waiting to snatch me up and do his bidding. But it's just the bustling servants who accompany us in the hall.

If he's talking, I'll keep him talking.

If I can figure out how much he knows then I can warn the others before he destroys me. We're still walking down the hallway, and Killian's hushed voice keeps those bustling around us from noticing the clear danger I'm in. To them, we just appear to be brother and sister—arm in arm—enjoying a stroll. They don't see my shaking hands or how I try to slow his long strides, but he does. In response, his grip tightens on my elbow so he can pull me along. To everyone surrounding us though, he's all smiles.

Suddenly, this feels like more than a brother questioning his sister. I've watched as he moves his pieces around his maps, mumbling under his breath the strategy he's working out. Now, I'm no longer his sister, but merely a pawn on a board.

His pace is quick, and he continues dragging me along down the hall toward the gardens. There are less eyes in the gardens. If we make it there, who knows what he'll do with this anger rolling off him. I don't have long before I lose the safety of those around us, so I square my shoulders as best I can.

"I'm not sure what you mean, brother." I try to be coy, managing to get the words out in between strides too long for me. My elbow aches from where he's pulling. The shaking has subsided, but now I can't decide if I'm more terrified or angry at him.

"Don't do that. You don't play games. Licia is the one to talk me in circles, not you." His grip tightens and I try not to wince.

"You're right," I pause, unsure how much to offer him, but knowing agreeing with him will at least put me on the same side. "I just don't know what else to do. I'm not used to this, you know. I've spent the past ten years on my own, basically. You knew Avicii..." I lead.

Good, yes, the truth. Or at least, a version of it.

"Yes, Avicii couldn't have been easy to live with. He was my truest friend, but Father had him travel all over the realm. I still don't know for what. But each time he came back, he was harder somehow."

My breath catches in my throat as I remember. Remember the feeling of dread when Avicii returned. Would he be the doting husband I thought I married? Or the worst version of himself?

Killian's grip loosens and he pauses, thrown off guard by my mention of Avicii.

The sun warms my face with our position just inside the doorway to the garden. His features slowly soften, turning from calculating to pensive. There's the brother I grew up with. I exhale a deep breath, knowing without him speaking that we're okay for now.

"I know this is all moving quickly, but this will be good for you. This will be a good match. Etos is a land known for its beauty. And Sturdevant is a strong king, like Father. He's done great things for his people. It's your turn to do great things for your people."

I straighten, looking up at him and holding my chin high. Some of his words frighten me. But there's also truth to them.

It is my turn to do great things for my people. Just maybe not in the way he thinks.

CHAPTER THIRTY-SIX

I blow into the steaming mug of mint tea warming my hands causing swirls of steam to kiss my cheeks. The breeze tousles my hair, a slight chill makes its way through the warm blanket I've wrapped myself in. I burrow in deeper, allowing it to tighten around me like a warm hug. The majestic Parisarret Peaks loom over the gates of Merula, their snowcapped tips are as unforgiving as jagged teeth.

The encounter with Killian was close, too close. And if I continue training, and preparing to leave, the growing gap between me and my family will only widen. Until I can't even see them from where I stand. The thought of losing Killian and Licia is unbearable. And the thought of what Hadeon will do when, not if, he finds out is terrifying. I'm under no illusion that he will spare me in any way.

The snow covered mountaintops remind me of Thaddeus. Even all that way in the distance, the fresh scent of frost tickles my nose and reminds me of him. Of the way he pressed me up against the library books, wrapping my legs tight around him. And of the night he came to me in my room. A ghost of his gentle touch haunts me as I take a sip of tea, the warmth covering my chills.

But with him, I can't help but feel I wasn't myself. There was something about him that was too alluring, pulled me in too quickly. His eyes, the way

201

he looked at me like he lost me, drives a knife through my heart. But I can't be with him to make him happy. That small voice within, it's growing. And I need to hear it. Breaking off things between us not only makes it less confusing to Etos, who has the eyes of a hawk, but it also allows us to leave here as friends. On a mission. Nothing more.

Despite all of this, despite my feelings, Killian is right. Just not in the way he means.

It's my turn. Somewhere within me is a primeval power, and if I can learn to harness it, perhaps it will be enough to do great things for my people. All my people, of all different races across Everguard.

CHAPTER THIRTY-SEVEN

The morning has flown by. The healer's wing has seen more patients than usual and there continues to be a steady flow. Between Thaliya, the handful of other healers on duty and myself, we've met the needs of every patient. I worry the winter will be a hard one for the people of Merula. With Hadeon's attention purposefully elsewhere, those in town have barely enough food and are terrified to ask or attempt a solution.

"Why hasn't anyone done anything? Why haven't *you* done something?" I swallow, knowing that once I turn down this road, there's no turning back. "You've had all this power all along, there have been Fae here all along," I lower my voice toward the end, and Thaliya's eyes narrow. "This could've been avoided."

"Are you done?" Thaliya breaks off my rant, her tone part reprimand, part hurt. "There's more at stake here than just you and me. The lives on the line are countless, and between me and the handful of Fae here, we're not strong enough yet. We had to wait, knowing the time would come. Know yourself, know your path."

The last part, something she's said to me over and over again as I've grown up here in the healer's ward, strikes differently this time. But I still don't understand why it's taken this long. So much time has been lost.

"You were scared." There. I said it. And just as quickly I wish I could suck the words back in. Thaliya's features drop in disappointment and I know I've gone too far. Even the room seems to darken as she shakes her head and turns away from me.

I'm disgusted with myself for lashing out. At the same time, I don't think I'm wrong. If she and the other Fae would've done something sooner, there would've been so many more people to save. Now, there's so little to salvage and all the races have separated. There's too much to fix at this point.

With embarrassment rising on my cheeks and nothing left for me here today, I gather the last of my supplies and head back to the shelves to hang up my apron for the day. After the last of the clean bandages are in their place, I straighten my dress and try to tame my hair. Just as I walk through the doorway, a familiar figure straightens.

Surprised that he'd venture down here again after what happened yesterday, I don't know what to do. I freeze.

Not a hair on his gorgeous head is out of place, but as he stands from leaning against the wall, he runs his hands through it anyway. Giving his chin length waves a tousled look. "It's going to take more than a paramour to scare me off."

I try to stifle my smile, but I can't help it. He's relentless. And knows it.

He'll take me anyways? He's not disgusted with what I've done? He's not bothered by my other relations?

He strides toward me, an air of confidence and strength surrounding him as he offers his elbow. I look at it, still unsure of what his game is and where I stand. Do I play along?

"Honestly, he can come to Etos with us if it'll make you happy. But I don't think you'll need him." He smirks at the shock I must wear on my face. His words are so bold, so honest. His bravado is more refreshing than off-putting. I don't want to cause friction where it's unnecessary, and he's come all this way just to be disappointed. I don't want to upset him. Until I must. I reach out and once again link my arm in his. The solid feel of him beneath my fingertips grounds me after such a long morning.

"And how was your morning?" he asks, and then listens as I recount some of the more exciting moments of the day. He's attentive all the way down the hall. Very few people are down this way, but as we draw closer to mine and Thaddeus' small office space, I can't help but peek in to see if he's there. Sure enough, I see his boots up on a footstool angled toward the fire. The tall-backed chair blocking the rest of him from view.

I wonder if Thaddeus, because of what he is, has heard our entire conversation. I think back to his reaction to Gryphon's hand in mine. Would our conversation unsettle him? Especially because with this one conversation, I think this king and I have exchanged more words than Thaddeus and I have in our weeks of knowing each other.

"What's so funny?" Lysander asks. I realize I've completely lost the thread of our conversation. I quickly try to school my features, scrambling to remember what we were talking about.

At a loss, I realize I'm the one who does most of the talking between us, and while he's gotten to know me fairly well, I still know little about him. And then I remember I don't want to know anything about him because I'm leaving soon and will never see him again. It's better for him if there's nothing between us.

But I can't help it, now I'm curious. "You've listened as I go on and on about my days, but what do you do back in Etos?"

"You mean besides run the country?" he replies, but I can tell he's thinking about the question.

"Yes, what does the King of Etos do in all his spare time?"

"I like to sword fight," he begins.

Of course he does. That makes it easy. Just another man with a sword.

"I'm quite fond of dual wielding."

I cough, almost choking on my surprise. "Two swords?" I ask, as he nods in confirmation.

"Of course." He's trying not to enjoy my surprise, but I can see the way he stands a little taller, puffing out his already impressive chest. "What would be the challenge in the one? I've trained all my soldiers, making sure they can wield two blades before they even see the field."

I think back to my recent sessions, the one sword giving me problems enough. But somewhere deep down, I promise myself after I master the one, I won't stop there. I'll somehow figure out a second. "You'll have to show me the basics some time."

He glances at me, and I see him weighing my words, wondering if I'm really interested or just placating him.

"Yes, I'd like that." He smiles his charming smile. "I usually train as the sun rises, if that's not too early for you?"

"Of course not. I'll meet you out in the training fields if you'd like?" I say, even as I do I wonder if Patton will allow something like this to cut into our training time.

"Oh no, I don't practice with your father's men." He almost looks offended that I'd assume as much. "I've found there's a small plot on the far eastern coastline, it's a bit out of the way, but..."

"I know it well," I say. "The land you speak of was one of Gryphon and my favorite hideaways, once upon a time."

"You're full of surprises, Princess." I do a double take, that title has never sounded so foreign as it does coming from his lips. I've grown too used to someone else calling me by that name.

"Oh, please call me Roe."

"Well then, Roe, shall we walk down together tomorrow? Make a morning of it?" he suggests as a light smattering of color hints along his cheekbones.

"That sounds divine. I'll have a basket packed for us." I manage to get the words out smoothly, but inside, I couldn't be more excited. Even though it's just for the morning, we'll be going on an adventure. Something I haven't done since I was a child and something I've been dreaming of ever since.

He must like what he sees as he looks at me because he continues with hesitance. "I also like to spend some of my free time..." he pauses, still adorably unsure whether to share what he's about to say, causing me to lean in closer to him. "...in the ballroom."

I'm not sure what I thought would come out of his mouth, but it was certainly not that. A laugh escapes me before I can help it, and I look at him, horrified that I've embarrassed him. "I'm so sorry—I didn't—it seems I'm not the only one full of surprises."

We walk a few strides in silence, arriving where the hallway to the healer's ward meets the rest of the castle. The bustle is greater than usual, workers moving with purpose, some carrying vases, others with stacks of silver platters.

The reason becomes clear to both Sturdevant and me at the same moment. Our eyes meet and a blush creeps up his neck, matching the blush I can feel rising along my own features. The comfortable conversation we'd fallen into is replaced with an insistent hum of what the future holds between us.

His confident facade slightly cracks with the realization that this, between us, will become much more permanent in just a few short days.

Is supposed to become more permanent.

Won't become more permanent.

Just as his features falter, so do mine, but for a completely different reason. It's all becoming real and very quickly. The fact that Sturdevant is so real, and that he's a good person, makes my insides twist knowing he's someone who perhaps I could even grow to love. I blanch at the implications.

"It's all moving so fast." He pats my hand wrapped around his bicep with a tender gentleness.

"We both have such different lives, and it's all going to change. But maybe it doesn't have to be a bad thing?" His voice rises with vulnerability, doing all sorts of things to my core and my mind at the same time.

Wrecking me entirely.

So much so that we walk in silence while I try to tame the turmoil writhing within me.

Sturdevant keeps watching me out of the corner of his eye, his dark hair falling across his brow each time. And each time, the movement shakes me from my thoughts, swirling over and over between him, the man I'm to marry to strengthen my family's hold on this realm.

This realm that is not their own. For a family who is not my own.

Each time I think my choice is solidified, a new piece gets thrown at me. Just days ago, it was Ombretta, my sister by birth. And today it happens to be this beautiful, kind man in front of me.

This man whose been nothing but nice to me since his arrival. A man who can take me from this realm and we can start over in a new place. Where he is king and I am queen, with my controlling father far away across an entire ocean. He could save me from this place.

But after these past few weeks, I see it now—I'm not the one who needs saving.

I've made it this far in life. And I've tried before. It didn't work out so well. Avicii was supposed to be the man to save me from this place. Instead, our idyllic cabin in the mountainside became just another prison.

I've learned my lesson and I have the scars to prove it. Sturdevant may be beautiful and kind and say all the right words, but that's just on the surface. He could be as much a monster as Hadeon, and I wouldn't find out until we arrived on his own shores, days, maybe years, later.

My blush from the wedding preparations has vanished and my nerves are replaced by a firm decision. A hint of my thoughts must cross my features because as I turn to thank Sturdevant for the company, his features harden into something unreadable. He's still smiling, but it no longer reaches his eyes.

"I look forward to the morning," I manage to get out before turning back the way we came and rushing down the hall. I don't even know if we decided what time or where to meet. I just know one minute we were talking about his ballroom dancing hobby, and the next I was desperate to find a way out of our conversation. Shades of white press on me from all sides as the servants rush out of my way.

Chapter Thirty-Eight

The morning's mist swirls around my ankles as I approach the eastern side of the castle walls. I wave at what must be Lysander in the distance and he waves back. Even from here, I can see his open smile.

As I close the distance and get close enough to greet him, he lifts the basket in my hand and in its place, offers his other arm. I wrap my hand around his offered arm and we follow the worn, dirt path that winds back and forth along the cliff face down to the sparkling water below.

Cattails whip lazily in the breeze while the sunlight plays across the approaching water. As the path narrows, he takes the lead and I can't help but notice the twin blades strapped to his belt. They're like no other blade I've ever seen. Of course, I'm no expert, but these look especially deadly with their long, curved blades hidden within their scabbards. I can't wait to see them in action.

"I haven't been down this way since my youth," I offer as most of our trek has been in silence.

"I don't suppose even the castle walls could easily contain someone like you," he replies.

"In what way do you mean?" The words almost sound like a compliment.

"You seem... different from other women I've met." He looks back at me and takes my hand, guiding me around a particularly rocky part of the path. "It doesn't surprise me you've been down this way before."

We arrive at the small beach and I instantly kick off my slippers, which are certainly not ideal for the trek, but Marlys wouldn't let me wear my boots.

He laughs, a sound full of warmth, like he does this often. "See? You dive right in."

It's odd having someone who knows nothing of you make observations. I suppose since I've been back at the castle, I've been more spontaneous. I've had to be. And the feeling it gives me feels like the sand that squelches beneath my toes. "I suppose I do." I smile as another piece of myself unlocks.

He shakes out a blanket and motions for me to sit. As he joins me, I don't miss the way his guards post up around us. As if anyone could reach us down here, we'd see them coming from a mile off in any direction.

I settle in, fluffing out my skirts beside him and in one smooth movement, he sits beside me, his swords cast off to the side. Our conversation is light as we snack on the fruit and cheese packed for us. He sets a canteen between us to share.

As we pack up what remains, I say, "I seem to remember you mentioning some fancy sword work." I blush and hope he doesn't read too much into what, in my mind, sounds like a clear, very innocent lead into him showing me what he knows—but could easily be misconstrued into something else entirely.

He busies himself with packing away the last of the meal before turning toward me. "I did. But I don't want to bore you, so if you'd rather just sit and admire the view, that's okay, too.

"No, I'd actually love to see your work. If it's not too much to ask."

At that, his smile widens and he moves to stand. Before grabbing his swords, he pulls his shirt over his head, folding it neatly before setting it atop the basket. Without a glance at me, he replaces his leather scabbard around his hips and draws the blades.

"I've never seen curved blades before."

"They're called shamshir." He holds them for me to look at.

I trace my fingers across the cold metal. The intricate carvings all the way to the tip are beautiful. "It's odd that something so beautiful can be so deadly."

"Truer words were never said." He moves outward, closer to the water, and begins moving through his technique work.

His movements are precise and the blades move as if an extension of his body. I can only dream that one day I'll have a fraction of his speed and grace. He moves over the sand as if he were dancing across the water behind him.

I can barely take my eyes off his swift slashes and strikes, but I also can't help but admire the way his muscles flex as he transitions. A dance in and of itself, the way his muscles tighten and release, the way they ripple as he moves smoothly from one movement to the next. And as the time passes, the glimmer of sweat reflects the sunlight, causing him to shine like a star himself.

After a particularly intricate set of movements, he sheaths his swords. He takes a few gulps from the canteen and looks to me, almost sheepishly awaiting my approval.

"That was beautiful." I would hate to come up against him in a fight. There would be no chance for me. "But why, may I ask, are they curved?"

He tilts his head, surprised that this is the question I have after all of that. "Shamshirs are best for cutting. While swords are for stabbing." The difference of the two are lost on me. And I think he realizes it. "In Etos, we have to cover a lot of ground. So we often ride on horseback. A shamshir is made to cut down your enemy from above, and the curved blade allows for the most direct contact for the most amount of time."

A chill runs down my spine. Beautiful and deadly indeed.

CHAPTER THIRTY-NINE

After my morning with Lysander, I ask Patton to fit in some extra sessions. Luckily, he was too happy to oblige.

"Brilliant! Yes!" Patton remarks as I drive toward him, slash after jab, even blocking some of his parries with the dagger in my left hand. After Lysander mentioned he requires all his soldiers to learn the skill, I decided that was my new goal. "Where has this skill been these past few days?"

"I guess it's all starting to click," I say, knowing that's just part of it. All of my training has been with Gryphon, today is the first time it's just Patton and me. Lately, Gryphon hasn't progressed as quickly, so I hold back, not wanting to upset him knowing that he's just doing this for me. But today, I let it all out.

"Whatever this is that you've found, learn this feeling. So you're able to find it again," he says, striking back, hard and fast. His movements have become harder to guess as he falls into full warrior mode.

With each practiced movement, my limbs feel more alive until both blades become an extension of my arms and my awareness of my surroundings heightens to where Patton's next movement is ringing in my ears and I become one step ahead. My senses are able to take in everything at once—both overwhelming and exactly what I've been missing all this time.

"Yield! I yield!" Patton's words cut through my concentration and all at once, my senses return to what I'm used to and I quickly drop my dagger from Patton's neckline. "Where'd that come from?" As soon as the danger of my blade lifts, he's visibly vibrating with excitement, at least as much as a leader of warriors could be expected to show. His voice rises and his eyebrows have found his hairline, but other than that, he still mostly resembles a hardened warrior.

Still shaking myself out of whatever warrior haze is still lifting, I look up to Patton, still slightly unsure of what just happened myself. "I felt as if I was everywhere and nowhere all at once. All of my senses were thrumming with energy. It's like I was aware of everything all around me."

"That's remarkable." Is all he says at first, placing a thumb under his chin and resting his forefinger on his nose, deep in thought. He shifts and squints down at me as if seeing me for the first time. "That is a trait of the oldest Fae warriors. A state that is desired by many, but acquired by few. To the point it's almost unheard of between the few Fae who remain. The question is, where has this been all this time?"

I shift on my feet, looking from the stone wall where I'd just cornered an ancient Fae warrior, and back to him. "I may have been holding back a tiny bit," I begin, unsure where to go from there. Was it because of Gryphon, and his inability to progress? Or because I still haven't come to terms with what Patton, Thaliya, and Thaddeus have shared with me?

"But why? The only people down here in this glorified casket are me and Gryphon—"

My eyes drop to the floor at Gryphon's name.

"I see." Patton's eyes flick over my shoulder and I cringe because, like he said, the only other person who comes down here is Gryphon.

A silence falls over the underground space and I don't want to turn around.

"You've been holding out because of me?" His face contorts in irritation.

"No," unsure what to say, my answer falls flat. He turns and starts back to where he came from. "At least I didn't think so until now." He pauses, looking over his shoulder just long enough for me to see the set of his jaw.

"You're supposed to be better than that. You've always been better than that." He continues walking down the hallway, the darkness swallowing him up as he goes.

I look at Patton, but he looks as surprised as me at Gryphon's outburst. "We're done for the day." He nudges me toward the yawning passageway, where I can barely make out Gryphon's retreating form.

"Gryphon, wait." I finally catch up to him, touching his elbow in hopes to stop his forward movement.

"What's left to say?" He yanks his arm out of reach and turns, but I can't make out his features. Neither of us have a torch, neither of us need one, except for at this moment it would be helpful to see his face, see how much damage I've done.

"I didn't mean to—I didn't realize I was—" I can't tell if I feel more stuck or caught. So I try another tactic. "What did you mean back there? When you said I've always been better than that?"

He looks behind him, caught between leaving me here in the darkness or explaining. His arm settles on the back of his neck, both stretching and rubbing, weighing his next move.

"We've always been—you've always been your true self with me. We've never had to be anything but ourselves with each other. Which, in this court, is refreshing to say the least." His growing disappointment is clear in the hardening line of his lips.

"I can't believe you're throwing this in my face. You of all people." He stills at the words, the only movement being his eyebrows raising in confusion. "You who, since I've returned, has not even let me back into your world the slightest bit."

"What are you talking about?" To his credit, his surprise appears earnest.

But that moment in the library flashes back through my mind. The sound of heavy breathing and soft murmurs and the exact moment when I realized who those sounds were coming from. The moment I realized how much I truly lost when I left the castle.

Does he really think I don't know? That I'm so swept up in my own world that's continuously turning upside down, that I wouldn't have time to notice?

"You and Licia." I cross my arms, unwilling to supply more information. My breathing is steadier now. A fierce calm settles over me as I face him, certain that no matter what he says next, it will disappoint me.

He searches my face, but I leave it expressionless, making him sweat at least a little. "You're not jealous, are you?" His tone is incredulous.

"No! Of course not! I can't believe you'd even think that." Anger continues to rise, unbidden. "You're my oldest friend and Licia is my sister. I couldn't be happier for you both. But I thought you both would've told me. Be excited to share something so special with me. I'm still stuck on the outside."

"We didn't realize."

There it is. They're a 'we' now. And I'm left discarded amongst the weeds.

Forgotten. Superfluous.

"You wouldn't have." I bite back before I have time to think.

"What is that supposed to mean?" His shoulders slump and I realize I'm just warming up. There's so much that's been left unsaid and now the gates are open.

"It means, I came back hoping we'd be able to pick up where we left off." I shove him backward, throwing all my weight behind my two hands as I push against his chest. "But I see that's impossible." Each word spit like venom that I can't call back, even if I wanted to. He stumbles backward a few steps but maintains his balance.

"Of course it's not going to be the same." He shoves me right back. I balance precariously on my heels and scrape at the walls with my fingertips, trying to find my balance before falling. I didn't expect him to retaliate.

"You were married." He jabs me in the chest with a pointed finger.

"You left." Jab again.

"You've been gone for ten years, Roe. Ten years is a long time. And Merula didn't just fall into a hole while you were gone." One final jab.

My chest stings and feels hollowed out at the same time. My hand comes up to rub at the spot he hit repeatedly. Right above my heart.

He brushes his hand down his face in frustration. "Although, it seems maybe you might've thought as much."

I flinch, his words hitting harder than any jab ever could. My whole body tenses, waiting for more and too stunned to respond.

"You can't live your life like this. You can't be the person you need to be, and still do this." He motions back and forth between us.

Maybe he's right. In the end, this is something I'll have to do by myself. There's no point in keeping those I love so close to me.

We'll have to part in the end.

"You're right." I stand taller for a moment, taking a deep breath and willing the tears not to fall until I'm alone.

The look of hope he gives me cracks something deep inside me, exactly where he'd been prodding just before.

But it fades just as quickly as I shake my head at him.

My mind's made up. And he's right.

Knowing this and whatever just happened between us escalated way too quickly but not knowing how to mend the massive canyon that's grown in my absence, I do what I must.

I can do this alone; I've done it alone these past ten years.

Just because I'm back at the castle, surrounded by family and friends, doesn't mean things should change now.

Especially where I'm going.

I square my shoulders and adjust the sword sheathed at my side, resting my left hand on my dagger. I step around Gryphon and continue up the path alone with my footsteps guiding me into the darkness I know so well.

CHAPTER FORTY

I come here to escape.

To escape myself.

The mild late autumn breeze tousles my freshly cleaned hair and wipes away all the thoughts plaguing my mind. The last rays of sunlight highlight the peaks, where the remaining Fae have made their home, the peaks I know so well, at least from this distance. Not for the first time, I stand on this balcony willing them for answers I don't have.

These past few days have been too much. I just want to go back. Perhaps if I marry Lysander, everything could go back. Licia and Gryphon don't need me. I won't have to figure out what I want. I'll have Lysander and his court to do that for me.

I let my mind wander, playing with the idea of getting on a ship tomorrow with my new husband. How would it feel to leave all this behind me?

"Princess Rowandine? I'm ready for you now," Marlys' voice cuts through my thoughts.

"I'm ready."

I follow Marlys' voice back into our chambers, the low glow of candlelight warms the room. Licia's moved from her perch before the mirrors toward the couch before the glowing fireplace. The warm light plays off her pale-yellow dress and highlights all of Marlys' careful work, from her carefully painted face to the gems sparkling in her hair.

I obediently take my place upon the pedestal before the mirrors. A slight excitement thrumming through me. Despite the occasion, I've always enjoyed this part. Shedding my daily skin while Marlys carefully molds me into the princess I'm expected to be.

"Tonight's the night, dear sister." Licia's pretty face is reflected in the mirror before me, her eyes light at the thought of all tonight will bring. By her careful tone, I can tell she's spoken to Gryphon about our conversation, but she keeps the conversation light. "Are you ready?"

How does such a simple question churn my insides into knots? Marlys senses my hesitation and speaks for me, "Tonight will be a night to remember."

Her answer seems carefully veiled, but her features and movements don't betray she knows anything more than tonight is my last night as a single woman. Again.

Her words remind me I still have a part to play, even here in the safety of our chambers with Licia, who needs to remain in the dark of my plans. I envy her obliviousness to what's about to happen tonight. It makes it both easier and more difficult to play this part. To walk away.

"I'm nervous. And excited, but yes, I'm ready." Both of which are true. "The celebration will be—"

"Bigger and more grand than anything! It'll dwarf your previous wedding and perhaps even Killian's. Which is probably the reason for his recent glumness."

"So you've noticed it, too?" His mood lately has been unnerving, to the point I thought he was on to my plans. But if Licia's picked up on it, then he's probably just annoyed Hadeon is making such a fuss over my nuptials to foreign royalty.

"His constant brooding and lurking around every corner? It's hard to miss. But I suppose you have an excuse. You've been so busy keeping King Sturdevant entertained, as well as the bard if I'm not mistaken."

Sometimes her awareness surprises me. But then again, how else is she supposed to keep entertained here? Besides riding upon the ever-growing wave of gossip?

"And tonight is just the beginning. Tomorrow, the actual ceremony will be—" I can't bring myself to finish the thought.

After Marlys pulls my hair up into loose curls, framing my face, she braids black pearls through the remaining pieces of my hair. Licia is long gone, and too excited to sit still a moment longer.

"Once upon a time, the Fae who watched over the land here used to wear thick braids in their hair, pulling it away from their face before going into war. They used pearls, such as these, to denote not their conquests, but how many they had saved along the way."

I watch her reflection in the mirror, the raspiness in her voice at odds with the strength and skill with which her hands work, as if she's done this a thousand times. But Licia nor I would ever sit still long enough for her to do this when we were younger. Perhaps Licia's grown more patient in my time away.

"It was a sight to see. You could hear the queen herself before she even set foot within a room, her beads and trinkets resting heavy, weighing down her curling locks, but not her spirit. She had enough of that to fill an ocean."

"She was a warrior? The Fae Queen went to war?" I ask, attempting and failing to mask my eager interest. Patton had mentioned she was good with a sword, but no one, besides Thaliya, has ever spoken of the Fae Queen, my mother. At least in a positive light.

"Queen Bronwinn was a force to be reckoned with." Marlys' gaze is far away. I study her features. The way she's careful to keep her hair combed just right so her ears never show, and how, no matter how far I cast my mind, every memory of her has her looking exactly the same as she does now. Could she be one of the Fae hiding in plain sight? I've never even questioned her loyalty to my father before. But the way she speaks of my mother, it's as if she knew her, herself. "She believed her people, all her people, not just the Fae, would do great things for this world. And that, along with her equally strong partner, King Azullian, kept her going."

"Roe! It's time," Licia's sing-song voice echoes from our chamber entryway. "Are you coming?"

"You're ready." Marlys, who's in front of me now completing her final ministrations around my face, gently touches my cheeks, still with mist in her eyes, kisses the ring on my finger, and motions me to meet Licia.

Chapter Forty-One

At the caller's announcement, those already gathered in the ballroom stop. The weight of their eyes roaming over every detail before I even complete my entry is heavy with judgment. The merry atmosphere, guided by the sweet, lilting tones of a small group of musicians, is at odds with the sideways glances I receive as I move farther into the room.

Hoping for a friendly face, I look toward where the music is coming from. But Thaddeus isn't among the players this evening. The king must be saving Thaddeus and his epic songs for later.

And then I remember, even if Thaddeus was here, he wouldn't be the friendly face I need. We haven't spoken in days, not since he told me of Ombretta, and the real reason he's here. The real reason he got close to me. The reminder is a heavy weight on my chest. The hurt mixes with anger at his actions.

And then fear rolls in, dwarfing the two other emotions. Will he still be there tonight? To aid us in leaving the castle? Or will we be left to our own devices? Does Baylor know the way? Or where we'd find Ombretta once we get to the north?

My steps falter and those around me move to help, steadying me and guiding me back to my feet. These are all questions I should've answered before tonight. Thaddeus hasn't even crossed my mind recently. Not unless I'm comparing Sturdevant to his impossible standards.

Moving through the crowd toward me as if summoned by thought is Thaddeus. He moves stealthily, watching me as a wolf watches its prey. And I suppose that makes me an unthinking rabbit because I find myself drawn to him despite how angry and confused I still am with him.

He pulls me around a pillar and the floral bows wilt under our movements. We move deeper into the dark shadows of the celebration, and his firm touch sends a thrill of memories through me I've missed too much these past few days. I grab onto my resolve like a lifeline. Despite this, all our rendezvous flood my memory. The memory of his touch, this touch, other places on my body. From my neck, drifting along my curves, down—

"I don't see your betrothed." His tone makes it clear he's not interested in anything other than talking, which is exactly what we need to do.

I wave his comment away with more disinterest than I feel. "Are we—" I'm not sure how to ask all the questions I have; I can't decide which ones are most important.

"Yes," he says, his eyes intently on me. "Despite what you may think, I'm a grown male and I can separate my feelings from the task at hand." His words are a slap across the face. Of course he's able to separate the two as should I. So much rides on our leaving Merula together that I can't believe I've spent so much time worrying about what's happened between the two of us.

"Of course. I just wanted to make sure—" The air around us crackles at our close proximity. How can I be so drawn to a person and so angry at the same time?

"The plan. Just stick to the plan. We leave tonight." And for a brief moment, I'm not sure if he's saying those words to himself or to me. His fingers brush a stray curl behind my ear and, before I can respond, he's gone.

I slowly make my way back into the crowded room, both comforted by Thaddeus' reassurance and emboldened now that I know, tonight is our night.

With a renewed sense of purpose, I make my way through the crowd, and this time, the side glances and whispers don't weigh as heavily as before.

A beautiful spectacle, but a fairly uneventful one. The evening passes slowly, and at every moment I have, I replay instructions for tonight's events. I've barely spoken with Sturdevant, even though tonight is for us, it seems more like a celebration of Hadeon.

The king merrily directs the musicians and the dance floor, sometimes he joins in but mostly watches from his perch up on the dais. The nobles of Merula and the surrounding towns celebrate yet another conquest under Hadeon's belt. For sure this last piece will help rid our realm of the other races, and magic forever.

I'm relieved when the servants begin to bring out plates of breads and meats. As we dine, Killian leans over to make conversation. "Don't worry about the pre-wedding jitters, they'll pass." His smile is kind, but as I look up, I realize there's no light in his eyes.

"Thank you. Yes, I must admit, it's a lot to take in, in such a short time." The way he watches me, waiting for me to say more, I swear he knows more than he lets on, which is nerve wracking, but we just need to make it a few more hours and his assumptions won't matter.

"Did you hear?" he asks off-handedly, and I swear I can feel Licia lean into our conversation. But the look of glazed adoration on her face suggests otherwise, so I turn back toward my brother. "The stable master was taken today. He'll be executed tomorrow."

"The stable master?" Baylor. Oh. *Executed?* A sense of dread spears through me at the shocking news. If what Killian says is true, there's no way we can leave without Baylor, especially if he's to be executed. I try to take command of my features, but something must show.

"Are you alright, sister? You're looking a little pale." And his lovely brotherly smile fades into something grotesque. A look I swear I've seen before, but can't place it right away.

And then I do.

On Hadeon. It's the same look Father gets when he knows he's backed someone into a corner.

"Executed? What could the stable master possibly have done to gain the king's attention?" My concern for one's life is sincere, and for Hadeon to be so quickly drawn to Baylor, part of our plan must have fallen into their hands. Suddenly, the outcome of tonight becomes hazy.

"There's talk of revolt," he says, and he quickly becomes more animated, fisting his knife and fork in either hand and slamming them on the table for emphasis. "Which is absurd, these people have nothing, there is no way they could successfully rise against us now."

Which is as good a reason as any to rise up, but I don't say that. "And what does our stable master have to do with anything that happens within the town?"

"He's the one who's been rousing the people. If we squash him, the rest will return to themselves, and if they know what's best, they'll be more hesitant the next time someone questions their betters."

This does not sound like the Killian who ran after my carriage with tears in his eyes ten years ago. Nor the Killian who used to run through the streets of Merula with me, racing as fast as he could but always stopping to help if he overturned someone's basket along the way.

What has Father done to you? Is what I want to ask, but instead I can only nod while my thoughts race, trying to figure out what needs to be done and how I get word to Thaliya without raising suspicions in such a short time. "It sounds like you've taken care of everything. I just hope an execution does not overshadow the happier events of tomorrow."

Killian's face falls, his disappointment in my response is clear. Was he hoping for more? How much does he know? "Indeed," is all he says, then turns his attention to his daughters.

If Baylor is now imprisoned, then everything is ruined.

Inwardly, I frantically search for a solution. There's no way we can leave Baylor to such a fate, beside the fact there's no way we can do this without Baylor. He's the very one Thaliya trusts to deliver us safely to the north. And while Thaddeus knows the way, and is good company, I'm not sure Thaliya would let us leave with only him.

I have to let Thaliya know what's happened. She'll know what our next steps should be.

I excuse myself but the crowd, seeming to work against my progress out of the ballroom, pushes me further in rather than out of the vast room. The music is louder here, the musicians vying for the attention of the onlookers. Thaddeus still has not taken the stage, which he'll surely do before the night's end. I have time.

Suddenly, an arm reaches out, gently but firmly halting me in my tracks. I jump, but the grip isn't aggressive, just strong. Not Killian come to arrest me then.

"May I have one last dance with my betrothed?" Sturdevant's hand grazes down my arm, tentatively possessive. His smile is warm and genuine, like he's having the time of his life tonight and he can't wait for tomorrow to come.

His words register, though. "Did you say 'last dance?'" I ask, a nervous tremor in my voice.

"I haven't seen much of you tonight. I know your family occupies you. And now, you appear as if you're fighting the crowd to retire to your chambers. You must be exhausted with all the festivities of the day, and I'd imagine you expect a full night of sleep before tomorrow. Would I be asking too much for your last dance before you go off to bed?" His smile lights up his eyes as he reaches out a hand, hopefully expectant.

I look toward the open doors and then to his expectant face. I have time. Baylor is in prison and I have to reach Thaliya. But I can't leave so suddenly. It would raise suspicions. I have time. That's all that registers in my thoughts as I take his outstretched hand. "I *have* heard you know your way around the ballroom floor."

As soon as he expertly twirls me onto the dance floor, I'm torn between worlds.

In the here and now, I follow his steps smoothly, two royals moving as one. I can sense the crowd smiling and nodding their approval. These nobles eat this pageantry up.

Previously, I would've smiled and played along. Nudged into this marriage by their smiles and cheers. Herded like cattle into the role I'm supposed to play. Now, I see what they're doing. Or, what they hope to do. And although I smile along, I will not play the game by their rules.

Lysander continues smiling, his hand low, but not too low, on the small of my back. Gently claiming what's to be his. This close, I can smell the allspice and birch sent on him, no doubt a soap he brought from his homelands. He smells like the warmth promised by a blazing fire on a snow stormy night. If I'm not careful, I'll settle right into his warmth.

"You're quiet this evening." A statement, not a question. After so many of our walks, I suppose comparatively, I'm rather quiet. "You don't have any tales of who you healed today? Or thoughts to share? Or the latest gossip?"

"Yes, I apologize, I'm quite tired and my thoughts are all with what's to come tomorrow."

"I can't fault you for that. These days have been long ones. I look forward to returning to Etos with you by my side. We'll have plenty of time to ourselves before I'm expected to return to my duties."

With each word, I crack apart a little more, knowing that I'll be the reason he returns to his lands empty handed, and knowing that he is such a good person and I am doing such a terrible thing to him. It doesn't help to know that he will find another wife, there are even many women here who'd gladly step up in my absence. It doesn't help that I'm leaving for a good reason. For something bigger than him and me.

If I keep this up, someone else will have to come behind me and pick up all the broken bits.

Luckily, the song slows and ends. He twirls me once more, swinging me back into a daring dip. When he returns me upright, his lips press against my own for a breath of a moment. His kiss, full of promise of our future together, ends with admiring applause from those around us. He bows and kisses my hand. "Enjoy the sweetest dreams, my bride. I'll beg the sun to rise again with haste."

With one hand to my heart, I curtsy to him and take my leave. I don't think anyone has ever said anything so charming to me in my lifetime. I don't even think I've been witness to something so hopelessly romantic. Tears threaten as I turn to go, but I swallow them down as I ascend the stairs to my chamber.

CHAPTER FORTY-TWO

The room is dark, but I don't bother to light a candle. Everything I need I can find by touch. I don't bother changing, the dance with Sturdevant cost me time. I need to gather my pack and get to Thaliya. From there, we can figure out how to get Baylor out before tomorrow's sunrise.

My bag, already packed with a change of clothes and some fruit and cheese I've pilfered from the kitchens these past few days, is still under my pillow. On an afterthought, I grab the small book I've hidden under my bed, the one I copied the runes down in. It doesn't take up much room and I still find myself flipping through the pages when I can't sleep. On our way up north, I'll have more time to decipher what they mean. I add my sword belt, and know Patton will have my sword and dagger for me as we set off.

Looking around in the darkness, I mentally check everything off my list. Everything is as it's been for a lifetime. The made bed is piled high with pillows to my left, where Licia and I would talk through the night about everything and nothing at all.

Lightning flashes from the terrace, outlining my room in light one last time. The proximity of the thunder that follows makes me jump. It's close, too close. The ride will be a wet one.

The fireplace, burning down to embers now, throws tall shadows across the room, causing the warmth I've always felt here to shrink away into the corners. The lurking shadows cause me to turn and make haste toward the chamber door. I must hurry. There are more lives than one on the line here.

With one last glance around the sitting room where Licia and I have gotten ready for countless dinner parties and dances, my fingers hesitantly graze the doorknob. Deep down I know as soon as I leave this room, there's no turning back. Before exiting the room, I stand in the dark, gathering courage around me like a shield.

"Know yourself, know your path," I whisper into the darkness. But before I have a chance to open the door, the knob turns unbidden beneath my fingertips.

CHAPTER FORTY-THREE

A small shriek leaves my mouth as a dark outline fills the doorway, the light from the hallway casts shadows around the figure. Willing my eyes to adjust, I take a step back. The figure is tall, but not as tall as Gryphon so I ready myself for what's to come.

"You thought you could just leave?" a voice I know as well as my own. One who used to be full of comfort and tell me stories of battles, making them come alive in the firelight late into the night. "You've never been this selfish before."

Another flash of lightning outlines my brother. My heart sinks and his words sting, despite their untruths.

"I can't marry Sturdevant." The simple truth leaves my lips before I can fabricate anything more.

"You will marry Sturdevant." Killian takes two steps into the room, closing the space between us. I want to take a step back, but I plant my feet and stand like a triumphant weed in a rose garden. "You failed in your first marriage, probably bringing on Avicii's death yourself. You'll not disgrace our family when all eyes are on our next move." He looms over me, the sour ale on his breath reminds me that to make any move against him right now would be a mistake. Thunder punctuates his last words, "And just to be clear, *you* are our next move."

I can do this; I can go along with his plan and figure the rest of mine out later. He doesn't know what I'm planning, at least not the entirety of it—and I thank the lucky stars for that.

"You're right." My gaze falls to the floor in submission. "I was being selfish. I'm just so scared of leaving again, and you and Licia moving on without me. Look at you, married with two beautiful girls, what will I miss if I leave for another ten years?" I appeal to his grand sense of pride, and I can see the subtle shift in his stance. He softens just a little.

"It does seem unfair, perhaps this time we can call on you more frequently. I'm sure after your first son is born, Sturdevant would not mind if you came home for a period." He nods as if this idea holds promise. When I know once my feet hit the wooden boarding plank, there will be no return for me.

"All I can ask is that you, Father, and Sturdevant give a thought to my request. Thank you for that kindness." I move further back into our sitting room, perching on one of the chairs. My yawn is not wholly contrived as it's getting late and I could very well fall asleep if I didn't have such a night before me. "I beg you leave me to rest so I'll be refreshed for my wedding day. Thank you for talking sense into me, brother. You always know what to say to make me feel better."

Killian puffs out his chest at my flattery, but his smile falls flat. "Don't think for one moment I trust you'll remain in your chambers for the entirety of the evening." And without another word, he strides from the room, slamming the door behind him. The noise reverberates around me in this dark space.

The candlelight from the hallway outlines the doorframe and the sound of metal-on-metal clinks across the darkness.

No. He wouldn't.

My footsteps are the only thing I hear as I move quickly after him to the closed door. Grabbing and trying the doorknob, but it doesn't budge.

"Killian!" I yell into the heavy wood in front of me. "There's no reason to lock me in here! I'm not going anywhere!" But my words fall on unhearing ears. As far as I can tell, there's no one left in this hallway, let alone our entire tower.

Tears slide unbidden down my cheeks, my hands cling to the doorknob as if I willed it enough it would open. But it doesn't.

I slide down to the ground, every bone in my body failing me, no longer able to hold me up.

Tears fall more quickly now, tangling the curls that have fallen around my face. The cold stone floor and the firmness of the door at my back confirming the feeling of a prison. I stare into the darkness of our chamber sitting area, unseeing.

My prison.

This room has always been my prison and the only way out is always marriage.

There's nothing left. I can't save my people; I can't even save myself.

Baylor, at daybreak, will be executed because of my actions.

I'll have to marry Lysander Sturdevant of Etos now. I'll never see my family or my friends again—those who've fought so hard for me and been there for me, even after all this time. I've ruined everything. Rain beats a steady, incessant rhythm on our turret roof, trying to calm the terror rising within me.

A pit forms in my stomach with each thought, heavy with the burden of so many lives. My hand rests on the pit, rubbing gently but it doesn't dissipate.

With my hand resting on the pit in my stomach, memories surface, growing the sickening feeling in my stomach from a pit to a stone.

A garden bed of rocks. That's what Avicii always said about my body. How is it I can bring anything to life in a garden, yet my body refuses to produce a life. Every month like clockwork, the weight in my belly would not be of a blossoming new life, it would be the weight of yet another disappointment.

Another failure.

And every time, Avicii would remind me it's my fault. My failures.

How is it I keep ending up here? When all I do is for those around me?

The pit, now the size and weight of a boulder, hurts so much as if I'm being cleaved in two, causing me to slide onto the ground, wrapping my arms tightly around my knees. As if all that's left of me, I have to hold on tight to. The ground presses against my tear-stricken face, bringing a welcome chill to my burning cheeks.

The darkness pressing in around me finally wins out, swallowing me whole.

CHAPTER FORTY-FOUR

*H*is blood. Everywhere.

All over my hands.

Heaving, gulping, deep breaths of air, trying to make sense of what just happened.

Avicii lays prone on the ground before me, flattening the heads of lettuce and spinach with a thunk where he fell.

But around us, the birds keep chirping. The breeze caresses the loose strands of hair that have fallen out of my bun in the struggle. The cloudless sky above is the same bright blue of Avicii's unseeing eyes at my feet.

The vines slowly retreat. The thick, leafy trunks wind their way around Avicii's ankles, tugging his dead body along with them. Away from me. As he's pulled across the field and toward the edge of the forest, the rays of sunlight glint against the gold of his hair for the last time and he's already forgotten by the setting sun.

A sob escapes me, and I crumple to my knees in the dirt now mixed with Avicii's blood.

Chapter Forty-Five

A grunt and a shove startle me from sleep. "Princess Rowandine, is that you?"

Slowly, recognition dawns on me. I push myself up, apparently I fell asleep on the floor, right beside the locked bedroom door.

Which is now open.

Marlys' gentle voice once again prods me, now fully awake, and my situation comes back in full force. Killian knows, or knew of my plan, at least some parts of it. He locked me in here and Baylor, "Stars! Baylor!" I sit up straight and look toward the windows where rays of sunlight stream through.

"Baylor lives." Marlys is able to push the door open around me.

My entire body relaxes at her words. "But Killian said—"

"Yes, but I believe your opinion about how it would look to begin a wedding day with an execution, it got to him. Baylor is safe, at least for today." She looks pointedly at me as if there's something I can do for him in here. "Up and ready, child." She gives a light kick to my side.

"What do you mean?"

"It's your wedding day, isn't it?" She smiles sadly down at me as she folds out the mirrors in front of the pedestal.

"Sturdevant didn't call the whole thing off? Does he know?" Hesitancy in my voice, unsure how much Marlys knows.

The distance between Marlys' ministrations and the open door is only a few strides, but it may as well be miles.

Do I dare make a run for it?

But all the fight has been sucked dry from me. There's nothing left. This is all my doing to begin with. I just need to leave here and everyone will be better for it. And if Sturdevant will still have me, then that's my only option.

"He only knows he'll have a blushing bride come this afternoon. Killian shared nothing of what was spoken between you two last night. I'm not even sure he enlightened your father with what transpired." Yet Marlys knows. Even the walls have ears in this castle, that's what Licia and I always said about this place.

But that Killian kept this to himself surprises me. What is he playing at? The question plays through my mind as I rise to meet Marlys in front of the mirror.

"The floor did nothing for you, you know. You should've at least grabbed a pillow if your plan was to sleep in the doorway," she scolds lightly.

"Spending the night pressed up against a locked door was not my first choice," I begrudge, but even though it's Marlys, I'm not sure if I should say more.

"You had plans to be gone, to be sure." Startled at her blunt response, I watch her features for any hints of where she stands. She dips her head back to the work of removing last night's dress and starting anew with tying up my corset, causing me to jolt and grab for the side of the mirror as she pulls it tighter and tighter.

"I couldn't do it. I tried to get out, but I couldn't." Finally satisfied, she ties it off and moves to pull out my dress. I say to her back, watching her unbox the dress in the mirror's reflection.

"Couldn't? Or wouldn't? Seems to me there's a difference there that you would benefit from figuring out." She looks pointedly over her shoulder before she pulls my dress from the box with a flourishing shake of her wrists.

The movement causes my gaze to travel up, which is when I notice another maid has joined us. Her saucer plate eyes tell me she's surprised we've noticed her so soon, but she covers it up easily enough by stepping farther into the lighted part of the room and curtsying. "Beg your pardon, Princess Rowandine, but Prince Killian's sent me to step in for Marlys."

Marlys, for once, remains quiet as the young maid steps forward with her arms outstretched, ready for Marlys to hand her the dress. In one quick movement, Marlys hands it over, bows to dismiss herself, and steps away, all while the young maid continues to shake out the dress. "I'll go tend to Princess Licia." As Marlys steps around her with a barely contained fire behind her eyes, I wonder how much of our conversation was overheard.

Marlys leaves me alone with this child maid, quietly closing the door behind her.

As the mounds of fabric unfurl like a grand mast of a ship, the billowing layers of tulle and a bodice of sleek velvet begin to settle and take shape and redirect my attention. I hold my breath as the young girl holds it up to me.

Another white dress, another wedding. This one is so different, more elegant. Fit for a soon-to-be-queen of a faraway land.

She speaks first. "It's a dream!" A smile stretches across her face as she gazes at our reflections. "A perfect dream."

Not my dream, is all I can think. Missing Marlys already and knowing this is not an appropriate response, I attempt to match her enthusiasm. "The beauty of the dress is unmatched. I'm unsure I'll be able to do it justice."

The young maid grabs a handful of tulle as well to help me step into the over-the-top gown.

"Oh you'll make a beautiful bride, this match will be much more fitting," she says, and then looks as if she'd like to swallow her words.

"What do you mean?" I keep my tone light, but I know there's more to her comment.

"Oh everyone says so, Princess." My opinion of the child is sinking as the minutes pass between us. "Prince Killian was speaking to his wife just this morning, saying how you'll make your family a proud match this time around." Meaning he knows I've already fallen so far and if I want to stay in Hadeon's good graces, I can't mess up this time.

"And you certainly look the part, now." She steps back so I can see my full reflection. Her hands are clasped at her chest as if an angel stands before her.

But viewing myself as a bride again does not reflect the excitement and hope I felt for my first marriage. I've lived through one marriage and come through worse for the wear. So now, in this ornate dress, all I see is dread. This dress does not belong to me, this life being thrust upon me, is not my own.

In this small amount of time, she's also tamed my curls and left small sections of them cascading down my back. A small knot of them rest at the nape of my neck, causing my reflection to appear unfamiliar to me. The effect is striking, but I wish Marlys would have been able to stay because she knows what my preferences are. Maybe that's why this young maid is here, because she knows King Sturdevant's style. What use is my own opinion here? I don't have one, and this is what my future holds.

There is no other way out of here. Killian has made it very clear what he and Father think of my leaving in any other way besides as a new bride and on a ship sailing west.

There's no choice here, not really, despite what Marlys seems to think. It could be worse. Sturdevant doesn't appear to be another Avicii. While his looks shout of masculinity, there's more charm to him than brutishness. He shows an attentiveness that would melt the heart of any woman, but for some reason he doesn't make my heart race nor flutter as it does when I'm with Thaddeus.

My heart remains my own.

So, with a heavy heart I nod approvingly to let this young girl with hearts in her eyes help me down from this pedestal and lead me forward to my impending marriage. All the while trying to puzzle another way out.

"Prince Killian will come to collect you when the king is ready," she says, motioning for me to sit and hands me a cup of wine. "For your nerves, Princess. I'm sure you are all but jumping out of your own skin at the moment with excitement." She turns then pulls a small key out of her pocket as she closes the door behind her.

Instantly, I lunge forward to stop her, but the wine in my hand slows me. The cunning child knew I'd instinctively try to save the dress. Too bad the hem is now soaked in a fine layer of red.

The clink of a lock being put into place fills the silence.

I attempt to sit but think better of it when the bones of the corset threaten to dig into my underarms. I give a silent cheers to the locked door before me and pour the rest of the wine over the layers of tulle while walking a circle around our sitting room, wondering where Licia was made to sleep last night, and if Marlys has found her.

A soft rap comes from the far end of the wall. I could slap myself for not thinking of it before, but in all honesty, between the pure exhaustion, surprise of how last night went, and the speed at which things are moving this morning, there wasn't time.

Until now.

The passageways!

"Roe, help me with this, will you?" A shudder of relief goes through me as Gryphon's muffled voice meets me at the passage doorway.

I tug and pull at the picture frame that guards our secret space. My mind moves quickly, planning our trek down the tower to where we'll find Baylor. It'll be so easy using the tunnels, if only I would've thought of it sooner.

But my relief is short lived. Nothing moves, even with Gryphon pushing from the inside. A sharp needle of dread pierces through me as realization sinks in.

"You don't think—" Gryphon mumbles between grunts.

"I do. I think Killian knows. But how could he have figured out the passages as well?"

"He's a king in training, Roe. I think it's time you give him a little credit where credit is due. At least a little."

"I should, especially knowing how his mind works. But I just didn't want to see him as the one who would do this."

"Ten years is a long time. A lots changed while you've been gone." Gryphon, still fumbling on the other side of the wall, points out the

FAE QUEEN RISING

obvious. "Don't worry, we'll get you out of there before it's too late."

"Gryphon," my voice is low. "It's too late. I'm in my wedding dress, Killian will be back any moment now."

I can hear him still at my words, but he keeps his voice light as he responds, "It's not over yet. We're still working on it. This is just a small set back. Don't give up yet. I'll be right back."

Before I can ask him to stay a moment longer, I hear his heavy footsteps moving quickly down the stone passage.

Alone again.

But am I? Gryphon's still working to get me out, and it sounds like maybe Thaliya is helping.

Was it wrong to push them away?

I need to fix this.

And Thaddeus. Oh stars, Thaddeus.

Stepping onto the balcony is a small feat in the layers upon layers of tulle, but I manage. The way the sunlight reflects off the peaks far off in the east creates spears piercing the building clouds above. But the sun is making its way toward the highest point of the sky. The day is still young but my time is running out.

Could what Thaliya says be true? That way up in the foreboding peaks, Fae are waiting for their moment to return to Merula, to their land. That they're rebuilding and waiting?

And that Thaliya, and so many others, know that the moment they've been waiting for is right now, with me—it's more than I can bear. I've always been the passed over one, the youngest in a royal family full of bright personalities. Where not only was my future planned carefully and handed to me, I gladly accepted what was decided, with not even a thought to my feelings, how I truly felt or what I really wanted. That voice—the one that's been whispering to me—sounds from deep within myself. Only this time, it's louder, and sounds like me.

So, is it more than I can bear? Or is this just what I've been told all my life? That there's no way I could want, let alone do, something as big as this.

And I remind myself this impossible situation is more than just me. And for my people, the ones who believe in something more—something good—I'll keep trying, keep fighting. My newly manicured fingernails dig into the thick marble railings and within the stone, a small hum answers the rage I feel for the people of Everguard. For my people.

CHAPTER FORTY-SIX

In answer, a rumbling runs through the stone beneath my feet and greenery begins to snake its way up the terret. It startles me at first, causing me to fall back in a nest of tulle. This dress is hopeless, and as I rise again to see what's creeping up toward me, I step on the edges and the bottommost layers tear away.

The satisfying rip of tulle is only matched by the instant freedom I feel from its confines. Layers continue to peel away as I pull forward, leaning back over the railing. Unsure what I expect, vines making their way up the balcony isn't it, but here they come. First thin as if tentative in their answer to my rage. But now, they spread over the railings in heaps as thick as my fists. As they land, cracks spread in thick plunks through the balcony stone itself.

Skittering back into my bedroom, the vines follow, summoned by me. The thought is a heady one, that this much power truly flows through my veins.

Looking across my bedroom, toward the locked door, I question whether the vines are strong enough. Only for a moment, though.

They churn around me and over the furniture toward the locked door, already aware of my need to leave this prison. They curl into thick waves, winding up like a snake before it strikes. With full force, they slam through in one blow and wooden splinters fly across the room at the impact. The sound reverberates in my soul and my heart brims with belief that this is happening. I can do this, just as Gryphon said.

I follow the destruction out of the newly demolished door and met with a sleepy and confused guard. His stricken face takes in my appearance, then the vines. His hand moves with a practiced grace toward his sword belt. He does not hesitate, but instead, makes quick work of unsheathing it, and then attacks.

But I'm not the threat. At least he must not perceive me as such. With the way the vines continue to wreath around the hallway, I must look like I'm running from whatever is happening within this room because he attempts to go after the vines. In doing so, unfortunately for him, he puts himself between me and my looping vines.

A flash of a memory strikes just as the vines begin to wrap and twirl around the guard. Except for a moment, it's Avicii staring back at me. But I shake my head and just as quickly, the nameless guard returns, just as the vines make their way up his body.

First, his ankles and then slowly up his thighs to his torso. He looks from the flora to me with a look that goes from incredulity to fear and whispers, "What—?"

"Not what. Who," I reply. His confusion only grows, but the dawning that the vines are with me, and for me, begins to bloom across his features.

"Unhand me! Prince Killian must know. Merula will know—" His eyes bulge just as his words are swallowed by a vine sliding with ease into his open mouth and down his throat.

I wince as his body goes limp, quickly disappearing under the swaths of green flowing farther down the hall. That was not in my plan. The fewer casualties the better, but this man would've set off the alarms. And for as long as I can, I'd like to remain in the shadows. Before the vines can swallow his sword up as well, I lunge for it, knowing it will be better than nothing with whatever I'm about to face.

Just as that thought of remaining in the shadows crosses my mind, I look over my shoulder to the splintering sounds following me out the door. Our room, or what's left of it, is cracking apart under the weight of the continuous climbing vines. They coil up the terret, over the marble trellis, and are now serpentining down the hall around me. The old power of the earth within them hums and reverberates through me in answer. I realize I'm no longer a part of the shadows. Just like the vines surrounding me, I twist and curl in search of sunlight. I will climb until I'm seen.

For a brief moment, I remember the fear and pain in Avicii's eyes in his last moments, when he realized there was no taming me and no breaking me.

I will rise and grow like a seed rises from the dirt; I will overcome. This, I will do for my people.

Know yourself, know your path.

Chapter Forty-Seven

T haliya's words echo in my mind, clicking and churning into place.

I pick up my pace, following the trail of vines down the turret stairs, wondering yet again if I'm too late.

Know yourself, know your path.

All those times before, I thought I heard her words, thought I knew what she meant. But now, the ray of meaning hits more directly. And my heart sinks, knowing that they've tried to tell me this whole time, and even though I thought I was listening, I wasn't hearing them. And now, everything is a mess and could even be too far gone to fix.

Knowing that sooner than later, the vines will be noticed and traced back to my chambers, I need to make every moment count. As I approach the ending of the staircase, I have a strange awareness that someone is close. The vines. They move ahead of me. My attention heightens in the same way everything heightened that one day I spared with Patton. What did he call it?

With bare feet and light footsteps, I reach the bottom of the stairs and try to peek through the ever flowing vines. It's impossible. I can barely control them. Instead, I hold my breath as footsteps turn the corner, readying the sword in my hand, no longer a foreign weight in my arms while I try to make out friend or foe.

I could almost laugh out loud with relief. Coming around the corner is Gryphon and Thaliya. Gryphon with a ridiculous look on his face and his sword out at an awkward and completely ineffective angle and Thaliya, who I do a double take at. Her aloof posture completely replaced with something much more severe, almost animalistic, honed from unseen ages of things I could not guess at. But the look in her eyes tells me she knows what she's doing.

I half leap half fall from the last of the steps, reaching Gryphon and Thaliya as they turn the corner.

"Roe, I was coming," Gryphon bursts, relief evident on his features. His sword clatters across the floor at the same moment he throws his arms around me.

"I don't need you to save me," I say, and it comes out harsher than I mean. I don't think the lack of breath and the blood spattered across my clothes does anything to help my tone. But he looks at me hurt still, no doubt upset about how I misled him with my sword play all this time. But I pull him back to arm's length. "But I am so glad you're here."

He smiles and hugs me tight. "I'll always be here."

Beside us, Thaliya whistles low and tosses me a pack. My pack. The one Killian took before locking me in my room. They've been busy.

As she does, she also pulls a sword belt from over her shoulder and hefts it toward me.

I smile at her. "You've brought me Ivy's Embrace." I smile as the name flows easily from my lips. Patton was right, I just know. I sheath my own sword at my hip, ready to move on and then shove my dagger into my belt on the other side.

Thaliya smiles, but it fades as she looks around us. "You have to get control of your vines. Ground yourself or we'll never get out, either because they've found and cornered us or our vines have done the work for them." Her words come out in quick, low huffs with her attention constantly scanning the hallways around us.

"Yes, but how? Ever since they've started crawling up from the garden, they've only gotten bigger, more destructive. I can't control them."

"You're thinking too much." Her hand wraps around my wrist finding my pulse in one practiced motion. "First control what's in here." Her other hand points to my mind and then my heart. "Then you can control this." She does a sweep with her head toward the twirling, climbing chaos behind us.

I try to calm my breathing, but nothing changes. I can still feel the hum of the vines within me, under me, everywhere. "It's not working."

"Don't worry about what's working. First, this." She does to me what I've seen her do with her patients a thousand times. She gently brushes my sweat-plastered curls away from my cheeks and my forehead. Her eyes meet my own, and without a word, I know she's asking me to focus on myself.

I close my eyes, aware that both she and Gryphon wait.

At first, there's nothing but darkness and the sounds of the weight of vines snapping wooden hallway furniture and pulling down chandeliers. But the hum is still there, so I follow it. First in the vines, but then deeper and deeper into myself until I find the root of the seedling glowing and bright within me.

Now, the hum becomes more of a melody, something sweet and lilting and flowing. It surrounds me, engulfs Thaliya and then Gryphon. I can feel our heartbeats become part of the rhythm, each calling and echoing the tune. I pull a little at the edges and the tune changes. The difference is small, but there, so I pull again. Suddenly, I can feel the vines bending back toward us.

My eyes open slowly, glancing around between barely opened eyelids, worried what I'll find in the quiet surrounding us. The vines, now calm, retreat. Climbing back up the turret stairs, back to my chambers.

"Good." Thaliya nods at my work as if it was a simple bandage dressing. And maybe that's what she's been training me for all along. She gets up, and then helps me stand on my now unsteady legs and brushes me off. "All this tulle and velvet is a damn shame, child."

I look down at what's left of my dress. "I tripped," is all I have to offer, but she laughs and pulls at what's left of the topmost layers of tulle. What was once a full, floor-length skirt that would've brushed the doorways as I walked through, now barely brushes the tops of my knees.

"I'll say. We'll dig you out of your hole yet."

"I love dress alterations as much as the next guy, but did we decide what's next? We have Roe, so now to Baylor?" The tension in Gryphon's shoulders defies his light tone as he glances around the hallways again.

I swallow the knot of worry at the mention of Baylor and what I've caused him, nodding in agreement that to save him is our next move. "Thaliya," I begin, knowing I have so much to apologize for and knowing even if we weren't up against a clock, there wouldn't ever be enough words for how grateful I am she's remained by my side.

"I know, love." She pats my hand and gives a knowing smile, one that forgives and forgets before the words have even been uttered.

"Baylor is still in the dungeons? Or have they moved him to preparations?" I cringe as I ask, trying to catch up on everything I've missed while being locked up in my own cell.

"As of this morning, they plan to keep him in the dungeons as long as possible. Killian was hoping to draw information from him before his sentence plays out. Damn fool." Thaliya rolls her eyes, as if she's used to this behavior. Maybe she is as I think back to her role these past thirty-five years.

"Thaddeus will know. He's been keeping track of movement between Killian's men and Baylor. Nothing out of the ordinary, at least not yet." Gryphon gulps at Thaliya's explanation; his eyes wide, no doubt imagining in what state Baylor will be in when we reach the bowels of the castle. I'd have to agree with Gryphon's assessment of Baylor's predicament, but at the mention of Thaddeus, my heart sinks. He said he was with us at the ball, but there's been too much left unsaid between us. I don't even know where he stands with me. Or helping with us. Or with him and me.

We move in silence, hiding ourselves against the shadows of the walls and splintered furniture. Although I know the way to the dungeons, I can't say I've ever stepped foot in them. But even my worst nightmares don't prepare me for the sounds that meet my ears as soon as the stone steps end.

"Watch out." Gryphon shoves me against the algae-slicked wall just before my bare feet are sliced open from broken glass, from the looks of it, wine bottles, but in the dim light streaming in through the window slits at the ceiling, it's hard to tell.

There's an insistent drip-drop and I can't tell whether it's my imagination or if everything down here is really darkness tinged with crimson. With care, we make our way down the narrow hall that opens to rows of ironclad cells. Moans and cries reverberate through cell after cell, most with just one occupant who doesn't even look up as we pass. There's no hope down here.

"Bay! My sweet Bay." Thaliya runs ahead of us into the darkness. And what we find is shocking. If I could give my life to forget the horror in front of me that is now Baylor, I would in a heartbeat.

When we all catch up to where Thaliya's gentle whispers mix with a sound somewhere between a sob and a child's cry, each one of us is frozen to the periphery of the cell for a moment.

In the faint darkness of the dungeon, Thaliya's fingers gently trace his face, but with all the bruising and blood, only a mother would be able to tell her son is somewhere underneath. I've seen her work hundreds of times, but the look in her eyes—something between rage and a brokenness—will haunt me forever. She doesn't stop, though, so I come to my senses, looking for anything resembling a clean rag to help.

There's nothing. Everything down here is coated with layers of varying stages of dried blood and dirt. I bite back the bile rising in my throat at the smell of death and despair that permeates everything surrounding us.

Down here, the white flowing layers of my dress practically glow, so without another thought, I break into the motion of a healer. A healer who's able to separate her feelings and surroundings from the task at hand. I rip more fabric from the layers of skirt and take three long strides into the middle of the room, where Baylor's arms and legs are strapped spread eagle to a wide slab of wood.

I mechanically catalog each of his many lacerations, tying off the ones still bleeding. All while Baylor's pulse, there but too faint, beats in answer to Thaliya's whispered song echoing off the empty walls.

A shadow crosses the only light seeping in from the small window slats causing everyone to jump. But while Thaliya is lost to Baylor, Gryphon who hasn't moved since laying eyes on Baylor, rushes to my side with his sword at the ready.

"There's not enough time," a familiar voice, a balm to the terrors surrounding us, sounds in the darkness.

"There's nothing here we can't fix." Thaliya's head of ward voice cuts Thaddeus off.

"Yes, but there is no time. If we want to live—if we want Baylor to live—we must go now." Thaddeus looks toward the stairs as if his Ancient ears pick up sounds approaching we can't. Judging by the way Thaliya's jaw clenches, she hears it, too.

In a quick movement, Thaddeus crosses to Thaliya and Baylor. Gryphon's eyes widen but he valiantly moves to step between Thaddeus and the others, only to find Thaddeus pulling his dagger and slicing deeply across his own wrist. A hiss escapes his lips and he offers his wrist. Even in the darkness, I can smell his fresh blood, mingling with the other stale scents in the room. "Here." He offers his wrist to Baylor.

Thaliya looks to Thaddeus' proffered wrist and tsks. "There's no need for blood magic here. He's immortal. He will heal."

"Yes, of course he'll heal." Thaddeus' tone tinges with urgency. "But if we're to all leave here alive, he needs to drink. And now."

I watch as Thaliya's will battles with Thaddeus' urgency. What was it that Thaddeus said about an Ancient's blood? If they share their blood with another, it will heal all wounds instantly, but the two will be bonded for eternity. Is that what Thaliya fears? Her son becoming bonded in some way to an Ancient? Isn't that infinitely better than the alternative?

"Thaliya," my voice breaks on her name, but she looks away from Baylor's broken face to me. "This can help. Thaddeus can help." I nod toward her son's prone form.

She looks from me to her son then to Thaddeus' outstretched and bleeding wrist, blood already dripping to the floor while fear and distrust mark each one of her features. But also love. She nods and moves to rouse Baylor enough for him to drink.

"Sweet Bay." Thaliya ever so gently prods Baylor in the shoulder, angling herself under him enough to lift his neck and head. Gryphon falls to his knees beside the table and angles Baylor's body against his chest. His movements are strong and practiced while his eyes scream to be anywhere but in this moment.

Thaddeus moves his wrist to Baylor's mouth, wrapping his other hand around the back of Baylor's head. "Drink." Underneath the urgent demand, there's an Ancient strength that even in his blood loss and nearly unconscious state, Baylor responds to. With Thaddeus' help, he manages to close his lips around the bleeding wound, lapping at the blood.

But as soon as Thaddeus' blood crosses Baylor's lips, a new fervor awakens within him. His wrists buck against the ropes tying him to the block of wood as he tries to taste more, drink more. Thaddeus' concentration buckles only a moment as he winces, adjusting to Baylor's thirst.

He's giving himself to Baylor so that Baylor can live. The lines of his face are hardened against the pain. The lines of his arms bulge against the struggle of holding Baylor close enough to get what he needs, but making sure Baylor doesn't take too much.

In this moment, I see it. He doesn't present the selfish, take-all air he usually does. In fact, he's so selfless. And I ruined it between us. He's been here this whole time, risking everything to find me and reunite me with my long-lost sister and I overlooked that. All of it.

Tears flow freely down Thaliya's cheeks. Her gaze flits back and forth between her son's growing thirst and building energy to Thaddeus' controlled stoicism. "Enough." Thaliya's tone leaves no room for argument, but Thaddeus allows Baylor a moment longer before he breaks Baylor's hold on him.

A moment passes as my mind attempts to catch up to what just happened. But before any sense can be made, Baylor groans loudly, too loudly. Thaliya sobs and moves to untie the ropes binding him. Gryphon and I are faster, and the work is done before Thaliya has left Baylor's side.

Thaddeus rises, a little ashen, but no less wobbly from what just happened. With a preternatural tilt of his head, he listens to sounds too far off for my ears. Apparently unsatisfied with what begins to close in on us, he sweeps Baylor into his arms and heads out of the cell. "If we hurry, we can still make it. They're closing in quickly now, though."

I gather my sword along with the one I picked up from that first guard, which now seems like eons ago.

Gryphon and I lead the way up the stairs and as we take the last stairs, I turn to ask him if he's ready. The question dies in my throat at the look I find on his face.

CHAPTER FORTY-EIGHT

I join Gryphon at the top of the stairs where we're greeted by a dozen of Hadeon's top guards. At first, I'm startled out of my mind and my shaking limbs don't do me any favors as Gryphon and I stand, swords poised at the ready, waiting for Thaddeus and Thaliya to join us.

The guards, some smirking while some openly laugh, dare us to make our move. As I meet their gazes, I notice Patton at the head of their crew. Shaken, I realize this is what he's trained us for. This very moment.

His slight bow of his chin is all the encouragement I need.

So, while the guards still laugh, waiting for the true fight to arrive, we strike as one.

Gryphon and I advance fast and hard, remaining with our backs close while driving a wedge between our enemies. Patton pivots and is able to strike three of his own men down before anyone is the wiser. And while another stands slack jawed watching Patton expertly cut down guard after guard, I step in, blade striking true to the collar bone before they're able to comprehend my wrath. Gryphon drives two at once into the wall, using our surroundings to distract and trap, just as Patton taught us. He catches my eye, his courtly smile bright from ear to ear with delight.

I heave my sword through the belly of one young but skilled female guard and step back, the clanging of swords overcome by silence as the last guard falls. I step into Gryphon, our shoulders brushing against each other, confirming we both still stand. He's blood spattered from head to toe but still smiling, eyes scanning the carnage before us as if it's the finest sight he's ever witnessed. And with the more than sheltered court life he's lived, maybe this is what he's been waiting for.

Thaddeus sets Baylor down behind us. "I carry the injured and miss all the fun?"

Thaliya and I quickly rush in to catch Baylor. His eyes are open but distant, as if he's fighting to gain control of his thoughts and movements.

"Next time, I'll leave you one or two," Gryphon says as Patton claps him on the shoulder, a look of pride shining in his warrior eyes.

"He's coming around." Thaliya looks to me and I nod in reassurance. Baylor keeps trying to hold his head up, but he's not quite stable yet.

"It'll come fast and hard," Thaddeus responds. Our eyes meet for a moment and in that completely inappropriate moment, everything snaps back into place. A million memories flash unbidden through my mind, moments we shared together trading breaths and kisses in dark hallways and stretched out across the office carpet, fire blazing in the background. His songs, both dark and hopeful, play in the background of every moment passed between us.

"Grrrter rrmmm," an incomprehensible breath escapes from Baylor and there's laughter. Laughter full of light in the darkest of moments.

Thaddeus looks up and as he does, another rush of guards head our way. Gryphon resumes his fighting stance, readying for the next onslaught.

"Keep him walking." Thaddeus loops Baylor around my shoulder and kisses my forehead. "We've got this."

I look up at him speechless. We're fighting for our lives and he offers a forehead kiss? The very least romantic of kisses? "We'll meet up with you at the stables." And with that he's at Gryphon and Patton's side, advancing to give Thaliya and I time to escape with our still woozy Baylor.

Still in a daze, I help pull Baylor through the hallway, trying to remain inconspicuous amongst the people who have begun to notice not all is right within the castle walls. It seems as if those we run into help us in our plight, blocking us from the many guards searching the passages. We're lucky enough to elude anyone who'd sound an alert all the way down the main hallway.

"We can run down and grab a few more supplies, then start our way toward the stables." I look hopefully at Thaliya, staring down the steps that lead to the healer's ward.

"No. The others will come this way looking for you. You must go straight to the stables." She points toward the stables as if I hadn't already realized I have to make it to the completely opposite side of the castle.

She looks at Baylor and a silent communication passes between them as she weighs the options, and Baylor in our arms. "Can you walk?" She nudges Baylor in the side and he stands, swaying between us.

"We can make it to the ward, the two of us." The confidence in her words, at a time when everyone's searching for us, makes me think they have other things they haven't told me yet. "We'll meet you at the stables." She gives my hand a quick squeeze and shifts her attention to her son.

"I can make it," Baylor huffs out as they turn toward the staircase. They shuffle off, slowly descending until I can no longer see them, Baylor leaning heavily on his mother's shoulder. Thaliya is a pillar of strength.

Chapter Forty-Nine

"P rincess Rowandine, behind me!" As soon as their heads dip below view, I spin to make out my next threat. Not moments later, King Sturdevant runs toward me, determination set in his jaw. His body presses against mine as he assesses threats around us, dual swords at the ready.

Even at this moment, after the day I've had, I can't help but admire the way his shoulders flex beneath his pressed white shirt and the way he balances his two shimshar without thought.

"What are you doing out here? Haven't you heard, it's unsafe! You should be in your rooms until the threat is neutralized." He takes in my wedding dress, in tatters and covered in blood. "We need to get you to a healer." His face is stricken at the sight of me.

"I'm fine," I assure him, trying for a smile. He pulls us away from the main hallway into the corners of the ballroom. I'm not fooling anyone.

Flowers brush against my arm, and for a moment, I worry my vines found their way in here, too. But the roses brushing against me are not my own. The white roses and baby's breath are scattered throughout the ballroom in tall vases and twine around the archways billowing with bright white bows and pale yellow streamers.

After taking in my dress torn and tattered, covered in blood and now the sword in my hand, he takes a step back. "Rowandine?" Confusion and hurt warring on his features.

"I can't marry you." Which seems obvious, but I don't know what words will make this easier.

"I don't understand." He looks again at my dress and the mess I'm covered in as if he's trying to reconcile it with what he knows of me. With the woman who strode down the halls arm in arm with him, quietly laughing at his stories or telling stories of my own. "I thought we held the same views, believed in the same things. We both want a better world, and it can start with Etos." I don't know if he's aware, but even though he's sheathed his weapons, his hands still hover over his swords like I'm the enemy.

And maybe now I am.

"We do. Want the same things. But it has to start here, in Merula, in Everguard. With me." Meeting his eyes, I wait, watching his features while this sinks in.

He doesn't get upset and he doesn't respond with anger. I see the moment he moves from Sturdevant the man to Sturdevant the ruler, and somewhere within I admire that he's able to do such a thing. Like a true ruler, his feelings are pushed aside as he simply states, "You can't undo this."

CHAPTER FIFTY

I 'm not sure what I expected, but this response is harder to stomach. He's clearly surprised, but takes it in stride as if it's just a typical night and I've asked to stroll through the garden with him when the other option is to dance amidst the crowded ballroom floor. Is this how a ruler responds, all mind and no heart?

I take a breath and stand taller, trying, but failing to emulate this practiced ruler in front of me. "I am not asking for forgiveness; I know what I'm doing is unforgivable. But perhaps, some understanding?"

"But I don't understand, we fit together. I thought you were sent from the stars specifically for me. An answer to my prayers." His words are poetic, something that in any other time of my life would've surely unlocked my heart. He takes a hesitant step toward me, the shadows playing across his beautiful face, a face I've come to know so well. I take a step back, straight into a table behind us, and a crash sounds. I jump and swirl around. My sword still out and ready, but it's only a vase. The roses scatter across the floor and a sharp pain shoot through my foot. A shard of vase grazes my skin, and now the blood mixes with the water spilt everywhere, staining the white petals red.

As I look from the ground to him, each of our walks brush through my mind in one breath. Even from the start, I knew there could be no love between us, but somehow he broke through the walls I put up. His pointed questions and the way he listened, unmatched and unheard of in any man I've known before this.

If only there was a better way to do this. "I'm sorry, Lysander." The hurt and disbelief in his eyes wars with the set of his jaw, but he remains as if there's more to say.

His reaction hurts more than the glass shard grazing my foot. I want to take back my words, do whatever is needed to fix what I've broken between us. On the inside, my heart wants to bend, collapse into what he wants me to be.

But this time, I can't waiver. There is too much at stake. "I wish there was another way. Where we could make a go of this, and together do something good for our people."

"Then why?" He takes my hands, clasping them tightly as if he knows if I let go there'll be no future between us.

"Don't you see? Hadeon has made a mess of Everguard. I have to put the broken pieces back together before we can be of any help to the lands surrounding us. Otherwise, we leave ourselves a weak, broken realm for someone else to pick up. I have to do it before someone else makes it their mess to put back together. This is my land, in more ways than one." His grip loosens just a little. "This is bigger than me, Lysander, or I would go with you in a heartbeat."

I can feel him slipping further away as each silent moment ticks by. And I'm torn in two. It was so clear we would've been a good match. He knows it. I think I know it, too.

He searches my eyes, but whatever's reflected there causes him to sigh. The rims of his eyes redden and his blond hair falls into his face. Finally, he drops his grip on my hands and steps back; his expression unreadable in the shadows of the room.

"We're through. You have no ally here." He takes a step back, drawing a line between us. "And between our realms as well. You'll regret this, Rowandine of Merula." As he leaves the ballroom he brushes past me, his shoulder barreling through my own without a second glance. His footsteps echo through the empty ballroom where we were supposed to celebrate our nuptials hours later, the streamers and flowers seeming to wilt with his retreating form.

CHAPTER FIFTY-ONE

The tears threatening to fall blur my vision as I hastily make my way down the corridor. The colors of the tapestries smear together and the cold marble floor appears uneven until I swipe furiously at the stubborn tears with my palms. I could walk this castle blindfolded and dizzy if I had to, but in this race for my life? I'd rather not. At least I know if I can just make it to the end of this expanse and past the kitchens, the doors closest to the stables are right there.

I'm so close. I look at my aching foot, wishing there was some way to numb the pain for just a little longer. As I look back up, just before I turn into the last hallway, a voice stops me in my tracks.

"You thought you could just scurry down to the dungeons like the mouse you are and what? Come away with my treasure? I still have big plans for that one." Hadeon's voice sounds behind me and I turn as he motions toward the other end of the corridor in the direction of the healer's ward. My stomach sinks. He knows where they went. I sent Thaliya with her wounded son unguarded. If they're found, they have no chance. I've just sent the most important person to me and her son to their death. I can hardly focus on the threat before me knowing what I've done.

"You weren't even planning to execute him, were you? He was bleeding out on that sorry excuse for a table down there. There's no telling how long you'd have left him there to rot. There is no honor in that." Emboldened by my conversation with Lysander, the words come out before I have time to call them back.

"Honor? You ask 'what honor?'" Hadeon's keen eye hones to daggers as he casually strides toward me. His movement allows me to see Killian over his shoulder in his shadow. "Who would look for honor when such great power awaits to be claimed? Who would call on honor when there's entire realms ready for the taking?" Hadeon's warrior frame, rusty with years of royalty but honed still nonetheless, towers over me. His questions float heavy in the air surrounding us.

I drop my gaze; my bravado sinking fast. But as my gaze lowers, Killian's questioning look holds onto something Hadeon said, puzzling over his words. Does he not see the monster our father is? But before I can motion to him with some sort of acknowledgement, that small glint turns steely with the same resolve I've seen reflected in Father's.

"You realize now, there's only one way forward." He grips my wrist, twisting until I'm thrown off balance. "There's nothing left for you here. You're going through with this marriage, and you'll be off to Etos by sundown."

The rage emanating from each word scalds me. His weight on my wrist forces me to take steps back until I'm pressed against the wall.

Just as Patton always drilled into my head to avoid. At all costs. Warning bells sound in my mind and I realize too late I'm no better than a cornered animal.

The first moment I'm on my own and I'm as good as dead.

Know yourself, know your path.

It's better to go down swinging.

"No." The word comes out almost inaudible, but firm. A growl from the cornered creature he's pushed me to be.

"No?" His booming laugh is a painful contrast to the quiet surrounding us as if the entire castle knows to let Hadeon have his moment, and they'll come to clean up afterward, as always.

"No." I twist out of his grip and stumble before righting myself, but the movement throws him off balance as well, sending him backward into Killian who catches his arm and steadies him.

Hadeon rights himself, brushing off any aid from Killian and glares at me.

Unlike him, I've learned it's okay to ask for help. But there's no one around and I flounder for a moment. But I can feel the support of everyone who loves me. Everyone whose stood beside me, no matter the time, no matter the distance. And I look into myself as a tension builds inside me. Before I know it, my power drives down, into the marble floors surrounding us, causing the floor beneath us to shake and shift. Hadeon's eyes go wide and Killian grabs onto his father's shoulder for balance.

CHAPTER FIFTY-TWO

"I knew it." He looks me up and down with hungry eyes as if seeing me for the first time.

My concentration breaks the moment he says something.

He knew.

Just like Avicii said.

And for just long enough I lose my connection to my power. I grab at it, but the threads fall through my grasp and the king recovers before I do. He draws his long sword and Killian follows suit. He stands, weapon at the ready. "You're one of them," he spits out, disgust sharpening each word. "It's true, isn't it?"

"I am what you think I am," I answer simply. He has a mind for strategy, but how quickly can he work out the entirety of the truth.

He lunges, striking so hard. I have to block with both hands, both sword and dagger crossed, the vibrations reverberating up my arms. "I thought I weeded all of you out so carefully. But even my own wife betrays me."

He still thinks it is Tristana. My mind reels. Everything snaps into place. He's punished Tristana all this time for a betrayal she did not commit. He knows pieces, but it doesn't make sense.

"But Licia and I are twins," I say, searching for a thread to his logic.

"I don't know what dark magic is at play here, but *she* is clearly mine."

Licia's strong nose, the one she shares with both Killian and Father, flashes through my mind. "You, on the other hand, have never measured up. You don't look like me, you've never shared any of the same interests, and you spend too much time in your own head to notice what's happening in the real world."

Well, that's because when I stop to notice what's happening around me, my own father tries to cut me down and my whole world falls apart, starting with Avicii. His hands flash through my mind. His hands on me. The memories I've tried so hard to forget, resurface in a flood.

"Your magic is in there. Show me what you can do." His grip is tight. Too tight. My wrists will snap if his vice grip gets any tighter. My basket of vegetables and bouquet of flowers lie askew and forgotten. The cry that escapes my lips is too much. Instantly, I try to muffle the sound with a cough. But only another sob escapes. He throws me to the ground.

The words under his breath are almost inaudible but I catch a few. I can't possibly have heard him correct. "He said this was going to be a challenge... The magic should manifest if she's pushed hard enough..."

The bloodline. That's all that mattered, right? Continuing the royal bloodline, showing the strength to reproduce more royals, despite my being last in line, that was always the goal. That's why we're so out of the way. The farthest point north and east in Merula makes it easier for him to travel and return home. This is how we got to see each other between his travels.

But other pieces move into place. The random anger, the threats, the surprises. He thought if I was pushed, some kind of magic would manifest?

Something snaps in my mind. Or snaps into place. This is too much. I can't keep going like this. I will not survive. His anger and his flip-flopping emotions will be the death of me. To feel so loved one moment and discarded the next is exhausting— always on guard.

While he paces beside me, his shadow looms over my place in the dirt, light poking through each time he passes. The thought gives me pause.

There's light where he is not. How can I grow, how will I thrive if he's always blocking my light? As the dangerous thought crosses my mind, there's movement beside me.

Vines.

But not from my garden, nothing I've ever grown has ever been nearly as thick around. It's as wide as a zucchini left a day or two past it's picking day.

But I recognize it. There's something familiar about it. A part of me.

It's a part of me.

It pauses as these thoughts grow into my consciousness. As if before there was an unknown part of me that could reach out and connect. Something I didn't, or hadn't wanted to, pick up on until now.

Avicii's right. I look back to him as the realization dawns, but he's still pacing, muttering to himself. I try not to hear any of his words. When he gets like this, it always gets worse before it gets better.

But this time, it'll be different.

I can't take the storm before the calm. It's not worth it.

Strewn all around me are the vegetables. Only vegetables. What will I do, peg him with eggplant when he comes too close?

And then I remember my tools. I look around, but they're nowhere in sight. Where did they land? The basket. Avicii placed them in the basket before we started off.

It's an arm's length out of my reach. There's no way I can get there and grab the tools before he figures out my intentions.

Just as I'm settling in to withstand another verbal lashing, hoping he'll be satisfied to leave it at that, the same vine moves again. And this time, I mentally cheer it along as it creeps closer toward Avicii's feet, only moving when his back is to us.

I wish and hope with all my might that it'll wrap itself around him. If it could just hold him long enough, I'd have time to grab the tools.

And then it does.

Just as Avicii takes notice and tries to kick it out of the way, it strikes. With the speed of a snake, it coils itself around his ankles, up his knees, and over his thighs. As soon as he's taken by surprise, more vines appear growing quickly toward the first, grabbing arms and wrapping tight around his neck.

He's quickly thrown off balance, the vines causing him to fall to the ground, nothing to soften his landing. A cloud of dust swallows him for just a moment. But when it clears, he's staring directly at me. Not in fear, though.

His eyes are two daggers pointed straight at me. He struggles against the vines, but they only tighten around him in response.

"You are *Fae." The smile he gives me will haunt me to my dying day. In it, I see all Hadeon promised him if he could break me. I see what he imagines my future to be and what riches and titles will rain down upon him because of it all.*

A shudder runs through me at the calculation in that one look. It throws me into motion. I don't have much time. I don't know how long his living manacles will hold. I move as if the wind has filled my sails. In one movement, I fall upon my basket, the sheers resting just where I thought they'd be. And then I'm in front of Avicii.

I have to get on his level. One last time.

The ground is unforgiving and I swallow the pain in my knees, knowing it'll be the last time he's ever able to inflict such pain on me. On anyone.

"You better cut me out of here. This isn't how you're supposed to use your magic, Rowandine." He twists and struggles against his captor. "Get it off me!" He spits venom with each word. But as I bring the open sheers to his chest and aim one point just above his heart, his tune changes. "What do you think you're doing? You can't kill me! This isn't how it works. Put that down, Rowandine. We can talk about this."

My resolve waivers. He's never wanted to talk before.

"We can visit the castle." His voice rises as I hold the blade steady, weighing his words. "I'll take you with me on my next assignment!" Tears stream down his face and his eyes flick from the blade resting on his skin to my face.

The anger is still there, I can hear it just below the surface. He won't fool me this time. It's always temporary. His anger always wins out. And I always lose.

I lean into the sheers, allowing the tip to puncture his skin while the other side of the open blade presses into my palm.

The odd thought flits through my mind that this isn't like cutting into a vegetable. Not even a potato. There's so much resistance.

Avicii's eyes widen as my intent becomes clear—my mind is made up.

He continues making promises and threats, switching between the two, but his words fade into a gentle hum.

The hum of a bee.

This bee won't sting again.

I put all of my weight behind the sheers. I focus on the way they cut into me as well, there's no handle here, so my left hand grips only the blade. I breathe through the pain as blood blooms from under my palms. It doesn't matter, though. I'm almost there, almost through.

He lunges again, the quick movement and proximity shaking me from my memory. One I've pushed into the darkest recesses of my mind until now.

I'd forgotten. He knew. Hadeon and Avicii knew. Avicii tried to make me see, tried to force what's on the inside, out.

Hadeon's strike doesn't give me time to recover. My dagger flies from my hand with a hasty perry, leaving only my sword.

Killian tracks the volleys with both his eyes and his sword flicking between us. He's even more surprised than Hadeon, and more unsure of how to respond. He presses in, attempting to aid his father, but Hadeon pushes him off and he slides backward.

"No dark magic had a hand here, except your own." I try to wait him out, buying more time as I shake off the remains of that memory while simultaneously pulling the slim threads of my magic. The small roots I've put down have all but withered up since earlier this morning.

"You little brat." His swipes are furious and wild. "You've always been a brat. And even worse now, a half-Fae brat! You'll die, here and now. There are no remaining Fae."

"You don't know, do you?" I blow out a deep breath as I strike and spin to the side already knowing where he'll strike next. I shouldn't have said anything. Fear flashes in his eyes before the fury returns. But it was there, a brief hesitation.

Which does he want more, the information I have or my death?

I pull once more and a great surge of power rushes toward me. The sound deafening as the marble floor surrounding us bends and cracks. Great horned vines of the deepest green surface through the wreckage, curling over themselves. They slither around Hadeon and Killian's feet, waiting for permission to strike.

Both Hadeon and Killian begin hacking at the vines closest to them. And I can feel each strike like a small cut across my own skin. I try to pull the vines back, and they listen, moving out toward the periphery of the room, but so much damage is done and my body aches as if their swords struck at me.

"What's happening?" Killian looks to his father. "Roe is part Fae?" The last word sounds like a curse as it crosses his lips. He looks at the vines, still climbing across the room and then disdainfully at me. "*You* are doing this?"

The pain lashes through me as they continue to strike with their swords and the vines recoil, returning to where they came from. Instead of answering Killian's question, I try to hold on, but I can't hold the power through all the pain. Doubt rushes through me. I'm not strong enough on my own to take him on. I look down, expecting to see all the cuts they've made on the vines reflected on me. But my skin is clear from any marring. Or at least no worse for the wear than it was before the vines. So, it's just that I can feel their pain?

"You foolish child." Hadeon sees the panic and doubt cross my face as the vines retreat further. "You have no idea what you're doing. Your handful of weeds will do nothing." He stomps on a vine as it slithers too close to him. I try to hide my wince, but I'm not sure I cover it with my step toward them. The vine, lifeless and left forgotten, sprawls out against the white marble. The red, pointed petals leak from it like blood.

"Perhaps not." Sword in hand, I wipe my nose. It comes away bloodied. The pain and the power are too much. My body feels too heavy for itself, but I continue to perry against each of Hadeon's blows, thankful Killian still hasn't joined the fight but I know my moments to strike are limited. "But Everguard can't go on like this. We'll crumble in your hands."

"Ha!" He slashes across my body, grazing my belly with his blade. A hiss escapes my lips as the sting sets in. "And you'd do better? You wouldn't know the first thing about ruling a city, much less an entire realm. Why do you think it was so easy to sell you off to the highest bidder? Now though, knowing what you truly are, you are worth nothing to me."

"It's in my blood," is all the answer I can voice before he strikes a fatal blow. His sword comes too fast, the blade moving in slow motion as the realization creeps in there's no time to move out of its striking arch. I try to bring my hands up to protect my throat, but I'm not fast enough.

CHAPTER FIFTY-THREE

There's a tug on my ankle, yanking me off my feet, and before I can make sense of it, I'm sprawled out across the ground, my head aching with the aggressive contact with the stone floor. I look around for the cause of my lucky fall.

The vines. They yanked me down and saved my life. But I didn't come away without harm. My fingers trace along my collar bone, a sharp sting and a warm stickiness answers my unspoken question.

Killian and Hadeon stand over me, their forms blurring as my eyes fill with tears of defeat. "I'd say there's very little of your blood left at this point." I can't see him through the tears, but I can hear the smile in his taunting voice.

"Father. Her blood."

"Yes, I think I'll leave it. As a reminder." At first, I can't make sense of what he's saying. My strength continues to weaken and I can't hold both hands to my wound, it's too hard. One hand flings out to the ground beside me. It's warm, the ground is so warm. Somewhere in the back of my mind, I know it's because of my blood.

"No, Father. She said ruling is in her *blood*." Killian talks over me as if I'm no longer present. Which, in moments, I may not be. But I can hear the realization dawn as he repeats my words.

"But that would mean," Hadeon begins, slower to reach the same conclusion. "No. She can't be. I watched Queen Bronwinn bleed out, her belly still round with child." But I can hear the question in his voice as he kicks my ankle.

The world slows, but something is nagging at me, pulling at me. A thought?

No. A thread. A faint thread of my power is pulling back at me now. Trying to make sense of it, I blink the tears out of my eyes. But my timing is wrong because Hadeon thinks I'm answering whatever question he's just asked.

"You're Azulian's brat then?" he confirms. "Well, this changes a thing or two." Even in my blurring vision, I can see as he tips his gaze toward his son.

Where's the dagger? I use the brief distraction of them deciding my fate to try to recall where it landed. In answer, the vine Hadeon had stomped out, rolls toward me—the large, pointy red petals blooming to produce the very dagger.

"We can't have her alive." In these past moments my attention has been elsewhere, but I still at those words. I'm running out of time.

"She's the last of the Fae, Father. She could be useful. All she knows is us. If we can revive her, she'd be ours. We can breed her, make our own armies of Fae scum. Think how quickly they'll decimate an enemy if we have all this power behind us. Think how quickly we could mine Blagdenbeck. Don't you see all we could do?" Killian, ever the strategist, is going straight to using me for a military advantage. I'm not surprised, but it still stings. I thought he saw my side, could be on my side.

I palm the dagger before their attention returns to me, the hilt rubbing across my scar, reminding me of Avicii—no, of my strength in tough moments.

Hadeon kicks me again. "You there, child? How does that plan sound? We'll take you apart piece by piece to find out how that power within you works. Maybe distill your essence into tiny bottles and set you on a shelf. You'd see eternity yet, that way."

Fighting against the unconsciousness threatening to swallow me whole, I hold onto each of his words as if they're the roots holding me to this earth. I inwardly cringe at the not so discrete picture he's painted.

"Precisely. We'll neutralize her and use her Fae-like qualities to our benefit. This is even better than we could've imagined. Rather than decades, we'll conquer the surrounding realms in years, maybe even months. With drops of her blood, we'll uncover the remains of Glorixia, and all its treasures." Killian nods along with his own reasoning, rubbing his hands together in anticipation of what? My blood all over them?

"I don't know, son." Hadeon still sounds skeptical. "She's a loose end. One I should've tied off years ago. Leaving her alive could be beneficial, but it seems too risky." Without warning, Hadeon lifts his long sword with two hands, putting all his weight into driving it down, straight into me.

I move without hesitation. Before his arms come down, I pool all the energy left within me, just enough to bring me onto one knee. I meet his movements with my dagger gripped tightly in both hands, poised high.

His eyes connect with mine, but there's no fatherly love there. Just pure hatred and loathing. As his sword comes down, I lean into his weight, knocking his sword from his hand causing him to frantically grasp for purchase on something. He grabs my shoulder but my body is planted. I will not go down with him—not yet. My hands and all of my focus lock on my dagger—driving it into his chest. I let his fall do some of the work for me, and every inch he falls is met with an inch of my blade.

A gasp from Killian sounds, a small reminder he's bared witness to my actions. I roll away, aware that he holds the upper hand as I still can't see through the blazing pain engulfing me. I expect swift retaliation from him. My foggy mind tries to figure out the fastest way out of here without another confrontation.

I don't think I could do the same to Killian, my big brother. A little stoic and aloof, sure. But his late-night stories raised me, fostering my love for books and adventure. He was a father figure where Hadeon was not.

I wait as the seconds tick by, watching what he'll do. Surprising me, he falls to his knees beside Hadeon. His hands hover back and forth over his chest unsure what to do. He finally clasps his hands around the dagger still in his father's chest.

I watch, knowing I don't belong here anymore. I am not part of this private moment. I am the cause.

Hadeon's hands find Killian's own, gripping with what strength remains. Together, they pull the dagger from his chest and within seconds, the floor turns crimson beneath them.

Chapter Fifty-Four

Forgotten for now, I stumble a moment before finding my footing on the wreckage surrounding us. The room spins around me and my only thought is *I must get away.* I run as fast as I can but it feels like wading through mud as I trip over my own feet and make slow progress. The area surrounding the confrontation is completely destroyed. The stone hallway surrounding us is filled with holes where the vines pierced through stone now works against me, halting my progress as I step around holes wider than my waist. The vines themselves though, they're bigger than I've ever seen before. They have the same look of a cucumber vine, but the smallest sections are bigger around than my wrist.

I step carefully around the sleeping lianas, the carnage of my brave vines everywhere I look. But I try not to disturb them in their eternal slumber. The tapestry lined hall clears the farther I get from our exchange, but I can hear Killian's sobs from here. I can't bring myself to turn around or stop, but I know those cries will bring guards in droves.

The door to the stables is straight ahead. I'm almost there. But dizziness overcomes me, unconsciousness looming too close for comfort, and I fall smack into a solid stone wall. The sweet, heady scent of cake greets me, confirming I've made it as far as the kitchens. I try to lean back into the hallway to continue the most direct route. But the sight of what has to be my wedding cake stands before me, stopping me in my tracks. Layers and layers of fluffy white icing, so much that I can smell the sugar and vanilla from across the room. The cake is large enough to feed all of Merula.

I guess the news hasn't traveled as far as the kitchens yet.

Good.

For me.

I have to gather my wits about me. I'm so close, but so many things could still go wrong. There's a door in here leading out to the gardens. If I can make it through the gardens and to the stables, I know we'll make it out of here. Gone under cover of darkness.

A sharp pain washes over me, dizziness clouds my vision for a moment and I have to fight through the urge to pass out. The coppery scent of blood overpowers the sugar, reminding me that I'm bleeding—profusely. I have to stem the steady flow of blood before I pass out.

I almost lost my head today. I almost lost my life.

Grabbing a handful of flour-covered kitchen towels, I pat my collarbone, pressing more firmly after testing the area. If only I had time to stop and make a poultice. But I have to keep moving, there's no time to do anything other than staunch the bleeding with pressure.

It feels tight where he cut, and my optimism that it's not too deep dims slightly when the towel comes away bright red. Still bleeding then. I grab a few more towels, tying them awkwardly around my shoulders and back to keep the towels in place.

Just as I tighten the last knot, there's a shuffling of hurried footsteps, the sound getting closer by the second.

I must get out of here before I'm found. Killian must've snapped out of it long enough to have everyone in the castle searching for me.

The garden. If I can just make it outside to the cover of the sinking sun, I'll be safe. As I spin on my heels, I'm surprised by the amount of blood I've tracked around this small space, but I push the thought aside. If I can make it out of here alive, I can worry about poultices and bandages later.

The footsteps grow. It sounds like it's more than one person. The guards are close.

The door to the gardens—to my freedom—looms in front of me, but it seems so far. I step toward the salty sea air, calling my name, but instead of stepping out into the setting sun, darkness creeps across my vision, swallowing me whole.

A small nudge and a tug from deep within awakens me. Wait, that can't be right.

But the incessant poking is enough to wake me from the darkness. They're pulling my hand, no that's not quite right either. My ring. They want my ring.

I open my eyes enough to look around, clutching my hand to my chest to keep my ring safe. There's no one here. But I felt it. Felt something. Was it just the breeze coming off the bay? The open door causes me to doubt what I felt.

Pushing up on my elbows, I realize I didn't even make it all the way outside. I at least made it to the doorway, but must've fallen across the threshold before making it completely out of the kitchens. Did I pass out on the entryway from blood loss? The cut is bad, but maybe passing out on my face actually helped slow the bleeding. The blood beneath me makes it difficult to sit up without sliding, but finally I manage, leaning against the door jam, partially outside and partially able to use the lights from the kitchen to assess the damage.

I'm no stranger to a wound like this. And with this much blood loss, I'll be lucky if I can manage to stand again, let alone escape from here. Luckily, the guards passed me by this time, but I need to figure something out, and quick.

A red petal catches my attention. Another vine. That's what was tugging on me. It winds its way up my wrist, past my elbow, and shoulder of my left arm. Over the wound itself, careful not to disrupt my makeshift bandage, which is now as red as the flower trailing down my other arm, stopping only once it rests on my finger. The pearls of my ring sparkle underneath the movement of the vine.

"Yes, it really is a beautiful ring," I say to the vine, half amused, half worried about my sanity. "But now isn't the time to be admiring primeval jewelry pieces." I hold the ring up though, momentarily entranced. That statue, the one where I found the ring, isn't too far away. I mentally follow the path looking toward where she should be, in the back corner of the garden.

Standing tall, illuminated by the last of the afternoon glow, is the Fae warrior herself in all her glory. Squinting, I can make out there's something on her outstretched hand, the one that wore the ring. I look down at my right hand where the vine still sits curled around my ring finger. The flower blooming next to my ring matches the one in the distance, wrapped around where the ring used to rest.

My thoughts are interrupted by another sear of pain from the wound high across my chest. I need to figure something out, and quickly, or I'm not going to make it.

I'll let everyone down.

The disastrous thought is met with another—*know yourself, know your path.*

I know myself now.

I'm a healer. I can do so much good with my hands, helping others and bringing wonders to life. I'm Fae. And my people, the people of Merula, and all the people of Everguard, depend on me now.

I know myself. And now I know my path. If I could just heal myself—wait, could it be possible to heal myself? I don't have anything to create a strong poultice, but maybe I have something better—the power within me.

I tug on the now fragile threads within and they respond. I've never directed my power toward myself, and it feels overwhelming pulling it into so much pain. The power within bends away from my own pain, searching for a way out.

It doesn't work. There's no hum of energy. I can't do this. Even if I can hold onto the threads, I can't direct them firmly enough, my head's too foggy to be convincing. The wound is too large and I'm losing too much blood too quickly.

Just as the threads start to fade and the darkness threatens my periphery once again, the vine at my finger quivers, focusing my attention on my hand for a moment.

The ring. The Fae warrior's ring. I look back toward the statue and the last rays of sunshine play across the statue's fierce gaze.

I look back to my hand raising it, bringing the ring closer. I rest my hand over the bandages, placing the ring close to the bleeding wound. Hoping against hope for something to happen.

The threads of power within me come alive at the movement. More power gathers beneath me, pooling in the ground below, waiting for a direction to flow.

I gasp at the raw power that begins to flow through me and position the ring directly over my wound. It's as if pure sunlight shines straight through me. The smell of fresh grass on a summer day fills my senses as the light passes through, up, and around me. It's everywhere at once. The hum rises in my ears, like a colony of bees hovering around their hive.

As the humming within crescendos, I can feel the exact moment the bleeding stops. It tickles when the skin around the wound stretches and pulls back toward itself, regrowing and healing all at once. As the power thrums through me, the ring helps focus the swell of power. As I direct it, the ring pools it, like a warm blanket wrapping snug all around me in comfort.

Finally, it's done. There's no more pain. I collapse against the door frame, gulping down heaps of air.

CHAPTER FIFTY-FIVE

"F uck. Roe, what happened?" a familiar voice says beside me laced with panic. "What happened?" Gryphon repeats, his voice bordering on hysterical. I must look bad.

"I'm fine," I say. And I am. The power still thrums through my muscles, my veins invigorate me further and keep me alert.

"Where's it coming from?" He's grabbed a towel and has slid onto his knees beside me. "Where's all this blood coming from?"

"I'm okay," I exhale a laugh laced with a breath. "I'm okay," I repeat, still out of breath and unable to say much more I pull at the bandages I had wrapped haphazardly from my neck all the way to my chest. The blood comes away with the bandages to reveal a bright white scar stretching from one side of my collar bone all the way across my chest to my opposite armpit.

"Oh, Roe," Gryphon says almost reverently. "What happened?"

"It doesn't matter now. I'm fine." I finger the raised scar, wondering at my handywork. The wound is completely closed, and left in its place is a scar that twists and curves across my chest.

Just like a vine.

He looks at me like he wants to say more but footsteps sound behind him.

"Oh good, you've found her. What the—" Thaddeus slips across the floor in my blood, catching himself on the table. Unfortunately, the layers and layers of cake are the only thing to break his fall.

He looks distastefully at the cake covering his hands and tries to shake it off as he takes in the scene, from the cake covering him up to his elbows to the blood all over the floor, to me, still leaning against the door frame. "Who makes a pumpkin wedding cake?" He licks his fingers but quickly wipes the rest on his pants. "It wasn't meant to be anyways, Princess." His pet name does something to my insides, but my body hurts too much to respond in kind. He moves toward us, satisfied that I'm no longer bleeding out, and not needing any further answers. Thaddeus says, "We've got to get you out of here."

I can see the way it pains him to inhale the scent of so much fresh blood. The blown-out blacks of his pupils replace the beautiful green of his eyes. He licks once more at the icing coating his fingers in an attempt to mask the scent. He must be struggling for control, so I make quick work of rising and pulling myself together. With the help of both Thaddeus and Gryphon, we're out the door and crossing the garden in no time. Each of them supports me as I loop an arm around each shoulder.

Thaddeus walks ahead, and I'm not sure if it's to distance himself from my scent or to keep a lookout. Perhaps both. But the shadows grow longer as the sun dips below the tallest of the hedges. I can't help but squint into the darkness closing in around us at each little sound.

CHAPTER FIFTY-SIX

There's a collective exhale as we enter the warmth of the stables. The scent of fresh hay wraps its familiar arms around us. The soft chuffs of the horses are the only sounds. Everyone else must've headed to the castle to help.

"They must be taking a break since their stable master is out of commission," Gryphon voices my thoughts on the empty structure.

"Or Killian's called everyone directly to the castle," I respond, reminded of what passed between the three of us earlier. Both Thaddeus and Gryphon stop and look at me.

"Why would it come from Killian to move everyone into the castle?" Thaddeus asks, his question accentuated by the lift of his eyebrows and his slow words, as if he's unsure he wants to hear the answer.

"Hadeon's dead." I take a few steps toward our horses, effectively ending the conversation there. I can feel the shock pass between them but don't acknowledge it.

Gryphon moves ahead of me quickly toward the saddles, gathering what's necessary.

"Roe," Thaddeus' voice is low as if he's still struggling for control. And I can tell what's next won't be about Hadeon. "You almost died." A statement, not a question.

"I know." My answer seems insufficient, but I'm not sure what else to say. I search his eyes for a clue as to what he's thinking. Sea glass green has returned, my Thaddeus has returned, and I'm surprised to see fear reflected in them.

"I can't lose you." He leans in close, and I welcome his scent of a fresh frost that wraps itself around me. "You mean too much to me."

"Then I suppose you'll just have to keep me close." At the look in his eye, something dark and unrecognizable flashes before he smiles and whatever it was that I saw, is just as quickly forgotten.

"Not even dragons could keep me away from you." His lips meet my own. At first, soft kisses that say I miss you. But they deepen, and something between a gasp and sigh leaves me as his hands find my hips and his palms trace up my lower back until our bodies are pressed against one another. His arousal presses into my thigh, promising pleasure the next time we're alone. Gryphon and the horses forgotten, for just a moment.

He kisses my jawline, down my neck. He continues, unable to help himself as he licks at the blood remaining where Hadeon almost took my life and I feel him shudder as he tastes me.

"We don't have a lot of time." Baylor clears his throat as he steps out of the tack room, looking anywhere but at us.

With that, our embrace is broken. With a growl filled with promises for later in his throat, Thaddeus steps away from me.

But before I can be too upset, I turn to see Baylor striding toward us as if he wasn't on death's door just hours ago.

He moves to hand me a saddle, but it falls forgotten on the floor as I wrap my arms around him. As I do, I realize in the past weeks, Baylor and I have interacted with more formalities than a hug would warrant, and the last time I had my arms wrapped around him, we must've been sixteen and up in the hay loft above us. He follows my gaze and raises his eyebrows suggestively. "Once more, for old time's sake?"

Something changes in the air and Thaddeus growls again. Baylor instantly steps back, hands raised.

I look from Baylor to Thaddeus. "He's—" But *alive* somehow seems like too small a word. Baylor is absolutely glowing. His curls gleam as if the sun shines down upon him. His skin glows with an inner light, soft and bright at the same time. All the lines in his chiseled face stand out more, giving him an ethereal appearance. His ears have the tell-tale look of the Fae. And even though he hasn't grown one bit, his whole presence just *feels* bigger. I look side-long at Thaddeus, is this what happens when Fae and Ancient blood combine?

"I'll live to see another day," Baylor finishes. "As long as you don't hug me again." He looks pointedly at Thaddeus, who's now trying to cover up his response with clearing his throat.

"The blood of the Ancients looks good on you." Thaddeus smirks, striding over to fit the bridles over the horses' faces.

"Ah, yes. I suppose one of these days I'll owe you one." Baylor winks at Thaddeus and combs a hand through his blond curls, belaying the seriousness of what passed between them this morning.

The stable door opens and all four of us draw our swords. The two figures close the door behind them with urgency. When they turn, relief and happiness swell within me. Patton and Thaliya; their arms weighed down with burlap bags, move quickly toward the horses to load them up. The scent of freshly baked bread wafts through the air as they begin tying each bag onto the saddles.

"I wish we had more time. But they're right behind us." Patton is all warrior-leaving-for-battle, expertly tying down packs in the proper spots along each horses' saddle as if he's done this a thousand times before. While Thaliya cups my face, she whispers all the words she thought she'd have time to say, but we're running out of time too fast. All her rushed words and instructions go right over me, I hope later I'll be able to recall even a part of what was said.

"We'll have to go out the rear. Let's ride." Baylor, with the enthusiasm and buoyancy of someone who was not on the chopping block this morning, mounts his ride, followed quickly by Gryphon and myself. Thaddeus mounts behind me without comment.

"You don't have your own mount?" I turn in my saddle, unsure how I feel about this invasion of space but enjoying the closeness and scent of him nonetheless.

"As a bard? I would not. My own ride will catch up to us, in time." Thaddeus looks so amused; I only hear half of his answer.

"Will catch up?" I'm unclear how that makes sense, but I squeeze my mare's ribs with my calves, starting our movement forward.

We pass Thaliya and Baylor on the way out the back. "We'll keep them distracted long enough for you to gain some distance, but don't stop until you know it's clear. The surrounding lands will be crawling with guards these next few days," Patton says as he positions himself between us and the door.

"I don't need to tell you as much, but your parents would be proud." Thaliya looks at me with tears limning her eyes. "This is what Bronwinn would have wanted. And now that you know everything, everything else will start falling into place."

SCARLETT M. HONEY

If this is what she thinks falling into place looks like, then it's going to be a rough road ahead.

Just as our horses step from around the stable doors, they begin whinnying and backstepping away from the thick trees surrounding the back side of the stables. The sound of shuffling gravel and sticks breaking grows closer.

Frantic and unsure how to proceed, I turn around to see Thaliya's body stiffen at whatever's coming from their side, so I try to stay out of the light from the stables. We're closed in. Stuck between the guards coming in behind us and whatever this unknown terror big enough to rattle even the horses is coming straight at us. I look to Thaddeus for directions.

SCARLETT M. HONEY

SCARLETT M. HONEY

SCARLETT M. HONEY

SCARLETT M. HONEY

SCARLETT M. HONEY

SCARLETT M. HONEY

CHAPTER FIFTY-SEVEN

H is eyes are focused on the darkness in front of us. He's listening for something. To something.

Over his shoulder, the guards close in around the front and I can see Patton stepping into his head of guard position, angling his body in a way that will seamlessly mislead those who come in.

My attention whips back around. The snapping branches and shuffling gravel has me terrified for what will come out of the darkness. I pat my mare to assure her, trying to calm her and quiet her snorts of fear.

I brace myself for all our plans to come crashing down around us before we even begin our journey. I realize that despite my hesitance, I am ready to leave the castle walls. Now with something in our way, the disappointment seeps in. The thought of not being able to rescue my sister who needs me is suffocating, but even the disappointment is not as bone-breaking as the thought of all those we're letting down. I can't help anyone from the cell of a dungeon.

I was looking forward to discovering more of myself. The self I just realized was sitting right below the surface. But it's over before it even begins. I pat my horse, gripping the reins so tight my knuckles are white and brace for impact, while at the same time, trying to keep us in the shadows as the sounds of swords clanging behind us grows closer.

Thaddeus remains solid behind me, but Gryphon has already pulled his sword from his belt and fixes it toward the direction of our pursuer.

I wait, expecting guards at any moment. But instead of being dragged off my horse and carried back to the castle to await the wrath of my brother, the new king, in addition to the cold resolve of the man I was supposed to marry, a hooded figure steps out of the shadows, stopping just short of our horses, as if now that they've arrived, they're unsure of how to proceed.

Everything stops for a moment. I look toward Baylor beside us who's already notched his bow and taken aim. Gryphon looks as frightened as I feel, for he'd be as destroyed as I'd be if we're caught and returned to our family. But when I steal a look at Thaddeus, he just looks annoyed. I wait for the figure before us to make their move.

While observing the figure standing before us, I notice the lone person is shorter and more slight than any of the king's guards. Although I'm up high on my horse, so anyone would appear shorter. Doubt at my ability to read the moment seeps in.

At the same moment, I notice the spotless riding boots and make the connection, the figure slowly raises her hands, palms up to show she means no harm and pulls off her hood. "Hold your bow! Don't shoot!" Her eyes wide and pleading as she looks straight at Baylor's notched arrow.

Baylor holds his loaded bow for a moment, then slowly lowers it and returns the arrow to the quiver across his back. Gryphon heaves a huge sigh and his whole body visibly relaxes. As soon as Licia is sure her life isn't in danger, she runs toward Gryphon.

As she runs at him, he lowers his arm and in one swift movement, he lifts her up and she gracefully lands behind him. He twists in the saddle to meet her eyes and kisses her deeply. A kiss that says everything about how he felt leaving her behind.

I shake my head, but really on the inside I'm swooning. If only one day, I could be as lucky as the two of them.

Beside me, Baylor huffs and rolls his eyes. "What's wrong with everyone here? We're leaving on a perilous journey across the realm, not a night out at the village pub."

Once Gryphon and Licia resurface from their own world they look pleadingly at me as if I'm the one making the calls here. And that's when I notice the pack slung across her chest.

I shrug. "You want to come?" I ask my sister. My heart floats at the awareness that she's known at least a part of this all along. And she's along for the ride. I marvel at her little birds around the castle and her ability to keep secrets.

"Of course I'm coming. I can't remain here, without my two favorite people. And you've completely lost it if you think I'm sticking around to watch the fall out of all this mess." She winks at me as she waves her hand in the air and a quiet understanding passes between us. We're done with this life.

She notices my shoulders relax and her eyes narrow. "Don't think for a second I've forgiven you both for thinking you could leave without me, but I figure I have a better chance of riding along if I'm smiling and agreeable." She swats at Gryphon and flicks an eyebrow at me.

Rather than engaging, I lead my horse behind theirs and address Thaddeus under my breath, "You knew and didn't say anything?"

I can feel the shrug of his shoulders and chest against my back as he makes himself comfortable behind me. "Honestly? I never thought she'd actually go through with it once she realized what we were doing."

Chapter Fifty-Eight

A s we continue in silence out of the gates, I wonder if he's referring to Licia or me. But I realize my mind was always made up. As soon as Thaliya spoke the words of my past and Thaddeus told me about my sister, I knew my time left in Merula was limited.

There's a whole wide world out there, and now I know I need to be a part of it. The people of Merula have struggled under Hadeon's rule at best. A pang in my chest reminds me that now the crown will sit on Killian's head. I fear he'll continue in Hadeon's footsteps until there's nothing left of Everguard.

Know yourself, know your path.

With my power awakened, and my understanding of my origins, I believe we'll be able to reach the north and reunite with my sister in time so we can save the realm together. I just hope I'm not too late.

After traveling for hours and watching as the stars fill the sky, my body feels it when Thaddeus and Baylor agree that it's time for the horses to rest. It's all I have the energy for to unload my sleeping roll and spread it out along the ground beside our small fire. Muscles I didn't even know I had strain and pull as I do simple tasks like bending over and bringing food to my mouth. Gryphon and Licia look to be in the same shape as me, but Baylor goes through the motions of watering the horses with ease and Thaddeus already built the small fire and now weaves in and out of the trees with stealth, making sure our simple campsite is safe. They are no stranger to being in the saddle for hours.

Despite the pain shooting through me, I lean in close to Licia and Gryphon, sharing our warmth and our smiles, the only part of us not yet worn out.

We did it. We made it out. Together and whole.

Together. I don't know how I could've done it without them and I don't think I'll get far into my journey without them beside me.

And now, they also have each other. The way they watch each other, communicating without words, is beautiful. Something I never even came close to with Avicii and can't imagine with Thaddeus. I look at him, limned in the light of the full moon above.

He tilts his head toward the darkness surrounding us and raises his thick eyebrows in question. A smile tugs at my lips—this is the solid language we have between us. I nod, wondering if Gryphon and Licia will notice if I sneak away.

He's already up and disappearing into the dark tree line before I can peel myself off the ground. I lose sight of him as I struggle to rise from the ground, but I move toward the tree line where he just disappeared, the cold winter air kissing all the parts of my body that were just wrapped in the warmth of the fire and my family. But the pull to Thaddeus is strong and the promise of him pressed against me, finishing what we started earlier in the stables before our escape leaves me with a warm, heady feeling.

Waiting against a tree, I bite my lip in anticipation.

CHAPTER FIFTY-NINE

"I wouldn't do that if I were you." Thaddeus' voice fills the silence. I can't see him yet, but his words are a promise of pleasure. The trees block out all moonlight, but I turn toward his voice. I feel a rush of air and then before I can even comprehend what's happened, Thaddeus stands before me, leaning against me once again. My body responds by arching into him before my mind can even catch up.

I smile, thinking that him being one of the Ancients has some perks. I wonder what else he can do at high speeds. My thoughts are interrupted by his thumb lightly tracing my bottom lip while the rest of his hand rests against my jawline.

"Rowandine." My name on his lips is a breathy whisper. He kisses his way roughly down my neck, across my new scar. My hands twist in his hair, pulling him back up so I can answer his kisses with my own. "I almost lost you today."

Our lips crash together, my tongue eager to find his, and instead, brushing against those powerful canines he's been so good at hiding. His carnal desire mixes with his Ancient desire, which somehow makes me hungrier for him.

My hands travel down his muscled chest, lingering in question at the waistband of his pants. I can already feel his hard length pressed against my thigh.

"Is this what you want? Am I what you want?" He pulls back suddenly, his question taking me off guard. My hands quickly pull back from the tie of his pants as if it burns me. I pull back just enough to look at his face, but I can only see the outlines in the darkness that presses in against us.

"Yes. You're exactly what I want. What we have is so—" My fingers graze the stubble across his cheeks, unsure if they're trying to read his features in the dark or comfort him. Even as the words leave my lips, I try to place his hesitation. Trying and failing to pinpoint the strain in his voice. Suddenly, I can't finish my sentence.

"That's what I was afraid of." With those few words, the strain in his voice turns from unsure and searching to smug and relaxed, a tone I've never heard from him before. In one beat, his demeanor changes.

I no longer feel safe with him here. He looms over me, and it feels as if he's suddenly taking up all the space and all the air around us. I try to shrink into the tree at my back, but I'm only met with rough, scratchy bark pokes through my heavy cloak and digs into my back.

He breaks my frantic thoughts with a cold, low laugh that turns my blood to ice. I stiffen as I realize I'm cornered. I look up at him, unsure how we got here.

CHAPTER SIXTY

"Princess." He trails his cold fingertips over the twists of scar across my collarbone, along my shoulder, and up my neck. My mind wars with my body as I lean into him, despite his sudden coldness in both touch and tone. "You've certainly made your feelings clear. It's time I return the favor."

Confused, I step to the side, trying desperately to make space between us. The leaves crackle underfoot as if in warning. All my senses heighten as I ready myself for whatever is to come next.

He takes a stride forward once again. My sight blurs at his rapid movements. I shake my head to clear my clouding vision.

He isn't. He couldn't be. He's so warm and passionate.

I knew he was one of the Ancients, but he's here to warn me about what's happening to Ombretta, he's not the one responsible for the horrors my twin has been living through. He can't be one of the very leeches he's warned me against. Has he come for me now because my sister is wasting away? My thoughts race to catch up with the pieces I struggle to mash together.

All the small observations pull together now to paint a vivid image. The way he always said he needed me; he can't live without me. I thought he was being sweet, but he meant it literally.

My entire spine tingles with the realization I've let yet another snake into my garden.

Still in denial of what our entire relationship has been, I say, "But there's always been something between us." I try and fail to put into words the pull I've always felt when he's near. The familiarity I feel, like I've known him all my life. The comfort I've felt in his presence, in his arms.

"It's not me you're drawn to." He grips my neck, roughly dragging his fingers down my skin, across my collarbone, where dried blood continues to flake from all night. Pulling his fingers away, he lifts two fingers up so I can see the blood he's wiped from my skin. And then licks them, his eyes flutter close to relish the moment and emphasize I'm no threat to him. "It's the blood. Ombretta's blood coursing through my veins draws you in and keeps you coming back. I told you, you had no idea what it'd mean if I took your blood. Now you know. Ombretta and I are forever connected. She's a part of me. Your Faeness can sense her in me. *That* is what you've been drawn to all this time. Not me."

I struggle to push strength I don't feel into my next words. "You can't mean that. I thought—"

He cuts me off again mid-sentence, "I know what you thought." His words turn colder with each word he spits out. "You thought I had feelings for you. That I was here to carry you off into the sunset. That we'd arrive in the north and you and I would live happily ever after. With Ombretta safe by our side."

My head cants to the side. I guess that's exactly what I thought would happen. I just hadn't put it into so many words yet. But he's right. And it hurts. I'm not sure what hurts more, though—the truth or the betrayal.

I curse myself for how stupid that sounds now.

I had hoped that once we made it to the north and could pull my sister from whatever dangers she was in, we could remain there—safe and happy. Then, when the time was right, and Ombretta was strong enough, we'd set off toward the Fae lands together.

But I suppose that's not what Thaliya, Patton, and Baylor had in mind. Not if they spent their lives watching and waiting. Not if they've been training me for something bigger than all of us this whole time.

That's definitely not what Gryphon and Licia had in mind when we set off on our adventure—a quiet life up north. I know they would've been devastated if, after all we've been through, all we've learned, that was the future I chose.

Channeling strength from all those who believe in me, I square my shoulders and widen my stance, making myself bigger than I feel. "Well, you seem to know an awful lot about my future. What then, exactly, were you planning?"

"Ah, it seems the Princess has found her voice," he taunts as he circles me—a wolf circling its prey. "Although I'm not sure it's her own," he continues slowly, reveling in the fear rolling off me that I'm so desperately trying to hide and failing.

He smiles a roguish sneer, seeming to have even more to share. "My dear Princess, Ombretta is not the meek Fae in distress you've come to believe. She's, in fact, a queen in her own right. She's the ruler of the north. And if she has her way, soon the entire kingdom. She has quite the score to settle with all those who've wronged her, you know."

Still trying to reconcile what he's telling me with what I've been told these past weeks, my thoughts piece together slower than I need them to. I speak carefully, knowing I haven't got it quite right yet. "So she's learned of me and has asked I join her?"

His laugh cuts the darkness, and a chill runs down my spine. I have even less of a hold on the current situation than I first believed. "Don't you see?" He grips my throat, not restricting air, just asserting dominance. "You are to replace her."

"As Queen of the North? That doesn't make sense." And it doesn't match the triumphant tone in his voice. So triumphant, I wonder if Licia or Gryphon can hear him. Or if Baylor is close enough.

"No, Princess. As a decadent meal. Only the finest dining for my queen."

Not able to follow his twists and turns, I stare at him. In shock. Silently begging either my brain to comprehend faster or my feet to turn and run, now. Really, anything at all to happen besides this.

He mistakes my inability to move as an invitation to continue. "Queen Ombretta, your dear sister, is tired of allowing herself to be drained by the Ancients. She's had her fun and now she's done. She'd like someone else to take over in that respect."

"So when you said she was strong, this is what you meant." The statement rises and bubbles out despite the slight pressure he's started to apply around my air supply.

"Exactly, and unfortunately for you, we've grown accustomed to a very specific vintage, you see. Your Fae blood gives us a strength we've not seen in centuries. Those of us who share her, heal almost instantly and are currently nearly invincible. And as Ombretta is growing weary of being our plaything, I've assured her I'll be able to find another. And since the realm is currently rather low on Fae, especially royal Fae, it must be you."

Those last three words hit me, each one a striking blow to the chest. Now I see. I've swiftly gone from a royal Fae fated to return the kingdom to her people, to the very bottom of the food chain. Thaddeus isn't even close to who I thought he was. Who I had hoped he would be.

The revulsion of me so easily trusting him, of being with him, must roll off me in waves because the calculating smile that's grown wider with each revelation quickly falls from his face.

"So, you do hope to whisk me away, just not in the dreamy and romantic way of most bedtime stories." I try to match his venom, but my words are as much laced with anger as they are of fear.

And he can tell.

"Yes, in fact, we'll be leaving now. I know you'll do this for me. For us. You always say yes." He trails his fingers down my arm, the icy touch burns across my skin. He's been grooming me all this time? Playing with me to figure out just how far I'd go to make those around me happy? Rage boils within me. "I don't think we should make Ombretta wait any longer to be reunited with her dear sister, do you? And the Ancients are all eager to meet you, as I'm sure you can imagine." He nods his head again, just as he had back at the fire.

I realize that was the moment when he made his decision to follow through. That perhaps he's not as set on this decision as he seems. Maybe I can sway him. The vitriol he spits isn't all his own. Perhaps there's a part of him that I've touched.

CHAPTER SIXTY-ONE

He takes me off guard by spinning me around and pinning my back against his chest. His strong arms hold me in a mock of a lover's embrace. Ever so gently, he traces his fingers along my jawline and tucks my hair behind my ears. His warm breath caresses my neck as he breathes me in. "I already know how sweet you taste. I've enjoyed all our moments together. Almost so much that I haven't been able to contain myself."

His tongue licks up my neck; I can feel a shudder run through him as he runs his tongue over his lips—tasting me and taunting me. Just before his teeth sink into my neck, all my recent days of training with Patton flash before my eyes. It's been mostly hand to hand combat and sword play. He hadn't thought to mention how to untangle yourself from the grasp of a creature of the night. Only now do I realize that was stupid. How hopeful Thaliya and Patton had been that Thaddeus would deliver me to my sister without issue.

Realizing Patton's training would be of little help, I instead grab onto a gleam of a memory. When Gryphon and I would wrestle as children, and how I could often get out of his strong hold by distracting him rather than hoping to overpower him. I try the same tactics here.

I quickly bring my heel up and stomp Thaddeus' foot as hard as I can muster. He howls in surprise and pain. His grip loosens around my body, but his hand fists tightly in my hair, yanking me off my feet.

"Just be a good girl," he says as he twists my hair so my face meets his own. "I know you think highly of yourself, but there's no way you could outmatch an Ancient."

His words sting almost as much as his grip on my hair.

I think to scream. The others aren't that far off. They'll hear me. They'll come. But as soon as I open my mouth, he sends his knee into my stomach, knocking the air right out of my lungs. As I cough, trying to suck back air, he fists his hands in my hair, closing the distance between my scalp and his grip. Stars spin around me in the darkness, my mind drifts in and out of consciousness.

"You think if you scream, they'll come?" he scoffs, holding me up by my hair so we stand face to face. My sight blurs and there's two of him. "You're worthless. I'm doing you a favor by taking you up north. There's nothing for you here. And no one."

He might be right. The darkness threatens to close in on all sides. I can feel the pressure and the release, both just out of my grasp.

But no.

I try to focus on him, look into his eyes as he says this to me. It's all wrong. He's all wrong.

Weeks ago, maybe even days ago, he could've convinced me to go along with him. That my role to be played is a passive one. But now, I know my worth and I know what I'm capable of.

And I know this isn't it. I don't want this.

I want more.

I'm meant for more.

Know yourself, know your path.

Tears burn in my eyes as the fire along my scalp tears through me. But rather than allow his words to break me, I use the time he wastes describing all the terrible things he looks forward to doing to me to wrap my hand around the gold dagger I know he keeps just inside his jacket.

He's either too distracted by his own machinations or too confident. Either way, I have just enough time to unsheathe it and prepare to strike. If I can move quick enough, I can swipe fast and hard at his neck.

As I swipe upward, aiming to find his neck, he reads my intentions in my movements and I'm thrown off balance.

I sway in his arms and the force of my imbalance sends us both falling. He pulls me toward him and we fall hard to the ground. I try to put my hands up to brace my fall with my forearms, but—the dagger.

My hand still fists the metal. I cringe and close my eyes as the sound of metal meeting flesh pierces the silence.

My forearms did break my fall, but so did he. I land askew on top of him. My free hand hits the dirt just above his shoulder. I note how cold it is.

But that's because there's warm blood slowly seeping out from under my other hand. I can also feel his hair brushing ever so softly against the side of my hand.

Almost a caress. But he hasn't moved yet. And I haven't opened my eyes. I'm afraid of what I'll find.

Even though my intention was to kill. And he was attacking me.

My thoughts and emotions coil and twist together like a cucumber vine seeking out the sun.

There's a sharp intake of breath from Thaddeus, quickly followed by a string of curses. His fingers dig into my arms, trying to shove me off. I can feel my skin bruising from his grip while I gather as much strength as I can to finish this fight.

While my mind spins and reels, I keep my eyes closed tight. I don't want to look, but I know I hit something by the way he struggles to both keep me away and not let go. So I focus all consciousness and effort on driving the blade further into whatever flesh I've found. His grip on my hair loosens, and I use that moment to back away, pushing against his chest and the dagger.

My feet refuse to stand so I use what strength I have left to shuffle backward as fast as I can until I'm backed up against a large tree trunk. My palms scrape against the rough trunk as I struggle to pull myself up. My vision blurs as my nails break and skin tears against rough bark as I blunder to find purchase on anything at all.

As I finally find my footing, I venture a look down at Thaddeus, who lies unconscious on the forest floor.

He looks more peaceful than he has in days. So peaceful, I'm taken back to the night we shared in my room. How then, looking at him in the moonlight only made me want him more. But I quickly toss the unbidden memories away.

His hands lay palms open, inviting me back to him. His thickly coiled hair falls around his shoulders as if in a deep sleep.

My eyes then catch on the golden dagger—now sticking out of his left eye.

This immediately pulls me back into the present.

I'm glad he's gone.

The thought swims through the fog in my head as I stand over an unmoving Thaddeus.

There's a rustle in the brush surrounding us. I glance over, unwilling to take my attention off his prone form. Vines of the darkest green curl around the edges of the forest floor. Bright red petals wink in and out of the moonlight, reassuring me I'm not alone.

I take one last look at Thaddeus, knowing Baylor will know what to do with him. I turn, heading back toward those waiting for me without looking back. To my family, the ones who know me better than I know myself, and will fight for me to find myself.

To those who are ready to shake up our realm.

Know yourself, know your path.

Thaliya's words.

My words.

Want to know what happens next? Find Beneath the Fae Moon's Fire, Book 2 in the Crown of Evergaurd series here.

Remember that deliciously steamy scene in the library? Want to read it from Thaddeus' point of view for free?

Click here for your FREE spicy bonus scene.

If this story sparked a fire in your heart, please consider leaving a review on Amazon or Goodreads—it truly fuels my magic! Thank you.

Acknowledgements

As a reader, I love getting to the acknowledgements. Weird, right? But by reading all my favorite authors' acknowledgements, I figured out how many people it actually takes to write a book. Which led me to think maybe I could write a book, too. And here we are. My very own acknowledgements, and in true form, I have so many people to thank!

A big 'thank you' to my editor, Khloe Cain for her keen eyes. Her invaluable guidance on verb tenses, all things commas, and her continuous enthusiasm for my manuscript kept me going.

I'm forever grateful for Claire Bradshaw's belief in my story. Even when I doubted myself, she gave me the courage to keep writing—seeing my story for what it could be instead of where it was.

Fae Queen Rising's stunning cover is thanks to the artistic minds of Louise and Jemima at INK Designs—and I can't wait to share what they have in store for book two!

I learned a lot from my unknowing mentor, Helen Scheuerer, on both the novel side and marketing side—thank you for being you!

And thank you to all the mamas in the Moms Who Write group—the place I continuously go when I'm stuck, knowing I'll get good advice and plenty of encouragement.

The wealth of knowledge I drank in while listening to podcasts on my drive to and from my day job—thanks Fiction Writing Made Easy, Joanna Penn, SPA Girls, and If Only I'd Known Then.

A huge shout out to my friends and Beta team for braving the unfinished versions and being my cheerleaders—Jo Mason, Terry Corle, Rachel Dailey, Val Schein, Kristen Bouvier, MaryLynn Schaeffer, and a special thanks to my sister, Carrington Beasley, for enthusiastically reading the story in all its forms and whose insightful comments helped me clarify the motivations of Roe at her lowest. Thank you to my other two siblings, Ashley and Wrightly, for cheering me on every step of the way.

I also appreciate all the weekends Jo spent explaining Insta and TikTok over a glass of wine. I wouldn't be on the socials without her masterful guidance.

Rachel—I love talking all things books with you! From our latest reads to more ways to reach readers. You know A LOT about A LOT. Someone needs to just give you the reins to the world.

I'm eternally grateful for Lori Brousse, a true hair goddess, for asking the right question at the right time.

Thank you to my parents, Trish and Tom Reed, who, when I said I wanted to write a fantasy novel, nodded ponderously and even now, ask questions throughout this long process. They are always interested and wowed by all I've accomplished and are huge supporters of this dream.

A million thanks to my husband, Bryce, who, from the beginning, had more faith in me than I did. And for all the Sundays when I said, "I need to write," he always shooed me out the door with promises of endless mugs of chai and quiet.

Thank you to my kiddos, who have the patience of saints when I have my Chromebook in my lap. And for always having a solid answer to the tougher questions, like, "What color are dragons?" and, "What's the opposite of earth magic?"

ABOUT THE AUTHOR

Scarlett M. Honey is a dreamer, a writer, and teacher. After years of nurturing young minds, she decided to pursue her passion for storytelling. As a lifelong lover of fantasy and romance, Scarlett has always been captivated by the magic of happily ever after. After years of weaving tales in her mind amidst the chaos of diaper changes and meal planning, she finally brought her dreams to life with her debut novel, *Fae Queen Rising*.

When she's not lost in the worlds of her imagination, Scarlett enjoys embarking on adventures with her family, curling up with a good book by a crackling fire, or attempting to master the elusive yoga handstand. With a heart full of dreams and a pen in hand, she invites you to join her on a journey through enchanting realms and unforgettable love stories.

Connect with Scarlett on the web at www.scarlettmhoney.com.

www.ingramcontent.com/pod-product-compliance
Lightning Source LLC
Chambersburg PA
CBHW050017120726
47903CB00006B/1805